Cover Design by BespokeBookCovers.com

ISBN: 978-1-7752052-1-0

Table of Contents

WANT

PROLOGUE

It's supposed to be easy.

That first night—the one where they decided they were ready—they thought it would be. They lay together on their sides under a goose-down duvet in front of the glowing embers of a slowly-dying fireplace, having reached the bottom of a litre of full-bodied Spanish tempranillo with a wine-drenched buzz swelling their steadily-mounting eagerness.

She ran her lips along his jawline and then underneath his chin while his index fingers brushed along the grooves of her spine. Mouths tasting salt and tang, fingers tracing ridges and contours, pulses and gasps aligning. Then his thumbs hooked into the corners of her pelvis. Hot, shallow breaths. Wet expectancy. In the hearth, embers glowed orange through a layer of white ash. Engorgement to the brim of heart and loin, thinking conquered by sensation. One of her feet slid over top of his from toe to heel—a signal. She rotated onto her back; he rose to his knees and bent in feverish greed towards her welcoming inner sanctum. A grasping of her ankles and a gasping insertion, the jockeying for purchase and depth and rhythm, slippery and steady thrusts, eyes locked. *We're making a baby. You and I. A baby!* This. Just this, forever.

No more round estrogen dials, latex spoilers, copper apparatus. Instead, a barrier-free savouring of sinking delight in each other, closer and closer to the verge of obliteration, then her eyes closing and mouth gaping with familiar, babbling sighs rising to crescendo, and subsiding into a throaty purr as he spasms in a rumbling, grateful release.

Mmmmmmmmm.

They murmured to each other about how it felt different to have a higher goal in mind this time. They whispered and giggled. Midnight came. They slept.

Meanwhile, one privileged sperm would enjoy its leisurely sojourn through a fallopian tube, penetrate his egg of choice, and waltz with her for a few lazy days towards the uterine mothership.

Nine months later, the fruit of their ecstasy would arrive. Hospital or home birth? Cloth or disposable? So many logistical, happy decisions to make.

This is how it was supposed to go. The most natural thing.

For a normal man and woman.

After all, anyone can do this. Teenagers do it in the back of sweaty, beer-stained Mustangs. Royalty do it on beds of crested canopy and horsehair-filled headboard. Genghis Khan fathered over a thousand. Omkari Singh mothered a child at seventy. People have been doing this forever, and there seems to be little to distinguish them—be they presidents or mass murderers, Olympians or quadriplegics, millionaires or paupers. Anyone can make a baby, the word "make" implying creative work.

It's not work. Anyone can do this.

Mitchell and Sharelle can't do this. They are afflicted, the source of their affliction only a guess by urologists, ob-gyn's, and countless friends and family members with warm intentions and limited medical acumen.

The possibility that they will create a child on their own is gone forever. Instead, the only way a child will come is if artificially-induced ovarian hyperstimulation results in a successful follicular aspiration followed by intracytoplasmic sperm injection culminating in the transfer of multi-celled zygotes via trans-cervical replacement. With the assisted hatching option.

The multi-phases of in vitro fertilization. IVF.

IVF is not mmmmm.

IVF is decidedly ffffff.

Like fffuck.

Like leaking air.

fffffffffffffffffffffffff.

They are on their fourth, and possibly last, IVF cycle.

Mitch longs to peer into the eyes of a helpless little creature—the lantern light of those tiny eyes shining up at him from eternity, making him new.

He wants to crouch down and stare while the child sleeps in the crib. He'll put his finger between the slats and into the palm of a little hand, feeling a gentle squeeze of the fist.

When the baby wakes, he'll lift the radiating cocoon and cradle it in his arms, bending down to the soft, peach-fuzz head and inhaling the sweet, earthy essence.

It will be like breathing in the universe, his soul filling up like a balloon.

That dream is running out of air. fffffffffffffffffffffffffffffffffffffffffffffffffffffffffffffffffffffffffffffffffffffffffff fffffffffffffffffffffff.

STIMULATION

April 1985

You need a good half hour for the de-smiting treatment, so it's important to wake up at 6:30. Have a brief but efficient shower, then slide the wool hat onto your wet head. Put the tight headband over top, so it's pressed against the ends of your hair. Sit on the bed and listen to the clock radio for the next half hour, allowing the hat/headband treatment to work its magic. Afterwards, take off the hat and look in the mirror. Ah, limp and straight. Yes, it will curl again later in the afternoon, but for now your hair is at its peak.

Put away your regalia where your older brother won't get his hands on it. You call your straightening "kit" regalia because you're always searching for better, more elevated words to replace your old ones. It's all part of replacing the old Mitch with an improved model as you climb towards Tier 2 status on the social ladder at school. Of course, *Duran Duran* hair would look right at home in Tier 1, but a sudden change might invite ridicule and that would be far worse. A bold hair change would require the insulating power of a girl's public affections. No. One rung at a time.

Now back to the mirror for a physique examination.

Frontal view: Nice triangular build, though those pecs could use some filler.

Side view: The pecs seem rounded. Borderline boobs, actually. Tighten them ASAP. Push-ups tonight, for sure.

Back view: From what you can tell, those are some pert buttocks. You've avoided the globular, wobbly rump that afflicted Dad. Switching from boxers to briefs seems to have paid some dividends in this regard. Solid support and carriage. Well played, sir.

Face check. Skin seems good. No acne to speak of, though that ruddy complexion and those white eyebrows? Not okay. Perhaps some tanning this summer. Eyebrow pencil for men: Is there such a thing? Worth investigation.

Your nose seems more bulbous than usual. Be sure to study other noses today. Could just be your frame of reference.

Go with the mid-rise briefs, Levis, baseball shirt. Tube socks, red stripe. No, you have PE today. Blue stripe.

Okay, we are a *go* for launch. Maybe today is a new horizon. Everything could change. Go forth and flourish.

You, my friend, are fully prepared for the day.

Mitchell Van Laren's routine each morning in high school was steadfast. Mitch despised his curly hair. Mom had told him that women would die to have nice blond curls like him and, unbelievably, that hadn't helped. He had decided if God was going to smite him with sheep hair, he was going to take corrective measures—a wool hat being a delicious piece of irony. This modification would hopefully help him get noticed by Kylii, an astonishingly exotic girl whose family had recently moved to Canada from Finland. The way she had said her name the first day in English 10 class in a singsongy voice that seemed half German and half Irish made him spell it in his mind as "Kyle-Lee." Ah, the power that hyphen held! How seamlessly that sensual little stroke turned two bland masculine names into a feminine one shimmering in perfume. He hadn't noticed the true spelling of it until he'd seen it printed seven lines above his on the semester honour roll. Tikkanen, Kylii. He had been disappointed at first but then concluded that this spelling, the splendid double *i* coupled with her unusually black, short hair—unusual at least compared to his knowledge of Scandinavian women, which was limited to a documentary he'd seen once on the underground Swedish massage industry in Vancouver—made her almost unbearably exciting.

Even more compelling was the fact that Kylii was nice to him and, maybe with her unique cultural perspective and some opportunity, she might get him. She might even want to get with him. None of the other girls seemed to want to try. He was the go-to guy for a quick homework clarification or to ask for a no-strings-attached partnership on a Canadian history project. "You're safe, Mitchell," Andrea Carrasco, a quasi-confidante, had told him once when pressed about how he was perceived by the female segment of the student population and whom he might put on his radar for possible courtship and eventual accompaniment to the grade twelve graduation dance, twenty-six months hence. He didn't take "safe" as a compliment.

It was a shame, Mitch thought that morning as he munched on his Cocoa Puffs, because he had a lot to offer if you could get past his fleecy locks. He was, after all, reading the *World Book Encyclopedia* from *A-Z* and had learned some striking facts about French Guiana the previous night. Freud would be among tomorrow night's enticing offerings—Mitch having peeked ahead—and Freud's theories about the unconscious mind might provide insight into Kylii's id, ego, and superego as possible departure points into a wider understanding of the nuances of her soul and all the delights that lay therein.

Mitch perceived a four-tier social hierarchy at high school. The top tier consisted of various athletes and beautiful people who were as mysterious to Mitch as they were inaccessible: Those whose DNA had transmitted the culturally-favoured characteristics for this specific space and time in human history, the Southern Interior of British Columbia in the mid-1980s. Chief among these seemed to be the ability to bounce a rubber sphere on a wooden floor and propel it with enough force to accurately enter a metal hoop rimmed with nylon mesh, or to possess the right combination of pleasing bone structure, contemporary hair style, and extroversion. The second level was a collection of assorted kids who, despite a dearth of any discernible culturally-sanctioned skill set, maintained a tenuous but relatively intact relationship with those above them and, as such, could go about their days unmolested through the hallways, self-esteem and dignity intact. Next were those with varying degrees of defects and socially undesirable traits. These were the weak, the marginalized, and the misunderstood (like Mitch). The remaining fourth tier was comprised of the crippled and sociopathic. At the very bottom of this unfortunate group was Stephen Leopold, whose fastidious masturbation schedule was rumoured to be as precise and unfailing as the changing of the guard at Buckingham Palace.

Mitchell left for school from their small, post-war bungalow at 8:00 as usual, knowing that he would be running the Larson Whittaker gauntlet within the next seven minutes. *Bungalow with full basement. Full.* He had heard Dad say that one time about their house. He ran his fingers lightly along the rough, white stucco of the house's west-facing wall, a daily compulsion but nonetheless pleasing in its gritty texture. For once, today his older brother Trevor said he'd walk with him.

Trevor was in a good mood because he was graduating in a couple months and had been accepted into the University of Victoria, his first choice, for English Literature. It had been months since Trevor had walked to school with Mitch. Gone were the days of reading *Archie* comics together, listening to *Thriller* over and over on their shared cassette player, walking to the arcade for *Gorf* and *Asteroids*, collecting hockey cards, divvying out barbecue corn chips with the "You pour, I pick" protocol and then settling in for another ecstatic, racy episode of *Three's Company*—taking turns manning the remote control in case of Mom's unexpected entrance.

"Kind of cool to walk to school together while we still can," Mitch said as they headed out of the yard. He turned to see if Mom was watching them go as she sometimes did, but he saw only the abundance of red geraniums staring at him from the large bay window in front. He picked up a piece of spear grass that was poking through a crack in the sidewalk and began chewing it.

"Yup, won't be seeing much of each other after high school," Trevor said. He pulled a comb from his back pocket and ran it through his dirty-blond bangs, then returned the comb and fastened all but the top button of his jean jacket. They walked in silence along their street and turned onto an abandoned railway track towards Creemore Heights High School.

"C'mon, Trevor. Timing is critical here," Mitch said as he strode ahead. Trevor was five inches shorter than Mitchell and had to take extra strides.

"Come again?" Trevor said, coming to a stop. "You walk like a giraffe having a grand mal seizure, by the way."

"Larson Whittaker walks to school along Kensington Avenue," Mitch said pointing to the street that lay at a 45-degree angle to the track.

"So? Who's Larson? A friend of yours?" Trevor asked, catching up to him.

"A guy from school. If he sees us, he'll want to walk with us."

"And?"

"And, that's to be avoided at all costs. He suffers from this unique sort of physical...incapacitation," Mitch said.

Mitch explained how Larson's dad had taken off on him, like Mitch and Trevor's had. It was even in the same year: 1980. The year of the hostages in Iran. Larson's mom worked at Pricewise Shoes to support him and his little sister. Worse, Larson was born with skeletal dysplasia; this gave him a height of about four feet, arms that were half the normal length, and a right hand with stubs for fingers. His bright red hair and milky skin made him even more noticeable. When he talked, bubbles gurgled from his mouth and Mitch could see strings of spit filled with bread crumbs and other food. He would try not to look at Larson's mouth when he spoke, since the sight of it might ignite his gag reflex.

"That's pathetic, Mitch."

"Easy to say. You don't walk in my shoes, evidently."

"Evidently, you're a knob."

"Your vocabulary astounds me," Mitch muttered.

Mitch felt sorry for Larson. There was little question that Larson was doomed to languish in the purgatory of fourth tier for the rest of his high school tenure. Mitch wanted to help him without jeopardizing his own possible social ascension. Up to that point in the school year, he had tried to introduce Larson to the odd Tier 3 kid who might befriend him and improve his quality of life. And still, Larson walked through the hallways and down the street alone. Maybe it was his imploring demeanour and body language—the puppy-like tilt of the head and widened eyes that spoke encyclopedic volumes: *Someone please be with me. Walk with me. Let me in.*

It ached to see Larson so alone, but Mitch had done what he felt he could. He wasn't in any of Larson's classes, which made it less stressful not worrying about having Larson affixed to him like a remora. There had to be a balance between taking care of Larson and not losing one's spot on the ladder.

Once when he was visiting Opa, his very Dutch grandfather, Mitch had made the mistake of telling him about Larson. He had said that he tried his best to avoid him. Opa had slowly shaken his head as Mitch said this and folded his arms. He had leaned in slightly, emitting a whiff of sweet pipe tobacco.

"Mitchell, never treat people that way."

"I'm not doing anything mean to him. He's kind of a friend, in fact."

"You're holding back something that's needed," he had said.

"I'm not taking anything from him, Opa."

"You're refusing to share yourself."

"I can't. People will make a mockery of me," Mitch had said.

"Sometimes the right thing to do is the hardest. But you don't walk away."

"You don't understand. It's really complex and…problematic."

"That's part of becoming a man. Accountability."

"I know you're right," Mitch said, resigned.

"Do you believe that, Mitch? It's what a true man is. You need to believe it." Opa had put a hand on Mitch's neck and gently squeezed. "Someday, you'll need someone to walk with you," he had said. What Opa didn't seem to understand was that it wasn't about walking, but about drowning. And if one drowning man helped another, neither would make it to shore.

After that, Opa periodically asked him how it was going with Larson. Mitch would lie and say they were becoming closer friends. He wasn't sure Opa believed him.

"Humour me, okay?" Mitch said. "If we can make it past Mr. Baker's house on the corner, we can turn quickly to the left and be out of his sight."

"And if we don't?"

"Larson will kick it into gear and be hell-bent on catching up to us."

"And then what evils will unfold, you neurotic freak?" Trevor asked.

"Oh, nothing much, really. Merely the dismantling of whatever shred of credibility I still have at school." He adjusted the straps on his backpack. "It wouldn't exactly ratchet up your stock value, either."

"I have no worries in that department," Trevor said, snuffling. "It's blue chip. Always has been."

"Congratulations, Merrill Lynch. Now let's get moving."

"Nope," Trevor said. "You run on ahead around the corner. I'll face the Armageddon alone, I guess."

Mitch double-timed his steps. He could not be seen with Larson. He needed acceptance, not stigma. Even Kylii would likely not be able to reconcile this and give him a fighting chance. Once he was firmly ensconced in Tier 2, he could be kind to Larson, even friendly, without being mistaken for his friend. He knew what a sad testament this was, but there were limits to what one could bear.

As Mitch cantered towards the corner with Trevor keeping an ambling trot, he spotted Larson out of the corner of his eye.

Then he heard, "Mitchell!" It was Larson's voice. *I'll pretend I didn't hear him. I'm almost there.*

"Hey, Mitchell!" Trevor's voice now. "Wait up! Your friend is calling you."

He sabotages everything. Every freaking thing. Defeated, Mitch turned and stopped. Trevor sauntered over and gave him a wink. Mitch seethed at him with his lips drawn in a grimace, metamorphosing it into a fake grin hybrid of surprise and delight as Larson drew within a couple inches of him, his sense of personal space notable among his disabilities. Mitch took a subtle half-step back.

"Hey, Larson, what's new?" Mitch asked.

"Haven't seen you around in a while," Larson said.

"This is my brother." Mitch jerked his thumb towards Trevor. "Trevor," he added. The name *Trevor* in its original form meant "Shrivelled penis," he wanted to add.

"Hi, Larson. Mitchell talks about you a lot," Trevor said. He smirked at Mitch. The boys started to walk three abreast down the sidewalk.

"Did you see the last *TJ Hooker*?" Larson asked. "William Shatner has a new partner on the beat. I heard there's a lot of fighting on the set. Just like *Three's Company*. Suzanne Somers wanted more money. I wonder what Joyce DeWitt thinks about that. She's so nice..."

Mitch listened to Larson's steady monologue of program synopsis and celebrity gossip with what he felt should be grinding boredom but was actually a kind of enjoyment. This was a walk to be endured however, he convinced himself, not one to settle for and into. He flashed a glance at Trevor who returned his look, stroked his chin, and nodded his head in mock contemplation at Larson's commentary.

An absolute psychopath for the ages. Time to leave the nest, Trevor. I'll help you pack your bags.

They walked onto the school grounds, down the long sidewalk between the tennis courts and the soccer field. As they made their way past a set of bleachers next to the field, Mitch heard, "Hey Frizzy" above Larson's babbling summary of Friday night's episode of *Dallas*. He rolled his head to the side, looked up, and saw Pryce Shanahan sitting in the top bleacher with Miranda Dalton, two years his senior. He was facing sideways to them, mouth open and eyes upturned, his left arm curled toward his armpit with fingers squeezed together in a Larson mimicry.

"What are you *looking* at?" Larson said, pausing his synopsis, and following Mitch's stare. Pryce dropped his arm and studied the sky.

"Why do you let people talk to you like that?" Trevor asked.

"Like what? All he said was, 'Frizzy,'" Mitch said.

"I'd never let anybody do that to me."

"It's a one-time thing. Misunderstanding of sorts."

"It's not the first time. I can't believe you put up with it."

Larson continued, "So anyway, J.R. decides to go behind Bobby's back and talk to—"

"I'm sorry, Larson. Can we continue next time?" Mitch asked. "I want to hear about it. I really do." He turned to Trevor. "So why don't you do something about it?" he said.

"Sure, okay. Next time, Mitch," Larson said.

"You gotta learn to fight your own battles," Trevor said.

"He's a two-hundred-pound behemoth." Mitch started to walk ahead. "But you could stand up for me. There was a time when you used to advocate for me."

"That vocabulary of yours isn't going to get you any girlfriends, by the way. And neither will getting calling 'Frizzy' by a bunch of punks."

Mitch bet that Kylii would like his vocabulary. "I have a plethora of girls who find me attractive," he said.

"Really."

"Really."

"Is that why you walk alone to school every day?"

"That's by choice not design. I don't see a young filly on your arm today. And, by the way, you're as afraid of Pryce as I am," Mitch said.

"Why don't you stop putting yourself in this position?" Trevor asked.

He's probably right. "I'm right in the position I want. All systems are go," he said. Mitch stopped and retied his shoelaces tightly in double knots.

"Wow, I'd hate to see what failure looks like in your world," Trevor said.

"You guys don't like each other very much, do you?" Larson asked.

"It's fine, Larson. Brother stuff," Mitch said.

"I wish I had a brother," Larson said.

"It's overrated, Larson," Trevor said.

Mitch's shoulders tightened. *It's not overrated. We've just lost it. And now we'll never get it back.*

The three waited for the bell in the canopied entryway, Mitch sitting on a bench with Larson perched with dangling legs next to him. Trevor stood against the wall of the school and stared at them. The subtle shake of his head communicated everything: Pity, disdain, and shame for his younger brother. Mitchell the Failure.

"Thanks for walking with me, Mitchell and Trevor," Larson said as soon as the bell rang. He said that every time. *Thanks for walking with me, Mitchell.* Every single time.

"It was awesome. You guys should coordinate it so you can walk together every day," Trevor said. "You could synchronize your watches."

Up your ass. Why do you hate me so much?

"Mine's broken," Mitch said.

"Funny, it was working fine at breakfast," Trevor said. He gave one more shake of his head and then held the door open for them in such a way that they had to pass under his arm. Larson entered first and Mitch followed, ducking under the arm with an exaggerated crouch to highlight his and Trevor's height difference.

Walking into school with the shrillness of the bell still pinging through his ears, Mitch decided to set Larson free. From now on, he would take the longer route along Winston and Hetchken Streets to get to school. It would cost a couple minutes, but the inconvenience would pay off. Avoiding eye contact in the hallways was easy enough, too. Some tough love would hopefully force Larson to branch outwards and make new connections. In the end, Larson would be better off, Mitch told himself with a queasy rush of sadness he tried to brush off. And he could still surreptitiously keep an eye out for him. In any event, it really was time to prioritize Kylii, he thought, as he headed down the hallway towards his locker. *She really deserves my best foot forward.*

Opa wouldn't be happy if he knew Mitch had jettisoned Larson. And Mitch wouldn't want to disappoint him. He loved Opa with a fervour that filled the nuclei of his atoms; the sight of his six-foot-four bulk striding into the yard with one hand jammed deep into his pocket sent a flood of warmth through Mitch's body. Opa's left hand—appendaged by thick, calloused fingers pounded by errant hammer blows and squished between two-by-fours throughout decades of immigrant labour—was the one that reached down and swallowed Mitch's right hand when he was a boy as they walked downtown to do errands or mail a letter. Opa's right hand was the one that gave Mitch his annual birthday handshake—wrenching his arm up and down in a huge arc that made Mitch laugh so hard he couldn't resist it and leaving his arm feeling numb when it was done, Opa then pulling him in for a shoulder-crushing hug with the boom of his laughter throbbing in Mitch's ear. This was the voice that recited poets from the Klondike and marveled at how deer could find their way through the protective metal netting to eat his lettuce leaves ("Do you believe that, Mitchell? Isn't Creation a mystery?") and told him with reassuring confidence, "You're a fabulous guy, Mitch. There'll never be another Mitch like you." How deeply Opa peered into his eyes, how gently he swatted him on the shoulder, how unfailingly he circled school musicals and hockey games on his calendar, how brightly his eyes lit up in concert with the deep bass of his thick brogue when he saw Mitch: "Allo, Mitchell. How is it all with you?"

It was all fine.

Opa was in the house.

MARCH

Mitch has lived in the small city of Renfrew for all of his forty-six years. Opa and Oma immigrated to Chicago after Opa fought for the Dutch in the first half of the Indonesian War of Independence. Opa built houses, and Oma was a maternity nurse. They weren't there for long. "That was so busy in that Shee-Ka-Go," Opa would say. They stayed long enough to have fraternal twins (Mom and her brother Joop) and then moved to the Yukon for a while where he worked on a construction crew building travel lodges along the Alaska Highway. The Klondike didn't seem like a place to raise a family, and they chose to start driving south until it felt right and arrived here in the Amara Valley.

This is not the British Columbia of rainforests and softly lit coffee shops. It's the arid land east of the coastal mountains: a land of apple and cherry trees and vineyards. A place where in the summer a shower is an event, where it seems to evaporate before your eyes as soon as it hits the pavement. Opa missed the heat of Indonesia but not the humidity. He said he wanted to live the rest of his life somewhere dry and scorching in the summer, where the dampness would get sucked out of his Dutch bone marrow. He and Oma chose this valley between brown and olive mountains, and he spoke once of how the sagebrush quivers in an unrelenting wind and sometimes a fine dust from the mesa gets in your teeth. Many transients come here in the summer—picking fruit for piecework wages, smoking cheap and potent British Columbia weed, hitchhiking and screwing their way across the valley. Tourists come here too from Calgary and Vancouver, their sun-burned legs jutting from pastel saris and cargo shorts, peach juice running down their chins.

Meanwhile, the locals plug away. The sawmill shut down last year because lumber prices were low and the forests east of town sparse and difficult to log. The copper mine has been closed because it's environmentally unsound. The summer tourist season isn't enough. Some people have been foreclosed, others grind their way through the month. New neon signs illuminate Main Street now. *Payday Cash World. Quickie Cash Emporium.* Everyone is trying to find the way, but in the meantime the casino in town is busy and the bars always full, everyone dancing old moves to new music they don't know, music spun by nineteen-year-old DJs who chose to find jobs in town and drink on weekends with their buddies. Mitch feels like he knows every terrace of grassland and cactus patch, and he knows that even the grayest winter day will only send enough of a dusting of snow to cover the brown grass. He teaches middle school here. He's also trying to make babies. Neither has gone well.

Like Sharelle and Mitch, Trevor and Megan spent their twenties building their careers, taking backpacking trips, and going out to eat twice a week. While both couples were cocksure that they'd have babies when they decided it was time, their roads to parenthood have taken somewhat different paths. Mitch's plodding quest for fatherhood first took physical form in a urologist's office—where his testicles were squeezed and rolled to and fro between the blue-gloved fingers of a young and seemingly over-enthusiastic urologist as a primer for the eventual surgery for varicose veins in the scrotum (to let the swimmers swim) and every bodily fluid was tested and quantified into parts per million—and things haven't really brightened since then. Sharelle has endured a battery of exploratory procedures, fertility drugs, meticulous tracking of every aspect of her ovulatory cycle, and invasive questions from the specialist—the answers to which Mitch has had the chuckling pleasure of being regaled with afterwards by Sharelle:

"How many sexual partners have you had, Mrs. Van Laren?"

"Today?"

"In total please."

"Can I include myself to pad the numbers a bit?"

Pseudo-clearing of throat. "I know it's a personal question, but please answer."

"By sexual, you mean the insertion of Tab A into Slot B, I assume. That sounds so IKEA, doesn't it?"

Papers adjusted on clipboard. "Yes, intercourse."

"You're a tough nut to crack. Hey, maybe that's our problem. I have to crack Mitch's—"

"So, how many sexual partners have you had?"

Oh man, how funny she is! How did I manage to end up with her?

Meanwhile, Trevor and Megan have a three-year-old girl—Rachel. She's an outrageously generous gift: Beautiful, smart, and funny. She came a little earlier than they had hoped. "We so wanted to do Eastern Europe yet. I guess modern technology isn't foolproof," Megan said. They might have another one in a few years, depending on career and travel plans. "Maybe when Trevor's done grad school. It'd be nice for Rachel to have a playmate. And I'm not getting any younger."

"You've just got to keep at it," Trevor said. "It'll happen for you too. Science and perseverance."

Sharelle and Mitch have done three cycles of in vitro fertilization. They know the procedure by rote: first, a nasal spray and injections to stimulate the ovaries. After about ten days of the injections, as many eggs as possible will be retrieved from Sharelle's uterus and clinically united with Mitch's meandering sperm in a petri dish in order to incubate. Two or three days later, Mitch and Sharelle will move on to the embryonic replacement stage if the embryos have been successfully fertilized: The embryos will be given a grade (*B* is the highest they've ever reached), and the three best ones will be inserted back into Sharelle's uterus with a catheter. The rest of the embryos will be frozen—leftovers to be used for possible future cycles. Their leftovers have never survived the freezing process.

Two weeks later, there will be a morning blood test and the Phone Call at noon to hear the result. Stimulation, Retrieval, Incubation, and Replacement: It will all culminate in a phone call. There will either be genesis or anguish. There is no other outcome.

Is there a word they can borrow from another language, Finnish perhaps, that encompasses a crippling cocktail of jealousy, bitterness, rueful laughter, sorrow, and hope?

They're not giving up, though, because in vitro worked once before. On their first cycle, Sharelle got pregnant.

On the morning they found out, he was doing the very important work of organizing the spice jars in the cupboard above the microwave. Sharelle was methodically combining two partial boxes of Cheerios. She carefully compacted the emptied box along its folds and pressed it flat onto the counter, then picked it up and slapped it into Mitch's gut. "I'm not waiting till noon. This is torture." It was 11:48.

She picked up her phone and dialed the pre-programmed number for Zenith Reproductive Services. Mitch stood over the sink, his back to her. "You sure you want to call? I can do it, if you like," he said.

"No, I can do this. We can do this."

"Yes. We can." He turned and walked to her. As she waited, he ran a thumb along her jawline.

This moment. Please, please, please. If not, we can handle it. It's the first time. Probably didn't work. We'll be okay. Please.

Sharelle's voice was almost squeaky in its constriction. "Sharelle Van Laren's pregnancy results from her blood test this morning? Are they ready?" *Third person. Yes, third person. Distance. It's okay if it didn't work. Totally okay.*

Take her hand. Study her face. It'll be okay.

Her eyes are flaring, lips parting. Is it fear? It didn't work. I knew it.

She's biting her tongue. She's looking at me. Yes? Yes? "Yes?"

A nod. The nod.

This, this, this. Us. Oh God, yes. YES. YES.

Mitch thought she finished the call in some coherent way, but he really has no idea. He lifted her up as she erupted in sobs. He put her down and buried his face in her neck. "We did it, we did it. WE DID THIS."

"We did do this, Mitch. I love you so much. So incredibly much."

"I had this feeling, ya know? I just did. Somehow the universe was telling me it was going to happen."

"Oh love, really? I think I knew too. That is amazing. You are amazing. A baby!"

"Together, girl. A baby together."

This. Only this. All we need.

Then Mitch remembers being in the dingy, confined ultrasound room later in the pregnancy and hearing the splat of the gel being squeezed from a tube onto Sharelle's belly, a probe sliding gently along it. The technician, a short Filipino woman— "Analyn with one *n*"—turned the monitor so they could see, and Mitch studied the blue screen but from time to time stole a glance at Analyn, checking for signs of concern. "Now I'm checking the heart. See, there are the four chambers. Let's check out the heartbeat now, Sharelle." A pause. "148 beats per minute. That's good. Let's see the little one's head." The screen switched to amorphous membranes and squiggles and then an oval shape in the middle. Seconds passed as she studied the screen. More seconds. A faint clicking of a clock somewhere behind them.

Mitch realized that he needed to take some breaths. "How are things?" he said.

"Excuse me for a moment," she said and then left the room and returned with an older technician to scrutinize the screen, who nodded pleasantly at them. "This is Rod. We give each other second opinions." She nodded and smiled.

Rod's salt-and-pepper hair conveyed experience. His left arm dangled at his side while the index finger of his right hand ran back and forth along the surface of the screen. His eyes were squinting in concentration. He took raspy breaths through his nose. Grating.

"Feeling a little vulnerable here," Mitch said. "A tad anxious, ya know?" He gave a polite chuckle out of his throat to interrupt the tension.

"Yes, I really get it," Rod said, face to the screen. "A nerve-wracking business sometimes. Just being thorough here. Almost done."

Mitch leaned over and stroked the fine blond hair above Sharelle's temples.

My dear Lord, she's magnificent.

He picked up her right arm and stroked it, fixating on the naturally tanned hue of the skin. He kissed the top of her hand. He scanned the length of her 5'6" frame and felt a swell of tender protectiveness shoot through him.

Completely majestic. My queen. My gorgeous love. She chose me. Me. Please, give this to her. To us. Let everything be okay. It's what people do. They have healthy babies. Please. We're ready. Please, God.

"What's happening?" Sharelle asked. Analyn remained silent but continued to examine the screen. "Mitchell?" she whispered. She never called him *Mitchell.*

"This is all routine stuff, right?" Mitch said. *Take another breath.*

"Can someone say something? Please?" Sharelle said.

"So how does the head look?" Mitch asked.

"I have to step out for a second, Ann," Rod said and left.

"Easy does it. Just checking on something. Almost done." Analyn took measurements with the cursors and lines and punched some numbers into the computer. Clicking and clacking.

Talk to us. Please.

"Excuse me, what's—" Mitch started to say.

"Tell me what's going on," Sharelle interrupted.

Analyn stood upright. "You guys, we're noticing some anomalies here. I know this is really hard, but I'm not in a position to interpret exactly what it means. You'll have to have a chat with your doctor," she said. She walked to Sharelle and squeezed her arm. "You're doing everything right."

"But everything's okay, yes? With the head, the brain. It's all normal?" Mitch said.

"I know it's super tough, but I can't talk specifics of these ultrasounds. My job is only to get images of the fetus."

Everything is fine. She's being professional. We've put too much into this for it not to work.

"But you said the other things were normal," Sharelle said. "Why didn't you say anything about the head?"

"Sharelle, we'll get you in to talk with Doctor Amherst right away."

"Tell us what's wrong. Is our baby okay?" Mitch said and scoured the screen, feeling his heartbeat in his temples. None of it made sense.

Not this. Not now. No.

"I'm going to prep the information and send you downstairs to see her after this."

"Ann, Analyn. Tell us it's okay," Sharelle said.

The hand moved to Sharelle's shoulder. "I don't know. If it isn't, none of this is your fault. Go ahead and get dressed. I promise that the doctor will go over everything with you." She gave a thin smile, another squeeze of Sharelle's arm, and left the room.

No, Not this.

Mitch's face felt hot. A dull ache cramped his stomach. Sharelle sat up on the table and tried to say something to him, but it came out in a sputter, and then she was sobbing, and he put his arm around her shoulders.

No.

"It's okay, girl. I'm sure it's all fine. All fine, okay? " One of his legs began trembling. He reached down and hugged her chest and clasped an open hand around the back of her head.

Mitch smudged Sharelle's tears with his thumb as she wept, her arms reaching up and resting limply on his shoulders. He pressed his nose firmly into the top of her head again and ingested the grapefruit-shampoo scent. "It's okay. Breathe. I'm here. It's okay."

She dressed, and they went down to Dr. Amherst's office.

After that, it was like dominoes: a rushed meeting with a very busy but kind Amherst, the "expiration of the fetus," a D&C, and a cold, scientific lecture on fetal hydrocephalus from a specialist.

And smoldering grief.

May 1985

The first time Mitch ever talked to Kylii Tikkanen was near the end of grade ten, and he was sitting in chemistry class at his usual stool by the window. The one next to him was empty because a bunch of kids were absent. Mitch thought to himself that there were a lot of loose and emptied stools today, and then he covered his mouth with his hand to stifle a laugh at his pun but a splutter came out anyway. Several heads swung towards him. He wiped his mouth and turned away to study a poster of Dmitri Mendeleev on the wall.

Mrs. Trethewey liked to mix partners. She told him to pair with Kylii, who was also sitting solo. As he walked over, his legs felt prosthetic. Her raven-black hair was pert and glossy. *Chiseled* was the word that immediately sprang forward, but then he decided that was too mechanical. Her left leg perched on the leg rest of the stool, while the inside of her right foot rubbed up and down on a stool leg. Working with Kylii meant having to speak to her. He'd have to use actual words, and she was so inconceivably gorgeous that he started to blush and sweat as he shuffled over and sat down on the stool beside her. He flashed a glance at her and said, "Hello, how's it going?" but what came out sounded to him like a lecherous, deep-throated "Heh-lohh" followed by a rapid-fire, hissing "Howsetgoin?" His face blazed. Kylii smiled.

"Oh, Mitchell. Hi," she said.

Her ch-sounds are s-sounds. Mit-sill. And she knows my name.

Mit-sill. Mit-sill. Mit-sill. Mit-sill. Mit-sill.

And that interjection, "Oh."

Oh, Mit-sill. Oh, Mit-sill. Oh, Mit-sill. Oh, Mit-sill. Oh, Mit-sill. Oh.

Mitch's ears roared as the steadily falling Finnish intonation of her question asked him, "What did you do on the weekend?"

He searched for a cool answer to give because telling her he stayed home and watched *Dallas* on Friday night wasn't ideal, since everyone else his age was probably drinking wine coolers and engaging in various forms of petting—light to heavy—at the Murrayville Reservoir. "Hooked up…I mean hung out."

"Cool. With who?" He almost corrected her. *Whom.*

"Friends."

Please don't ask for names. Please.

Mercifully, Mrs. Trethewey began droning instructions on dissolving potassium permanganate and set them to work. They opened their log books, and Mitch tried to hide his from Kylii because it was meticulously organized with the date and title for each lab session underlined with a red pen and ruler—a blazing advertisement of his compulsiveness. He read the directions to her as they went, and it felt good to be talking to Kylii and saying something normal even if it was only steps to an experiment. They worked quickly together, talking through the steps and for a minute or so Mitch felt comfortable and even maybe confident; that is, until they were done early and there was nothing left to do but talk. That wasn't good.

"Seen any good movies lately?" Kylii asked.

He had seen a number of movies in the past month and couldn't remember a single one. "*Casablanca*," he stammered.

Casablanca? Are you kidding me? You're an idiot.

"*Casablanca.* My parents own that one. They say it's their favourite."

Mitch wanted to go home.

Casa-freaking-blanca!

"Actually...it was the only thing on. Pretty dumb. Black and white."

"Have you seen *Fast Times at Ridgemont High*? My parents just bought a VCR, so I rented it on Friday night with some friends. So funny," she said. He hadn't even heard of it.

"So awesome. Really wicked," he said.

"What was your favourite part?" she asked.

"There were many. I think the acting is so excellent."

"Hmm, yeah. Good actors," she said.

Suddenly, he remembered. *Risky Business*. I saw *Risky Business* and—" he said, but he was interrupted by the bell and Mrs. Trethewey's homework reminder.

As they got off their stools and gathered their backpacks, Kylii said, "It was nice being your partner, Mitchell." A smile glittered from her eyes.

"I really liked it too," Mitch said. He forced himself to give her an eternal micro-second of eye contact. They walked to English class together, and on the way he did an impression of Mrs. Trethewey saying, "Potassium Permanganate" in a nasally voice, and Kylii laughed in the most profoundly musical way, taking in one long deep breath and then exhaling in stuttering gasps. She did it three times: three sets of in-and-out. Then she asked him to do the impression again, and there were more gasps. They got to English and sat in their assigned seats, on opposite walls. He felt lit up. He pulled his books and pen from his backpack and glanced at Kylii. She was talking to Raymond Knutson, in whom she seemed disinterested. Mitch stared across the room at her until she caught his eye, and she smiled. His lungs were inflated to the hilt with oxygen. For the first time ever, he was truly alive and totally present. While Mr. McAllister talked about the assigned reading of *Beowulf*, Mitch replayed the last hour with Kylii in his mind: his new confidence, her beautiful laugh. Things were going to change for him.

"Who would make a good leader, and why?" McAllister's voice snapped him out. McAllister didn't like Mitch and would find ways to make him look stupid. Years ago, there had been an ugly two-week period in which the teachers went on strike for lower class sizes. A few teachers had refused to strike and agreed to teach, which meant that some parents decided to send their kids to school. Mitch's father was one of them, and he walked Trevor to Kindergarten to intentionally cross the picket line. He came face-to-face with Mr. McAllister, who was the primary school librarian at the time. McAllister took exception to this breach of their picket and let Mitch's dad know. A Tribune photographer had been there and taken a picture that made the front page: Dad walking across the line with Trevor behind him. The angle from which the picture was taken made it seem like McAllister was yelling in Trevor's ear, his face scrunched in a vitriolic grimace. That seemed to be a tipping point where the public started to turn against the teachers, and the strike ended soon after. Mr. Powell McAllister would never forget.

McAllister was a stout and gooey version of the Glad Man, so Mitch called him "Portly Powell" to himself and then it was "Double P" and finally just "Porter." Everyone else liked Porter because he was the cool teacher who made sly allusions to parties and how wild he used to be. The class was frequently reminded that he had a master's degree. Mitch doubted if Porter had had a stitch of exercise in ten years, except of course for his bowling. Walking by Renfrew Lanes once, he had seen Porter walking from his car to the alley with an ugly brown bowling bag in front of him—carrying it in his arms like it was the Ark of the Covenant. He walked the same as he did at school: a hunched, loping amble with his eyes darting back and forth like he was trying to itch them against his sockets.

"Who in this class would be a good leader?" Porter said again. "Think about that for a minute." He explained that for their class projects on *Beowulf*, each group of four would need a leader to move the project forward. And leadership was so important in life. Take him, for example. He was always such an effective leader in school, and that had really translated into his adult life. "We have to make a choice in life: are we going to be impotent eunuchs or are we going to take charge?" Porter said.

Impotent eunuchs? That's a redundancy.

Porter continued, "Take this class, for example. Who would you say has strong leadership skills?"

There was a long silence. Porter sat backwards astride a chair. It probably hurt his back and knees to stand anyway.

Raymond piped up, "A good leader would be Mitch, because he's smart." Mitch had let Raymond copy his biology worksheet answers once, and he was always grateful after that.

Porter wheeled his chair around to Mitch and leaned forward with his arms crossed on the chair back and his giant head perched over top his right wrist. His chin spilled outwards in shock waves of wattle.

"Mitch, huh? Okay, Mitchell, lead us."

"Pardon me?" Mitch asked with a squeak in his voice. Porter gave an imitative little squeak. A couple kids laughed.

"Come up here and lead us. I want you to demonstrate how you would lead your *Beowulf* group. Pretend we are all in your group, and I want you to be our leader. Raymond seems to think you'd be outstanding."

Raymond tried to save him: "I meant that in a small group situation, Mitch would be—"

Porter raised a hand and cut Raymond off. "Let's go, Mitch. Up and at 'em. Come to the board and lead us."

Raymond made a last-ditch rescue attempt: "I can be the leader."

"No, Mitch is on. If he's anything like his father, he'll show us what a big man he is. A man of action."

Mitch rose slowly and walked to the front, but he knew he appeared awkward because he was conscious of where his feet were placed when he was walking. He got to the front, turned a little too quickly to project poise, and stood in front of everyone. He lifted his eyebrows imploringly at Porter, who had turned his chair to the front while maintaining his chin-on-wrist pose. Porter closed his eyes for a couple seconds and then gave Mitch a little nod as if to say, "Work with me here," but he said nothing.

Mitch interlocked his fingers and turned his palms up with thumbs out. *What now?*

"Okay, Mitch, lead us."

Mitch could feel the burning sensation work its way from his temples into his cheeks. "Ummm, err. Okay, we should uh..." Everyone was staring at him—some commiserating, some smirking. Porter was one of the smirkers, but he also appeared somewhat worried like maybe this was going a little too far. He continued.

"Come on," Porter said. "Lead us forth."

Mitch folded his arms clumsily, trying to appear confident, but he couldn't find the right place to tuck in his hands. He felt sweat under the hair on his forehead, and he wiped it with his wrist. "Uh, we need to make a list of tasks to complete and a list of jobs for everybody to do and—"

"Who's we? You're the leader," Fat Freak sounded bored. "We don't need lists. Leaders make things happen. Come on, lead. *Lead*."

Mitch shrugged his shoulders. It was becoming too much now, and something had to happen, or he'd have to get out of here. His face was purple hot. He scanned the room. Kylii was whispering to the girl behind her. She was seeing how completely useless he was. Leslie Gallagher mercifully offered a suggestion about matching tasks to people's natural skills, and Mitch started to diagram boxes to write names in.

"You're stalling, Mr. Chairman of the Board. That's not leadership, that's Pictionary," Porter said.

Mitch put down the chalk and began to walk back to his desk.

Porter said, "Hold it, Winston Churchill, you're not done."

Mitch imagined walking over to him and driving his fist into his gelatinous face again and again, feeling the warm blood and loving it and students leaping from their desks and scurrying all over and some guys grabbing him and trying to hold him on the floor but it's nothing to get them off and then pushing Porter's desk over onto him, pinning him, and his chubby legs are bent at the knees kicking in desperation like he's pedaling a bicycle, and he's squeaking in a little voice, "Get me out. I'm sorry. Get me out."

What actually happened was that Mitch walked into the hall and down the stairs and into the fresh, moving air. He heard McAllister's voice yell after him, but he kept walking fast along the alley behind the gym and then onto the footbridge across the creek. Then up the hill. He didn't have anywhere to go, but it was at least away from school and Porter and Kylii and hushed giggles and whispering and sweat and awkwardness.

At the crest of the hill, he looked down, and Larson was trudging his way up the hill about fifty yards behind him. He was wearing gym shorts. As he got closer, Mitch yelled, "What are you doing, Larson?" Larson kept walking.

"PE is over. Got a spare now. Do you want to talk?" he called up.

"I want to be alone. Thanks, but I'm okay, alright? Please, leave me alone."

Larson stopped and stared at him for a second. Then he walked over to a large rock and sat down. He fixed his eyes on Mitch again and then turned and peered down over the valley. "What are you—Go back to school, Larson. I want to be here by myself."

Mitch walked further along the hilltop and, at 2:15 on a Monday afternoon, he sat down on his own rock. He picked up a small pine branch and scraped the dirt with it. K-Y-L-I-I. He stared at the word and then erased it with the clump of needles that clung to the end of the stick. Maybe he could die up here in the hills—sort of shrivel and decay, like a discarded banana peel. What would that be like to just stop being? What if you just didn't wake up one morning? To no longer feel the ache of anxiety and the fury of having your failures studied and jeered at? There was a certain joy in that prospect.

He swept his eyes over the valley, panning across the bone-dry hills and benches of the eastern horizon that baked in the sun. Amara Lake was glass. Twenty feet away, a chipmunk climbed the side of a ponderosa pine tree. Across the valley, a car wound its way up Valley Vista Drive, and a flash of sunlight bounced off its windshield in a pinprick. These and a thousand other little oblivious sparks of life went about their business.

Mitchell closed his eyes. He thought about how he would have to go back and mumble some excuse or apology. He'd have to walk down the hallway at some point and hear whispers about how Frizzy lost his shit in class, went postal, freaked out and ran off. But not right then. He would sit on this rock and make the time pass.

Why does the same cycle repeat over and over? You think today things can be different, but they never are. Never.

He opened his eyes. The chipmunk was standing on its hind legs at his feet.

He spent the rest of the afternoon on that rock, and Larson never moved off his. And when Mitch finally rose and walked back down, skirting him by 20 yards, Larson never said a word. He just followed Mitch down. In a way, that was really the last time he ever walked with Larson.

McAllister never talked to Mitch about that afternoon. No phone call home, no discipline, no acknowledgement of it at all. But from that day on, he left him alone, and Mitch became invisible in his class. He assumed that was as good as it was going to get.

MARCH

Opa is in palliative care. The melanoma that was diagnosed two years ago has shot its metastasizing tendrils around his pancreas. Mitch visits him at least every other day. Today is a Saturday, so Mitch goes to the hospital first thing when visiting hours start. He enters in the customary way—a full-speed march from the hallway to Opa's bedside with enormous, exaggerated strides. Upon arrival at the bed, he comes to attention with feet together and fists on hips.

Opa responds in kind by shutting his eyes and pretending to be asleep. He waits for about ten seconds and then jerks his eyes open at Mitch to startle him, and Mitch laughs. It never gets old. Opa is sitting upright, and the TV is on. On the table beside him is a black device.

"Whoa, Opa? Is that a—" He picks it up and stares at it in wonder.

"Get with the times, Mitch. Smartphone. Your mother forgot it last night."

"You've been tweeting, haven't you?"

"LOL," Opa murmurs.

"Wow, somebody's up-to-date with the lingo."

"I'm full of...surprises."

"You are. Think you can leave it long enough for a short visit? Or do you need to text somebody?" Mitch smiles.

"I only do sexting," Opa says and laughs, the booming bass replaced with a weak chuckle and grimace. *How Opa marvels at his own sense of humour, wallowing in it with a lack of humility. So un-Opa-like.*

Mitchell's laughter begins low, but soon he's breathlessly giggling, and his chuckles are feeding off of the mirth in Opa's eyes. Mitchell feels the tears trickling along his red-hot cheeks, and he bends over and splutters from his nose. He raises his head, certain that Opa is mimicking this sudden outburst like he always does: grabbing his hankie from his pocket and pretending to blow his nose ferociously into it. Instead, he has stopped laughing and is sitting back, his chest rising and falling in pants of fatigue.

Mitch feels his cheeks drain. "Sexting? Clarence Huisman!" he says with a counterfeit reprimand and stands upright.

"You can't call me that. Until I'm gone," Opa says.

"From the looks of it, you'll outlast me." Mitch gives a nervous laugh and stares at the window.

He's very weak. He doesn't want me to see it, but he is. He can see the sign across the street, the one inscribed with five words in black metal lettering in front of a white, two-storey building: *Zenith Centre for Reproductive Health.* He feels a whoosh of heartburn. He can tell that Opa is studying his expression and body language from the side. Nothing is hidden. "So, any new nurses you've got your sights on?" Mitch tries to sound extra cheerful and keeps staring out the window.

"What's wrong, Mitchell?"

"I don't know. Nothing. Heartburn. Why?" Silence. "Things are going fine. Teaching is good and the sun is shining and—"

"Mr. Van Laren. Eyes on me," Opa says. Mitch turns and faces him. *How does he always know?* "What's wrong?"

"We're embarking...starting our fourth cycle soon."

"That isn't nothing." Opa pulls on his own earlobe. "How's Sharelle with it all?"

"She's marching through it. It's hard. On her."

"Not on you?"

"That doesn't matter. It is what it is," Mitch says.

"Bullshit. How is he doing with all this? My Mitchell?" Opa motions for Mitch to sit down on the chair next to his headboard, which he does. Mitch puts a hand on the bedrail.

"Your Mitchell is trying to figure out why this is happening. For instance, why there are monsters roaming the earth breeding like rabbits and then ignoring or abusing or defiling their offspring while my wife and I parade back and forth to the doctor's office, begging God to throw us a bone. One bone. One."

"A child's not a bone. It's sacred. A sacred thing."

"Yes, that's not what I mean."

"I know, but I'm reminding you." Opa folds his hands together and leans his chin against them, like he's praying with his eyes open. "You are thoughtful, Mitch. Sensitive. You process everything, and you feel deeply. I love that. Makes you the biggest man I know. You must never stop," he says.

"I think I'm hypersensitive. It sucks. Things bug me more than they should."

Opa's thumbs stroke the stubble under his chin. "Your heart will break a lot in this life. Sometimes you have to let it because there's nothing else you can do. Hold your arms out and let the pain sear you, Mitch. That's where the gift is. The wisdom."

"We want to have a child, Opa," Mitch whispers the word *child* like it's an obscenity. "Is that such an outrageous request?" He takes his hand off the bedrail and sags in his seat.

"No. It's a natural desire. I don't know why you can't have a baby."

"Can't you throw me some bumper sticker platitudes, then? Like, 'Count your blessings?'"

"You know me better than that. No bones thrown here."

"Mysteries, eh?"

"Mysteries. So many...mysteries." Opa's voice trails off, and he studies the curtain beside his bed. "Today the doctor said it usually doesn't spread to the pancreas. Usually lymph nodes, liver, brain. I'm a special case."

"You can't do things the standard way, can you? Oppositional defiance disorder. Pure and simple. I've seen it before."

"Only goes to the pancreas two percent of the time. I feel very privileged," Opa says.

"I don't think any statistics apply to you anyway, Opa. "You've already kicked the shit out of liver cancer and melanoma. You're just working your way down the list." Mitch punches his palm three times.

"Do you know what the survival rate for liver cancer was in 1979, Mitch? Eighteen percent. I dodged that bullet, but this one's a little different." Opa slowly nods his head.

"Nope. It'll be history in no time. Boom. Done."

"I'm tired, Mitch. Heart's been pumping for eighty-six years, without a break of any kind. I want to slide into some new skin and bones."

"For the record, I am strenuously not in favour of that option."

"I want to hop into a shiny new pickup and hit the road. It won't be that old GMC either."

Mitch clears his throat. "You are not hitting the road. We need you here."

"You're all busy with your own lives. Why do you need an old stubborn Dutchman around?" He closes his eyes and blows a long breath through his nose, his arms folded on his chest.

"Merely for cosmetic reasons. You're my only proof to Sharelle that there's eye candy in our gene pool. Oh, *and* we'd miss you."

"Oh good, I thought it was for superficial purposes." Opa smiles and takes another long breath. Then he opens his eyes and frowns. "I see you cut your hair short again."

"Keeping the curls at bay."

"You and those bloody curls! The ladies love them, you know."

"Sure. The women were always beating down my door."

"They *were* actually. You were just too busy inside your own head to notice."

"So you've said. But curls just don't work for me." Mitch rakes a hand roughly through his hair.

"Mitchell, tell your brother to visit me sometime. I want to talk to him," Opa says.

"I will."

"I need to talk to him and iron something out. It's important, Mitch. Make sure."

"Got it, Opa. I'll make sure. I'd better let you get back to your sexting," he says. A corner of Opa's mouth curls weakly into a half smile. "I'll see you soon." Mitch stands and pushes the chair sideways, sending it sliding on its casters into the closet with a thump.

"Two things before you go. One, thanks for trashing my closet," Opa says.

"This room was already trashed. You're a freaking maniac," Mitch says.

"Two, most people don't get what these in vitro cycles are all about. They don't get the science behind them, and they don't get the hope and grief ping-pong. I, however, do get it."

"Thank you for getting it, Opa. Yes." Mitch takes Opa's hand between his hands. "You're the only one who does." The hand feels almost icy, and he presses his hands tightly together to thaw it.

Hope and grief ping-pong. Yes, ping-pong.

Mitch rubs the top of the hand vigorously. "You used to do this when my hands got cold on our walks. Remember?"

"You refused to wear gloves. 'Confining,' you said."

"Maybe I just wanted you to rub my hands. Now *your* hands are cold."

"I am cold, Mitch. Getting colder."

"I know."

Please, not yet.

"I probably won't warm up anytime soon."

Mitch exposes the top of the hand and kisses it. "We'll see about that, won't we?" He lowers the hand to Opa's lap. "Sweet dreams, stubborn Dutchman."

"Thank you for coming so faithfully, Mitchell. Really. And deep breaths, okay?"

"Deep breaths. Yes." Mitch walks into the hallway and towards the elevator. He presses the "Down" button.

Don't leave me here. You are my oxygen.

Don't drive away without saying goodbye.

The button lights up with a sharp chime.

Down.

It's the next afternoon, and Sharelle and Mitch are meeting Trevor, Megan, and Rachel at the Caulfield Caves, a local tourist attraction comprised of a series of caverns and rocky outcrops amid towering cliffs—a place shaped by heat and pressure over millennia. It's been unusually warm this week: a great excuse to have a picnic and let Rachel run around. She loves exploring in the caves. When they arrive in the parking lot and get out, Rachel runs up to them, and Mitch lifts her and perches her on his shoulders.

"Easy there. Hang on tight, Rachel," Megan says, putting her hands forward like she's ready to catch her fall. Rachel grips Mitch's ears and giggles when he gives a mock screech.

"Rachel, you're hurting Uncle Mitch so bad," Mitch said. "I think you need a clothesliner." He takes her off his shoulders, hangs her upside-down, and swings her around. He flashes a glance at Megan, whose teeth are clenched with apprehension. "It's okay, Megan. I'm a professional," he says, over top of Rachel's deep, guttural laughter. "Now, little parsnip, I'm going to give you a helicop—"

"Let's head to the caves," Sharelle says.

"Let's," says Megan, who locks arms with Sharelle, and they walk up the long trail towards the caves. Trevor takes Rachel's hand and walks behind them, with Mitch taking up the rear. As they cross some stepping stones across a small pond, he notices the way Trevor weaves Rachel's tiny fingers into his.

Mitch wonders if Trevor can even begin to fathom how colossally beautiful the arrival of a child is. Is Rachel simply a product of procreation, or does he see at least some of the awe of this? As Trevor lay underneath Megan (Mitch tries never to imagine the two of them together, but when he does he gleefully likes to think that Trevor is always on the bottom) on their $2000 hypoallergenic, memory-foam mattress and worked away in a uniform rhythm—while probably at the same time mentally debating the relative merits of early-nineteenth-century Romantic poets and then deconstructing Derida's postulation about the internal limits of structuralism—and then ejaculated midway through a conversation with himself about the pre-Raphaelite critics, did he stop to remotely consider that this act carried more weight than simply doing his duty by transmitting genetic material and carrying on his lineage? Did he for one minute think about the monument he was building? In the ease with which they had a child, can he possibly conceive of the cosmic weight of what it really means? How has he viewed each of Mitch and Sharelle's successive and increasingly desperate cycles—with pity? Relief?

Soon, the trail climbs steeply and the view extends across the valley and along the undulating ridges of the clay hills. The only other companions are a squirrel bustling through a pile of pine needles and a woodpecker swooping for ants in the wheatgrass that lines the trail. They turn a corner where the trail plateaus, and there is a clearing underneath some fir trees.

"Time to park it," Megan says, and she and Sharelle lay out a couple of large blankets, and everyone sits down.

Trevor hands Mitch a business card. "Take a gander at this. A little something for your fridge," he says. Mitch studies the card: *Trevor Van Laren, PhD (Candidate).* A little presumptuous, Mitch thinks. A little pompous too. Trevor will be Dr. Trevor soon: A PhD in English. He just has to finish his big project, his dissertation. He says that students like him are called *ABD*s. All But Dissertation.

"How's that *Big But* going anyway, Trev?" Mitch says, after leaning carefully forward and unsuccessfully trying to get Sharelle to sit between his legs. She is so unresponsive lately, in every way. Today, she barely has a thing to say.

"Plodding along. Maybe another six months yet."

"So you got an extension?"

"Yeah, but another grant came through. Plus, I got bumped to the next pay level in my teaching job."

"That's great, Trev," Mitch manages. Of course, he did. Every possible thing he's ever touched has turned to gold. He's always had the girlfriends, the perfect job, all the goodies. Mitch watches Trevor run a hand through his hair and cradle Rachel in his lap. Mitch feels like he's always paddling upriver and Trevor is leisurely floating down, watching him and shaking his head. There he sits—on his raft—perfect little child on his lap. Shaking his head.

"It's like I've told you before. You've just got to keep at it. In everything."

It's that simple, eh? Awesome.

"Hey Mitch, have you visited Opa lately?" Megan asks.

"Yesterday morning. His energy seems to be good."

"So, it's spread to his pancreas, eh?" Trevor says. "Shame."

"Shame? That's your assessment of terminal disease? Shame?" Mitch says. His temples start to throb.

"I don't know what else to say. It *is* a shame. A waste. What do you want me to say?" Trevor says.

"It just seemed not as sincere as it could be."

"Because I'm insincere?"

"Now, boys," Megan says.

"He really wants you to visit him. Can you do that? Soon?" Mitch says.

"Things are crazy for me right now. I'll visit him when I can."

"It's March. The college term is over fairly soon, right?" Mitch asks.

"Yes, but there are lots of loose ends to deal with."

"Mommy, can I climb that rock?" Rachel says, pointing to a three-foot high boulder behind them.

"Sure, Baby," Trevor says.

"I guess, but be careful," Megan says. "I wish she had her bike helmet here."

"Seriously?" Trevor says. "She's fine."

"I think she got her risk-taking side from her father," Megan says. "Go easy, Rachel."

"No, I think she's being three years old," says Trevor.

"No, she's definitely got your genes," Megan says.

Genes. With the waves of the lake white-capping in the distance, Mitch sits back against a rock and thinks about how Opa's blood flows through him and brings oxygen to all the cells in his body and about the journey that Opa's own cells have made through the millennia from Creation to his own formation in the womb to Mom and then passed into him—the DNA stamped in unfathomable complexity with his twinkling sense of humour, love for the smell of sawdust, and pathological desire for blueberry pie. He imagines the roar of Opa's lifeblood as it surges through his giant body, and then pulses through his hands, and metaphorically leaps into Mitch's fingertips, and his thrumming lust for life, raw and pure, and his yearning to care for his children and grandchildren and safeguard them—a yearning that runs through Opa like lava. Mitch imagines his own lifeblood coursing through the arteries, then into the veins, and filling the capillaries of his own child, flesh of his flesh. *Walk with others, Mitch. You'll need someone to walk with you.*

"So, what's your thesis called again? And I like the *candidate* thing. Makes it sound even closer now, yes?" Mitch asks.

"Dissertation."

Mitch murmurs, "Right, your dissertation."

"It's basically about how language can perpetu—promote certain elements, even unintentionally and—"

What's the whole title again?" Mitch says, despite knowing it verbatim.

I'm so glad he didn't use the word 'perpetuate.' I would have died from perplexity.

"I'll tell you what it's about. Again," Trevor says.

"C'mon, give me the working title. I'm not a country bumpkin." Mitch leans forward in anticipation. These are the moments worth living for.

"De-othering the Othered Others: Problematizing the Postcolonial Short Story's Positioning of Marked Body Inhabitants," Megan says.

Did I detect an ever-so-slight sigh at the end?

There is a long pause. Mitch purses his lips together in an ambitious attempt to stifle a smile.

In other words, racism and sexism are bad. What if the bodies of the inhabitants are unmarked? Have they already been de-othered? Where exactly are they on the othered/de-othered continuum? Mitch chews on a thumbnail to disguise the mounting delight at his inner monologue.

"Pretty complex subject matter, man. Ambitious, but you'll get there," Mitch says.

"Six years of my life. I'd better get there," Trevor says.

"So how did you approach such a huge body of literature?" Mitch says.

"He was searching for re-emerging patterns," Megan says.

"Are you citing Chomsky and Frye and all the other usual suspects?" Mitch asks.

"Yes, among many others. Many." Trevor says "Many" a little too loudly. Mitch notices that Trevor's forehead is sweating. This is shaping up to be a fine day indeed.

"If you ever need extra time, you know you can drop off Rachel anytime, right?" Mitch says.

"You totally can. Please do," Sharelle says.

"Thanks, you guys. I know. I just need to buckle down," Trevor says.

"Imagine being done. Getting tenure. Removing the albatross. Any way I can help, let me know," Mitch says.

"Totally. I am soooo ready to not be a student anymore."

And the student will become the teacher, and his students will in turn become teachers. And thus the circle shall remain unbroken, by and by. And so it goes, sayeth Kurt Vonnegut.

"What about you, Mitch? You've talked about grad school," Megan says.

"I'm happy to work with pre-undergraduates at this point. Our cash flow is a little tied up with other things at this point too. Otherwise, I'd love to—"

"Things are chugging along pretty well," Sharelle says. "Hey, you guys realize where we are, right? You two should go thread..." she says and then stops short when Mitch flashes her a clenched-teeth shake of his head.

"That's a great idea. Let's go, Mitch," Trevor says.

Shit.

Threading the needle refers to the squeezing of one's body through a fifteen-inch gap between two rock outcroppings. Tourists can buy a T-shirt at the gift shop below that says, "I threaded the needle." The problem, as Mitch sees it, is not only that he's claustrophobic. It's also that he has put on a good thirty pounds in the past ten years through the steady but rigorous delivery of liquid malt carbohydrates into his blood stream and a fastidious avoidance of physical movement. The result is that he has a bit of a paunch—a "roof over the tool shed" he likes to tell Sharelle. Trevor, by contrast, has pledged his support of Megan in her quest to shed post-birth fat, and they use a commercialized program of counting calories and tracking exercise minutes. Whenever the two families have a meal together, Trevor and Megan discuss the various food and drink items to assess their impact on the daily and weekly calorie allowances. It is annoying enough to bring you to your knees, and to make you open another bottle of pale ale. Sadly, the result is that they're both svelte.

"That's for tourists," Mitch says and casts his eyes over the lake again.

"I'd say that too if I couldn't thread the needle," Trevor says and grins with that slight lift of the chin he often does. Mitchell takes off his baseball hat and rubs his sideburns that are tingling with irritation. He puts the hat back on.

"Let's go," Mitch says, and they walk over to the gap. Trevor goes first, extending his arms and laying them flat against the inside rock while he grinds his body against the rock and through the gap.

"Like butter," he says.

"You ought to at least take that rock for dinner and drinks first. I hope you used protection, perhaps some spermicidal gel," Mitch says.

"Yeah, good one. Your turn," Trevor says.

"No worries," Mitch says and sticks his right foot into the gap. It gets stuck, and he tries to retrieve it. His foot pops out of the shoe, and he stumbles backwards and falls on his ass. He rolls to the side, and his hat falls off.

"A promising start," Trevor says. Mitch yanks his shoe from the gap, puts it back on, and decides to take Trevor's approach by laying his arms flat on the inside rock. He holds his hat in his hand, inhales deeply, and begins sliding his torso through the gap. The grooves of the rock push into his ribs. He feels a sharp pain in his navel from a pointy ridge but keeps sliding slowly through.

His right foot pushes through the gap, but the toe of his left foot gets wedged. He jerks on it, and now he is completely stuck. Panic oozes into his mind. He hears a chuckle from Trevor, and his heart thumps in his ears, his diaphragm paralyzed by the pressure, and now he can hardly breathe. He is stuck and may never move again, and this was a terrible idea, and he has to get out of here now. His right leg can move, so he stretches it forward while turning his left foot slightly sideways and wills his body to follow along, looking ahead to the other side where Trevor's chin is lifted in derision. He sucks in his stomach and slides along, creeping his way along the rimpled contours of the boulder with his jowls puffing in exertion. And then he suddenly finds himself free on the other side. He bends down to pretend to tie his shoe so he can take in some extra breaths to slow his heart. Then he rises, gives Trevor a wink and manufactures a George Jefferson strut back to the blanket. Trevor follows behind.

"Like hydrogenated margarine," Mitch says.

"I've got to hand it to you. You overcame your...handicap and squeezed through. Congratulations," Trevor says.

And that's what it comes down to, doesn't it Trevor? Mitch thinks. To you, I am handicapped Mitchell—cap in hand—squeezing his way through his life.

Why are you worthy of fathering a child and not me?

Trevor sits down beside Sharelle; Mitch beside Megan.

"How was it?" Sharelle asks.

"Wonderful. Haven't had that much fun since my last testicular examination," Mitch says.

Megan laughs.

"Just like a man to be so obsessed with his balls," Sharelle says.

"Mitch is very forthright," Megan says. "I like that."

"Why don't you marry him then," Trevor says and laughs.

"He's taken," Megan says. "Otherwise, I could do a lot worse." She puts her arm around Mitch.

"I know what you mean, Darling," Mitch says and kisses the top of her head. Across the blanket, Sharelle regards him so distantly that he checks behind himself to see if she is looking at something else. He wiggles his eyebrows at her for some sort of recognition, but she continues staring, lost in thought. He reaches forward and holds out a palm to initiate a high five: their customary sign of assurance that they are okay. She slowly reaches forward and gives it a short handshake.

RETRIEVAL

June 1985

Mitchell was fumbling with his locker combination after social studies class, which had been dismissed a little early. Pryce Shanahan would be coming back from his math class any minute, and there was time to grab the books for chemistry and hide in the library until class. In January, Mitch had given Pryce a low grade on a supposedly anonymous group self-evaluation in French class. Ever since, he had bullied Mitch relentlessly. He usually managed to avoid Pryce by carefully planning his trips to the locker.

Mitch couldn't get the lock open the first time, so he slowed down and matched the numbers. 43—25—16. Click. As he popped the lock and opened the door, he heard intentionally heavy footsteps behind him, the stomping of two boots coming to attention, and then blowing on the back of his head. Fear tiptoed its way along his spine and stood coiled in his neck. As Mitch started to turn, he felt the smack of Pryce's hand on his skull. Mitch's forehead thumped into the top shelf of the locker.

He turned and looked down at Pryce's black hiking boots and slowly brought his eyes up along the tangled fur of his bare legs, his jean cut-offs dangling with loose threads, his white *Kokanee Beer* tank top, his flat and pock-marked face, and his eyes—thin red slits, likely from a lunchtime trip to the creek to smoke weed. Mitch didn't want to enrage him further by staring into his eyes, much like you'd avoid staring down a Doberman Pinscher, so he glanced at Pryce's shaved and scabby head covered in a fuzz of new growth. Pryce was chewing on one of his knuckles like a dog gumming a bone. Despite his fear, Mitch tried to place him on the timeline of human evolution he had read about two months previously during his foray into the Volume E of the *World Book Encyclopedia*.

"Hi Frizzy, having a good morning?" Pryce said, pulling his knuckle from his mouth and wiping it dry on his cheek.

Australopithecus Man, likely. Although he lacks the elongated jaw, so maybe Cro-Magnon.

"What you done with your hair?"

He dropped the auxiliary verb: yes, definitely Cro-Magnon.

"What happened to the frizzy lamb hair?" he said. Mitch took out some books randomly, closed the locker, and started to walk away. Pryce put himself in his path. "Where you goin', Frizzy?"

"Chemistry class."

"Chemistry class," he said in a falsetto voice. "You mean, chem class?"

"Chem class," Mitch said. Pryce pushed at his books trying to spill them on the floor. The harder he pushed, the tighter Mitch clutched them. The pressure felt like an outlet for his fear.

"You're pretty tough, eh Frizz? Like a brick wall." Mitch gave a beseeching lift of his eyebrows at Pryce but saw no chance of his relenting. What he did see behind Pryce, however, was Trevor coming around the corner, doing an about-face, and leaving.

"Pryce, I need to go," Mitch said. "Mrs. Kennedy doesn't tolerate tardiness."

"'Tolerate tardiness?' Why do you talk like you have gravel stuck up your ass?" He poked an index finger in Mitch's chest. "Who you think you are, Frizzy? You're worth nothing," Mitch felt his face burn, and then two girls walked by, and one resembled Kylii, but then she turned, and, to his relief, it wasn't her.

Thank you, God. He smiled to them like it was all a joke, but Pryce was really champing at the bit. Kylii would be getting out of math class any minute, and she'd have to walk this way.

"I need to get going. To chem class."

"I'm not sure if I can allow that," Pryce said and planted one of his boots on Mitch's left foot.

Larson's right arm came from nowhere. It reached upwards and delivered a single stabbing-motion punch to the kidney, like he was knocking on a door. Pryce fell to his knees with heaving gasps. He wheezed and coughed, and a string of spit dangled from his bottom lip. "What the living shit?" he spluttered and glared up at Mitch, who assumed he was talking to him.

He braced himself. *Get out of here now. Run.* Mitch turned to watch Larson, who was rocking back and forth on his heels with his right leg forward. His left fist clenched, he stared straight through Pryce. Pryce rose to his feet, then hobbled to his locker and sat in it with his head between his knees. He glowered at Larson. Then he swung his head and slit Mitch's throat with his eyes. Mitch felt no relief or gratitude, only shock and terror.

"Larson, you can't...Pryce, he didn't mean to do that. I didn't tell him to do it."

"No, you didn't tell me to," Larson said in a voice drenched in saliva. He made a whooshing sound and sucked in some spit, then ran his tongue along the front of his teeth and seemed to take a big swallow. "And yes, I did mean to do that."

"What the...holy shit...what kinda...what was that?" Pryce wheezed.

Mitch felt like he was going to pass out. Mechanically, he walked down the hall, around the corner, and into the grade eleven biology class that was still in session. Mr. DeKalb, the teacher, stopped lecturing and said, "Can I help you?" and a few of the kids laughed and he shuffled backwards and continued down the hall. Everything was spiraling. His forehead and temples were awash in sweat. He found the bathroom and waited inside a stall until the bell went. He stayed put. After a while, he carefully made his way through the empty halls back to his locker. He grabbed his books and walked late into chemistry class with a mumbled excuse. Mrs. Kennedy didn't even question him. Her lecture on hydrostatic pressure created white noise that overrode his shuffled footsteps to a desk at the rear of the room.

"The weight of a fluid will cause pressure depending on density, gravitational acceleration, and height of the fluid above measuring point. The higher the fluid the greater the pressure and consider this example of the pressure in a fluid which..."

"The higher the fluid, the greater the pressure." Mitch repeated this in his head like a mantra. The higher the fluid the greater the pressure, the greater the pressure, pressure, pressure. Mrs. Kennedy's voice floated away, and the classroom walls dissolved. Eight years old, standing in the kitchen, your hand inching towards a plate of cookies, when the light from the open front door catches your eye.

Dad and Opa are shaking hands at the door, its hinges squeaking with Opa's foot still over the threshold. Squeak. Squeak. Squeak. Dad pulls away, opens and closes his fingers pinched by Opa's big grip. Open close open close open close, like a crocodile mouth. Opa swings the door open to get his foot out and steps inside, bringing the light with him. The screen door slams shut—*bang!* No more light—and Dad is talking fast, bragging, breathless. He's got big business deals, big ideas.

"I'm on the cusp, Clarence. On the cusp."

Opa clears his throat, a low rumble. Dad chews a thumbnail. You wonder what the dirt tastes like.

"Mitchell, fetch Grandpa a drink."

He loves how you make his instant decaf. Unleaded, he calls it. Start filling kettle.

"No need, Mitch."

Turn off tap.

"Mitchell, do it."

Turn on tap.

"No, Tony. Not thirsty. My daughter here?"

Fill, put kettle on stove anyway. Please stay, Opa. Walk to front hallway.

"Went for groceries with Trevor. If it's not too much trouble, maybe you could give us a quick phone call before you come?"

"Why would I need to? Is she feeling better? Missed her for coffee yesterday. Morning, Mitchell."

Hand reaches out, locks yours inside.

"Morning, Opa."

"Yes, had twenty-four-hour bug." Dad shakes head, eyes down.

"Has lots of those." Dad's lips stretched tight, yellow front teeth, stone eyes. Opa's eyes back and forth along walls. "Seeing a lot less of her."

"Life's busy." Opa's fists behind his back, thumbs tucked inside. Not himself.

Look at me, Opa. Be with me.

"Opa, come see my model airplane. Dad tried to build it with me."

"Love to."

"I got most of the way but couldn't figure out the last four steps."

"Don't show grandpa that mess." Cobra hiss on *mess*.

"Said I'd love to."

Walk to bedroom, Opa's hand around back of your neck. Heat waves of love.

"Here it is. Took me fourteen hours. Dad spent a half hour too."

"At the very end. When it was almost done, I bet," Opa says.

"Kind of," you say.

"Not true," Dad says.

Opa flips the prop. Studies the seams, under the fuselage. "Pure craftsmanship. Fabulous."

Tell him every step. He nods and grins, soft elbow to your stomach.

"Let's build one together soon, Mitch."

Dad's voice from doorway, "It's kind of Mitch's and my thing. So..." Kettle starts whistling. "Just didn't have time to finish the last one."

"Just thought it's something fun I could do with my grandson, if that's alright. I saw a B-52 in the shop window. Let's do it next Sunday, Mitch. You and me."

"Sorry, Clarence. Too expensive."

"My treat."

"Mitchell's busy."

"I am?"

"You'll have chores."

Steam climbing to full roar, at its zenith. Learned about sun's zenith in science class: the highest point.

"What chores do I have to—"

"I said chores." Dad shifts foot to foot in doorway. Sea legs.

"Some other time then. I'd love to build a treehouse sometime too."

"Could we do a birdhouse instead? I'm scared of heights, Opa."

"That's right. I forgot. We'll build a bird mansion then."

He swats your shoulder, turns, and walks to doorway. Dad is tense, moving aside, hands in pockets, eyes darting. Seems afraid of him. Opa twice his size. Your giant Opa.

"Tell Jeany I stopped by." Shrieking kettle.

"Will do, Clarence. Let's fish next Saturday." Holds up left hand in farewell. No ring. Hates rings.

"Okay."

"You'll never outfish me, Clarence. I'm one of the great ones of all time." Screen door rattles shut on "great."

Don't leave me here. Come back. I need you. Don't walk away.

Go back to kitchen. Turn kettle off. Whistle fades to silence. Teacher erasing board until nothing left but black. She turns and stares at you.

"Mitchell, are you with us?" Mrs. Kennedy asks.

"I am with us. With you. Yes," Mitch says. Scattered chuckles.

"Lovely. Welcome back."

Thank you for having me, Mitch thinks of saying. "Sorry," he says.

Don't leave me here. I need you. Don't walk away. Come back.

MARCH

It's Sunday. Mitch is sitting at the kitchen table with the laptop open. Yesterday was payday, so he's paying some bills online. He tries to steel himself every time he does this. The MasterCard bill is $3,500. The invoice tells him that it will take seventeen years and seven months to pay it off if they make the minimum payment each month. He taps in the minimum payment and hits "Confirm" with a soft press of his thumb on the mouse—as if that will somehow make it less real. Mitch can't remember the last time their checking account had a positive balance. They get close to zero on payday and then the parade of automated bill payments pulls them back down into overdraft. The line of credit keeps them going, but it feels like a tightening noose. He figures they can finish this IVF cycle and find a way to do one more cycle. Maybe.

Their in vitro bill for this cycle is $7,300. The drugs are another $2,100. Mom lent them some money for the third round after all their savings were gone, but things are tight for her too. Mitch and Sharelle have agreed that it's time for the absolute last resort: ask her parents for help. Sharelle pleaded with him to be the one to ask. She said that she's incapable of looking into her stepmother's eyes and asking for anything. Norman and Audrey are due here any minute.

As Mitch finishes paying the bills, his in-laws arrive. He considers leaving the laptop open to display their predicament but snaps it shut instead. They're on their way home after three days on Eckhardt

Island and want to stop in and see the rental basement suite that Mitch and Sharelle recently moved into. Mitch has given up trying to understand these people. When they lost the baby, they were the first ones over. Norman took Mitch for a beer and gently drew out his grief, sitting with him and listening. No advice, no pop-psychology clichés like he would have expected. He was just there. Yet any other time he's spent with them, Mitch has ended up feeling like shit. They understand grief but are blind to everything else. Why is death the only loss they understand? Was it about blood—that the death of their grandchild was the death of their own blood? Are they that primal?

Mitch and Sharelle welcome them onto the living room couch, across from where they sit on the love seat. Norman has his arm around Audrey, his hand dangling freely in front of her shoulder. He is short, stocky, and built like a tank. He has great hair for a guy of sixty-eight, and he carries a weird habit of pressing his hands on the line of his part, karate-chopping it, and then smoothing the hair on the sides with his palms. His voice is nasal, almost shrill. As usual, he's wearing a dress shirt. Even when he worked as a cabinet maker, he wore a dress shirt and polyester pants. The same goes for hanging around the house and doing yard work: Button-up shirt and slacks. "Dress for success," he likes to say. Audrey is tall and skinny. Her hair is thin and wispy, her voice deep. When she gets indignant about something, which is often, her bass voice deepens. Her lips are often busy forming tableaus of emotion: puckering to show disapproval, twisting to the side for bewilderment, stretching tight in pleasure or mockery—often both.

"Didn't see much of you last week, Sharelle," Audrey says, puckering.

"Things are tough at the travel agency, Audrey. People are booking everything online, so we have to fight to find new clients."

"I had some dizzy spells from an ear infection."

"Sorry to hear that," Mitch says. "How are you feeling?"

"I'm okay. Now," Audrey clucks at Sharelle. "Heather was a big help to me." Heather is Sharelle's older sister. Three kids, and one on the way. "She even brought over some supper."

"Sharelle's got a full plate at work," Mitch says. Silence. Audrey shifts in her seat. Then she gives Sharelle a slow once-over.

"Wow, Sharelle. Wearing Spandex. That's brave," Audrey says. Her lips are stretched wide and taut.

"Exercising later," Sharelle says, her eyes downward.

Norman asks why they're renting the bottom floor of a house. The market is right. Why aren't they buying?

"Dad, we have other priorities right now." Sharelle's back rises with an extra-deep breath.

"Like traveling through Europe?" Norman asks.

"Like paying for in vitro," Sharelle says.

"Your mother and I went to Europe when we had the money saved and the kids were out of the house. We appreciated it more."

"We went on air miles. We appreciated our trip too," says Sharelle.

"And we didn't come home to a huge credit card bill," Norman says.

"Neither did we," Mitch says.

"Everything's on credit now. Credit cards are modern slavery," Norman says.

"When you manage credit cards, they're perfectly fine," says Sharelle.

"Perfectly fine. Perfectly fine, Mom," Norman says to Audrey. Then he turns to Mitch. "Ever thought about finding a second job in the summer, Mitch? Or do teachers need the whole summer to rest?" Mitch doesn't even bother telling him that he's trying to find summer school teaching work. He needs to find a way to ask them for the loan. Norman undoes the sleeves on his dress shirt and rolls them up.

"Life is expensive. We do the best we can, Norman," Mitch says.

"I'm sure you are doing your best," says Audrey.

"So, yeah, life is expensive and—" Mitch begins.

"Now this in utero thing you've been doing—" Norman says.

"In vitro," Sharelle says.

"I get the basic idea and all, but how does it happen?"

"What do you mean, how does it happen?" Sharelle says.

"How do they get the fertilizing business done?"

"They use drugs to get the body to produce more eggs and then—" Mitch says.

"No, no. How do they get the stuff? Extract the sperm?" he says. Mitch winces.

"Norman!" Audrey says. "That's nothing to talk about." Her lips pucker and then twist.

"What?"

"Dad, it's not important. Why do you have to ask that? Make things awkward? We've talked about this so many times before." Sharelle says.

"I'm only wondering."

"Drop it, Norman." Audrey glares at him with a hand on her hip. Mitch's face is hot. Audrey turns to Sharelle. "You talked to Heather lately? So uncomfortable. Her ankles are swollen like a balloon. See what you're missing, eh?" She chuckles. Sharelle forces a smile. Mitch gives the small of her back a little rub.

"Can I get you a hootchie, Norman?" Mitch says. Norman smiles conspiratorially. Mitch goes to the kitchen and mixes him and Norman one of their usual drinks: two shots of Crown, a splash of ginger ale, two ice cubes. He pours a red wine for Audrey and apple cider for Sharelle. Then he puts on a pot of coffee and walks back with the tray of drinks and puts it on the table between them.

"Mitchell, a man who likes a strong drink is my kind of guy," Norman says. Mitch hates whiskey. He puts a glass in each of the ladies' hands.

"So, they call it a test-tube baby. What's the test tube have to do with it? How do the egg and the sperm get together?" Norman continues.

"Google it, Dad!" Sharelle says.

"Sure, I'll type the word *sperm* into Google. Next thing you know, every pervert and pedophile in the world has my address and phone number. No thanks."

Mitch takes Norman's glass from the tray. "Like I was saying, our last round was pretty expensive. Here's your drink," he says and hands it to Norman. Some of the liquid sloshes over the side and onto his pants.

"Sorry, Norman. I'll get a towel."

"No worries, Mitch. I feel bad for the wasted Crown. By the way, did I tell you about my new drink?"

"No, what is it?"

"You pour a bottle of Heineken in a glass and add Tabasco sauce. It's called, 'a Bloody Shame.'" Mitch laughs and a screech slips from the back of his throat. They all peer at him as he blushes. Sharelle studies the wall.

"However they create a human life in a test tube, I don't get why it's got to cost ten grand a pop. Can't you do it cheaper somewhere else? Like go down to the States or something. It was simpler in our day. We didn't have all those procedures and what-nots."

"So I guess no one had problems having children," Mitch mutters.

"Oh, sure, but they accepted the Lord's plan for them. Those barren couples ended up being excellent aunts and uncles. Some even adopted. Lots of unwanted kids around, especially the Chinese ones. And the blacks. Although, you wouldn't want that...lot of problems. Adopting's not the way to go."

"Not sure what race has to do with it. But we'd never adopt," Sharelle says.

"I don't know if we'd never," Mitch says.

"I do," Sharelle says. "We want our own child. Flesh and blood."

I'm not getting into this, Mitch thinks. Not here, not now.

"A child will always have a bond with their birth mother that an adopted mother can't duplicate. You really must give birth to your own child. Norman's right. Lots of extra trouble otherwise," Audrey says.

Sharelle starts to open her mouth and then stops and turns her glance to her dad—like she wants him to say something. Mitch sees heaviness in Sharelle's eyes like something is pressing on her forehead from the inside, and it instantly makes his eyes feel heavier. *Audrey is a sociopath.*

Norman takes a sip and then swirls the ice cubes in his glass. "Mitch, I'm going to tell you what my father told me. You need to wait on the Lord and let Him decide. You want to make God laugh? Tell Him your plans." Mitch wonders which billboard he got that from.

"I have a plan. Let's show you around our place," Sharelle says. There is no way Mitch is asking them for a loan right now.

Sharelle shows them the bedroom. Audrey likes the plaid pattern in the bedspread. Norman likes the texture of the unfinished dresser. "Natural and rustic," he says. "Cute little place you got here."

They walk to the bathroom. Norman points out that the door doesn't shut properly and asks Mitch for a hammer. A lump of inadequacy is growing in Mitch's throat. He strides into the living room, yanks open the closet, and feels around for the rubber handle of the hammer under the pile of winter scarves that got dumped there in the move. He brings it to Norman, handing it to him claw first. Norman bangs in the door plate and closes the door, and it's fixed. Sharelle seems to be studying her shoelaces, her hands in her front pockets. Do I embarrass her? Mitch wonders. They go into the living room and Norman notices that the footstool is tilting to the side. One of the legs has come loose. Mitch's head buzzes with annoyance.

"I've been meaning to fix it," he says.

"Good thing I came over, huh?" Norman says and smirks.

"Good thing," Mitch says, in a tone meant to convey sarcasm but resulting in an impotent half whisper. Norman gives a little grin, bends over to study the stool, and asks if he has a Robertson screwdriver. Mitch goes to the closet again. *Is a Robertson the square or the star shape? Square.* He pushes around the scant items in his little plastic tool box. There's a pair of pliers that he grabs and squeezes as hard as he can to vent his frustration. He releases it and rummages for the screwdriver. He probably threw it in the closet, and it's buried in there somewhere.

"No luck," Mitch says. "I'll have to take care of it later."

"You need to put tools on your Christmas list," Norman says.

"Yeah, well, I could swear I had it. I was working on a project."

"What kind of project?" Audrey says.

"Putting together some woodworking...panels and..." Mitch searches for a credible answer.

"The coffee must be ready by now. How about it?" Sharelle saves him. She goes to the kitchen and comes back with four cups.

"So, Audrey," Sharelle says. "How was the trip?" Mitch would rather go bankrupt than ask for a loan right now, so he sits back and listens to Audrey's mind-numbing description of friends that they visited on the Island and what their kids are up to now, the authentic Chinese-made plastic trinkets they bought, and the ways in which both commercialism and a permissive "hippie culture" have ruined Eckhardt Island. Norman rumbles in agreement as she speaks.

"Sounds like a trip full of paradoxes," Mitch says to the backdrop of Norman's clinking stir spoon.

"Yes, it was such a lovely time," Audrey says. The coffee is quickly dispatched, and she wants to get home before dark.

Mitch hugs her and gives her a peck on the cheek and then gives Norman a shoulder hug. Sharelle hugs Audrey, and then her dad lifts her off her feet and swings her in a circle. Mitch used to swing her like that. She's not in the mood for this; her rigid body is like a mannequin in his embrace. Why are they so oblivious to her pain? Mitch thinks. It doesn't whisper; it screams, the pain of enduring the cancerous departure of her joyful and softly hilarious mother and the arrival of the antithesis, stepmom Audrey—thrown into her life to belittle and exasperate at the most vulnerable time, hidden behind Norman's blind sense of dutiful husbandry and utter cluelessness about the complexity and disguises of evil, and the paradoxes and mysteries of life that defy Christendom and logic, this father who mocks the life experiences of others but has never spent a minute of his own trying to understand himself and his own brokenness and to even consider that there is life beyond religiosity, that maybe the infinite awe and mystery of God is not something to be buttoned down and mastered. This smug man with his unequivocal categories of people has sat in his easy chair, smoothing down his hair and sniggering at these modern people and their modern ways who don't understand "how simple life really is," oblivious to what is happening in his own home, oblivious to this Audrey whose sadistic genius is knowing the absolute most extinguishing thing to say to a teenage girl and young woman—*my how you've thickened in the thighs; you have your father's appetite; you'll never get a boyfriend if all you do is homework; my summer skirt is too big for me would you like it; older mothers have higher risks of birth defects; stress in your career can't help fertility*—and is surpassed only by her ability to subtly insert its knife edges with surgical precision into her stepdaughter's delicate psyche without detection by anyone else, leaving a hole the shape of a messianic child who will be the redemption to hold in Audrey's face, praising it and devouring it with hugs and kisses and play

Some women just aren't meant to have children, my dear. Maybe you just aren't the mother type.

Mitch walks them to their car and watches them drive off. Then he goes back in. Sharelle is in the kitchen, cleaning out the coffee grinder with a brush. "Don't let them get to you," he says and puts his arms around her waist from behind. She stiffens slightly, reaches down and gives his left hand a couple pats, and then goes back to cleaning. "I didn't have a chance to ask them."

"I know," she says. "Things didn't go the way I hoped."

"There was no way. I couldn't get a word in edgewise," Mitch says.

"There were openings. But you tried, I guess."

"No openings at all," Mitch says. "None."

"Maybe we'll write an email to send to them about it." Sharelle says. "You won't forget about our appointment tomorrow morning, right? The ultrasound?"

"I won't forget," Mitch says. "I already booked a sub to cover my first two classes tomorrow."

Sharelle tightly wraps the grinder's electric cord around the base. "We're ready for another round, right?" she asks, putting the grinder away under the sink.

"Let's do this," Mitch says, putting his hands on her shoulders. She covers his hands with hers, then lifts his hands off and places them at his sides. She turns and hugs him with his arms flat against his body.

"Okay," she says. "Another round."

August 1981

On the day Opa showed the boys the letter, Mitch had hopped on his bike for the twenty-minute ride to his house. It was like so many summer mornings before it, except that this time Trevor came. Mom had insisted; it was his Opa too.

Opa met them on the porch, took them to the pantry, and offered root beers as usual. "Have a beer on me, boys," he said and winked. Then he popped off the bottle caps with his teeth. They took their bottles and sat at the kitchen table. Opa gave them some fresh butter cake from the Dutch bakery and salty black candies called dropjes, potent enough to curl their tongues. Mitch liked to give dropjes to kids at school and watch them spit the candies into a cupped hand, their cheeks aching. In some small measure, that made him feel like a man: he could handle his dropjes.

Their bellies full, they went to Opa's small sitting room. He opened the closet door and pulled out a long, narrow wooden board with four slots in the end. He put it on a tabletop, stood back, and rubbed his thick hands together, nodding at the board. "You are about to learn how to play the best game of all time. A Dutch game, of course," he said. The goal of shoelbak was to slide small wooden disks (about the size of a tobacco tin) into one of the slots. One hundred points was a perfect game, and Opa announced the score after each turn. "Fordy-dree." "Fifty fife!" When one of the discs rolled on top of another, Opa called this a bokje (he-goat), and Mitch blushed at his lewdness. When the first game was done, Opa opened up a false bottom he had made underneath the board. "I used to hide my tobacco from your grandmother. Oma hated the stuff," he said. "But we all do things we're not proud of." That was one of his favourite expressions.

"With the exception of you, Opa," Mitch said.

"Mitchell, everyone does bad things. Your Opa has too. Very bad things," he said.

"Like what? You mean in your youth?"

"Everyone has flaws. I am no better. Trust me."

They played shoelbak for a couple hours until Opa wanted to stop. If he wasn't so tired from his liver cancer treatments, he'd probably play forever because Oma wasn't around to bring some structure and rationality to the day. Her photograph showed a short woman with long, loose gray hair, but she had apparently run a very tight ship. She had died from an aneurysm when Mitch was a baby.

He led them into his sitting room. The boys sat on the couch with Opa across from them in Oma's old armchair, which was upholstered in a floral pattern and was way too small for him. It was funny how high his knees came up. He still wore his wedding band, and he played with it constantly. He'd twirl it clockwise for a few rotations and then change direction, as if he were calibrating it to a specific setting. Opa used few words, but he liked to recite poems and tell stories—tales of the searing hallucinations from rheumatic fever on "The Boat from Holland," of crazed gold prospectors and grizzlies in the Klondike—that sent tingles through the small of Mitch's back. Trevor wasn't really into this.

"Can you do 'The Cremation of Sam McGee'?" Mitch asked. Opa gave a slow nod, reached into a drawer in the coffee table beside him, and pulled out his pipe and bag of tobacco.

As Opa prepared the pipe, Trevor asked, "Is that a good idea since you're doing chemo?"

Opa's eyes flashed from the stem of his pipe to Trevor, who shifted in his seat. "Moderation in all things," Opa said. "It's certainly not hurting. You should see my latest scan." He struck a wooden match, lit the pipe, and gave a few sucks to allow the tobacco to catch. He put the match in a glass ashtray and it slowly extinguished. Sweet velvet smoke rose in curls from a corner of his mouth, and he stared at Trevor until he knew he had his reluctant but full attention. Then he started in. One freckled hand gripped the pipe stem. The other grasped his knee as he began the Robert Service poem, "There are strange things done in the midnight sun by the men who moil for gold" and Mitch inched closer, partly for love of the poem and partly to allow smoke to seep into his nostrils and pores.

Strange tales. He had many. When Opa was done, Mitch said, "Opa, will you ever run out of stories?"

"Stories of good versus evil. Too bad life isn't that simple," Trevor muttered.

"I'm not following," Mitch said.

"People can change. There are reasons why they act a certain way." Trevor stopped when his eyes met Opa's.

"As long as you're listening, I will have a story for you," Opa said.

"Sorry, I want to believe your stories, Opa," Trevor said, rubbing his fingertips with his thumbs—the tell-tale sign that he was anxious.

Opa gave a polite smile and said, "All of them. True," he said.

"They're true alright," Mitch said. He wondered how this could be his brother. What was there to question about their magnificent grandfather?

Why don't you trust him, Trevor?

"There's a different side to every story. I can only tell my side of them," Opa said.

"That's true," Trevor said.

"I like your side of the story, Opa," Mitch said.

"I like your side sooo much," Trevor mocked in his ear.

"That's enough, Trevor. How about getting us some more beers?" Opa said.

Trevor sighed and shuffled off to the pantry. "Root beers," he muttered.

Opa leaned closer to me and spoke in a low voice, "Your brother is very skeptical and rational. That's good. We need that. Always. Just don't lose your love for stories. Your life is a story to pass down."

Trevor returned with their bottles and the opener. "And Mitchell, there are stories I haven't told you. But after I'm gone, they will be a part of who you are."

"What sort of stories?"

"For instance, did you know that your mother is a genius?"

"Details, please," Mitch said.

"See for yourself," Opa said. "Go upstairs to my bedroom and bring down that framed letter hanging on my wall." Mitch ran up to the room, two stairs at a time, and found a simple black 8" x 11" frame above Opa's bed. "No peeking," he heard Opa say, so he lifted the wire hanger from the screw on which it was resting and ran downstairs with the frame.

"What does it say?" Trevor was leaning forward on the couch.

"Yes, read it loudly and clearly. It's a very special thing," Opa said and closed his eyes. He laid his pipe—now extinguished—in the ashtray.

Mitch began: "'May 12, 1966. Attention: Miss Jeanine Huisman. 485 Pembroke—'"

Opa interrupted, "You can skip the address stuff. Just start at 'Dear Miss Huisman.'"

"'Dear Miss Huisman:

It is my very great pleasure to congratulate you on being the recipient of the Francis L. Campagnolo Memorial Scholarship. As you know, this scholarship is only given to one outstanding female candidate in the entire province of BC. This year, based on your academic record, personal interview, and application essay, you were chosen from over 1,200 applications for this scholarship province-wide. Needless to say, you are an exceptional young lady and have stood out from the 'rest of the pack,' as it were. This is no mean feat.

The scholarship amount of $15,000 will be paid directly to the post-secondary institution of your choice, once you have been accepted and enrolled at that institution. We hope that it provides much-deserved support for you as you pursue your academic goals and aspirations.

Again, our sincerest congratulations and best wishes in your future endeavours.

Sincerely,

L. Bernard Colefield, Director

Francis L. Campagnolo Memorial Scholarship Committee.'"

"What does this mean?" Mitch asked.

"It means Mom was really smart," Trevor said.

"It means your mother *is* really smart. She even talked about law school later on," said Opa.

"She never went, and she could have had a free ride," said Trevor.

"She gave it up. To get married and have you right away," Mitch said.

"That sucks," Trevor said.

"Why didn't she want to go to university first and marry and have kids later?" Mitch asked.

"She did want that," Opa said. He pulled a roll of dropjes from his pocket and peeled a long foil strip off of it to get to the core. The strip broke loose from the roll and helicoptered to the floor. He held out the roll to the boys and they each took one. Then Opa sat back, picked up the pipe, and banged it against the inside of the ashtray. He inspected the inside of the pipe and then reached into the tobacco pouch.

Slipping the lip of the pipe in the corner of his mouth, he looked at Trevor and said in a lilt, “Zo gaat het in het leven.” That’s how life goes.

APRIL 2

Hi Sharelle:

It was just so nice to get your Christmas letter a while back.

That in utero stuff! Crazy! Wow, thanks for your honesty and openness.

I'm being super forward here, but I just want you to know that I'm just thinking of you always and praying for you. Life is not complete without children. So I just want to love on you.

"What do you think so far?" Sharelle says, holding her phone at the top and bottom like a scroll. They are standing in front of a pile of clothes that sit on the dryer in the laundry room. Mitch is folding some towels.

"In utero fertilization? I take it she wasn't in the pre-med program."

"Social work. Let's read on. It gets more interesting."

Remember in college we talked about which guys in the dorm would make the most beautiful babies? I remember you saying once that you wanted twins. "Get it done all in one shot," you said.

I just want that for you so much. And I know how you've struggled, how your heart cries out for a child. I just want to hold your heart in my hands.

"Psycho. She wants to rip your heart out and hold it."

"Cut it out. I haven't gotten to the good part yet."

Here's the good news, Sharelle. We know that we will never be given more than what we can bear.

Here's the better news: In a sense, you're already pregnant. It's just that your body isn't ready to accept the gift of a child.

"I'm thrilled that you're in-a-sense pregnant. Congratulations, in a sense."

"Ok, Rebekah is a flake and dramatic. She was a good friend, though."

Let me tell you about Dr. Lyon Muzillo. I personally know three women who got pregnant after his treatments. It's not quackery, I promise. Kind of a mix of holistic medicine, including acupuncture and natural remedies to bring balance to your entire body. It's the most ancient of all practices: like God intended.

Just come to Chamberlain and check it out, Sharelle. Nothing to lose, right?

Say hi to Mitch, k? Blessings to him.

Your old roomie,

Rebekah Finlayson (nee Caswell)

"What do you think of that?" Sharelle asks.

"Not much. I count eight "justs." The lazy adverb of the chronically overearnest."

"Yes. Puke. But there's something about the idea that a woman has to be ready to accept a baby. Maybe there's a baby out there waiting for us, and it just needs me to be ready to be a vehicle, kind of."

"Let's peel back for a second and hold off on the needles. Are you okay, girl? That's a pretty heavy and...insensitive message." Mitch gently takes the phone from her hands and lays it on top of the washer.

"I talk to them sometimes."

"Who?"

"Babies. Sometimes it's a girl and sometimes a boy."

"You mean that you walk over to babies and talk to them. I know. You're terrific with kids." He takes a washcloth and folds it in half.

Sharelle takes her phone from the washer. "No, not like that. I talk to babies that are waiting to be born. They don't even have names. I just imagine them and talk to them. And I dream about them. A lot."

"That is really amazing, Sharelle. I like that. I love your mind."

"It feels like that's what's happening. Like the baby is waiting for me instead of me waiting for a baby."

"That is a totally gorgeous thought," Mitch says. He takes her phone again and slides it into her back pocket. Then he pulls her hands out in front of her with palms up, unfolds the washcloth that's still in his hand, and lays it out flat on her palms. "The idea that you're receiving a baby when the time is right."

"I know, isn't it? Thanks. That's a beautiful gesture." She smiles and folds the cloth in half again, laying it on the pile.

"In that vein, we need to talk about something."

"Yes."

"It came up again when your parents were over."

"Sperm extraction?" She laughs.

"Something more...controversial. No."

"I don't like where this is going. Controversial for whom?"

"You and I."

"I know what you're going to say."

"And?"

"It's not on the table. Don't even say the word."

"Not even as a possible contingency? Something to look into?"

"No." She pulls the phone from her pocket and begins thumbing through it. "Have you been listening to what I just said?"

"Yes. But explain to me why it can't be an option."

"I've heard horror stories. Mostly rejection and heartache."

"I've heard tons of amazing stories. It's an incredible gift for a child; maybe one of the greatest things you can do for someone."

"Tons?" she asks with lips drawn tight.

"Tons."

"I can't explain it."

"There are babies waiting for us. Even if they've been born already, they're waiting. Come on, I'll show you a site with amazing stories about families who did it."

"I'm not in a place to even look into it, okay. Please Mitchell, can we not talk about it?"

"Of course. We can table it. We both need to be on board."

"It's not something I can be on board with Mitchell. I'm sorry. And we need to focus right now on one thing: in vitro. Talking about this is like talking about radiation therapy before you even have cancer."

"You're comparing this option to cancer?" His voice starts to rise, but he whispers the word "cancer."

"You know what I mean," she says.

"So we can seriously consider a guy who uses needles and rosemary as a fertility treatment, but you won't talk about real alternatives."

"It's not that simple."

"You wouldn't have to sit in a harness and push for eighteen hours."

"I'd be thrilled to have that opportunity."

"Yes. In any event, if you're likening this to cancer, then I guess the discussion is over."

"I'm sorry. I think it is over." Sharelle holds the phone in front of Mitch, showing him Rebekah's email. "There's something mysterious about why things haven't been working."

Mitch picks up the stack of laundry. "I want to understand your aversion to adopting. I know it's a huge shift, girl."

"You do understand me, Mitch. I just can't explain this. Let's please not go here right now, okay?"

"I will never go anywhere you don't want to go. But I am asking that you be open to the possibility," Mitch says and walks to the door.

Silently, Sharelle flips her thumb across the surface of the phone.

APRIL 3

Mitch and Sharelle are in Dr. Williamson's office. Williamson wants to see an ultrasound before they do another cycle. He's forty-five minutes behind schedule, and they sit waiting to go in. Mitch reminds Sharelle that today's procedure is nothing too intrusive, and she shrinks him with her eyes. Not in the half-winking, quit-screwing-around way she used to, but detached. Almost bored. Her eyes seem to have changed with each cycle, shining like liquid opals when she talked about having a family, going to play groups, and hanging out at Megan's place during naptimes. She had winked at him that first time at the doctor, the whole left side of her face scrunching up. She was such a bad winker, but it was so cute. Her eyes now look withered and, with each failed cycle, the skin underneath them grows more sallow like week-old bruises. "We're building a life story, you and me," she told Mitch after their first unsuccessful attempt. "We're in this story together and we'll get through it." She doesn't talk like that anymore.

Clinics usually try to appease men in offices like this with three-year-old copies of *Sports Illustrated* but there is only *Cosmopolitan* to thumb through. An article, "25 Positions That'll Make Him Crazy," catches Mitch's eye, but it bores him with its lack of specificity. Lots of people are waiting for all kinds of scans and scopes and probes here, including two ladies sitting directly across from them. They both have swollen bellies and are talking loudly. One is tall and slim, and her neck stiffens when she talks, the sinews tight like guitar strings. A body like a chopstick.

How can she ever pop a baby out of that?

"I was already five centimeters dilated, and the doctor said we should induce. I could've gone a lot farther but he made the call," she says.

The other woman has long, straight red hair tied back in a ponytail and a fake crystal amulet that she keeps buffing with her thumbs and that hangs much too long on her neck—the spawn of a torrid love affair between Ozzy Osbourne and a thirty-year-old Anne of Green Gables, Mitch thinks. "On my third one, my water broke and, within an hour, I was fully dilated. I mean, fully." Both ladies laugh knowingly. "So the labour went three hours start to finish."

Sharelle is studying her nails with the fingers curled in towards her—the same gesture she makes when distracting herself from crying in front of him at cheesy movies. Mitch runs his index finger back and forth along Sharelle's wrist, tracing the natural horizontal lines in her skin. She gently pulls her arm away and grabs a brochure on mastitis. Her gesture gives him a dull ache in his stomach.

Chopstick leans in closer to her friend and says in a low but very audible whisper, "Heath and Gina are starting AI soon."

"Figures he'd be shooting blanks," the Buffer says.

"She's no spring chicken, though. Almost thirty-five."

"What's with that? Let me guess, she wanted a career first."

"I think it was more him than her," says Chopper.

"The chickens have come home to roost." The Buffer lets out a big yawn. "Play games with Nature and see who wins. Every time. Every freaking time."

"I don't know, maybe they were trying for a while. We don't know the details. Just saying," says Chopper.

"Trust me. Gina's a career woman all the way. Buy now; pay later. That's how she operates. Now she can pay the piper. Watch, they'll end up doing in vitro and the whole shootin' match. Cha-ching." The

Buffer licks the tip of an index finger, taps the air, and makes a sizzling sound. "See ya. Sucks to be her." She laughs and Chopper gives a fake little laugh too. She wants the Buffer's approval, like they're in junior high. Pathetic.

Mitch watches these very fertile ladies as their mouths move like two telemarketers reciting a sales pitch. He silently wishes them both forty hours of agonizing labour, followed by a last-minute C-section. He asks the Buffer for the time in order to provide a reprieve from their conversation, and she glances at the clock on the wall above her and says it's 2:40 without missing a beat and then segues into breach births and epidurals. Finally, Mitch and Sharelle are called in.

The appointment is surprisingly short. Sharelle's ultrasound appears positive, so they get the go-ahead for another in vitro round.

Ten days later, Mitch and Sharelle are at Brendan and Barbara's place for a party. They're a pleasant-enough couple who they maintain a tenuous friendship with—tenuous in the sense that Sharelle and Barbara were BFFs in high school, and Brendan and Mitch are their husbands. They have three cute, designer kids—Benjamin, Belinda, Brian: they apparently liked the alliteration of that. Brendan says he's a self-made man. He started the *Thirsty Esquire*, a "sampling lounge" where the bourgeoisie can nibble on imported cheeses and artisan breads while sipping obscure wines. It took off and he sold the business within three years, making an absurdly large amount of money. They've got a big post-and-beam log house with a wide driveway, which is full of minivans and SUVs when Mitch and Sharelle show up at 8:00. They know most of the people, but there are a few new ones that Barbara has recently collected. They ring the bell and no one comes to the door, so they let themselves into the foyer. They're faced head-on with a large portrait of the family posed in a pyramid—Brendan, Barbara, and Benjamin on the bottom, Belinda and Brian perched on top. Their laser-whitened smiles are straight out of a toothpaste commercial. They're all wearing jeans, the males with blue collared shirts and the females with yellow.

"How precious," Mitch says.

"It's a little much," Sharelle says, "but I'd love to get a professional portrait of us done sometime."

"Cha-ching," Mitch says.

"We'd have it for the rest of our lives. Not everything's about money."

"Really? I thought it was," Mitch says.

"Whatever."

"Whatev—forget it."

Barbara comes in and greets them with a soulless, department store, "Have a nice day" smile. She leads them into the living room, where most of the others are sitting. They find a spot on a couch and make small talk with another couple on the love seat. Mitch opens a can of root beer and Sharelle does a double-take to make sure that it's not a beer. Alcohol is apparently toxic to sperm. *Everything in moderation.* He could sure use a couple beers to help him relax among all these extroverts.

At 9:00, he gets the nod from Sharelle, and it's time to inject her with the medication. This is their last injection. Egg retrieval is tomorrow.

Sharelle walks to her purse in the kitchen and grabs the vinyl carrying case full of vials, syringes, and alcohol pads. Mitch gets up off the couch and walks with her down the hallway. On the wall opposite the bathroom is a portrait of a man and woman in an Italian courtyard. The man holds his coat over his shoulder with an index finger, and his other hand grasps his lover's neck. Their lips are an inch apart. Mitch turns and opens the bathroom door. Sharelle comes in right behind him, and they lock the door. The walls are painted in taupe and dark green. Earth tones. But they are two clinicians performing a scientific procedure. In a bathroom. A toilet.

Mitch begins mixing one vial of saline with the Repronex powder and draws it into the syringe, but he can only get two-thirds of it and now there are bubbles in the syringe solution. He injects it back into the same vial and there are even more bubbles. They're now fifteen minutes late with the medication, and Sharelle is getting nervous because she thinks the timing has to be precisely right, which he doesn't think is true. They've argued about that so many times. He tries mixing it again and the same thing happens. He flicks his middle finger against the syringe a little too roughly, and it slips from his fingers and falls into the toilet. He retrieves and throws it in the garbage can. Sharelle doesn't say anything, but Mitch can hear the rush of breath that she sends through clenched teeth when she's about to go apoplectic. He doesn't even want to see the expression on her face right now—an impatient fury that makes him feel useless. He starts again.

The next mixture attempt only has a few bubbles, and he taps the syringe a couple times to pop them out. Finally, it's ready and he swabs the site on her butt with an alcohol pad and then pokes in the syringe like a dart and peels on a bandage. They clean up all the vials and little pieces of wrapper and put it all in the case and then head back to the living room.

"Were you guys in the bathroom together?" Barbara asks, and people laugh.

"This isn't that kind of party," Brendan says.

"At least take her on a date first," some guy calls out.

"Don't we all have to put our keys in a jar for starters?" asks Barbara, and there are a couple of titters.

Mitch says, "Oh, Sharelle wanted me again," with a lurid roll of his eyes.

"Yup, a woman has needs." Sharelle tries to sound cheerfully lewd.

"Too bad it only lasted for ten seconds, eh Sharelle?" Brendan says.

Hey Brendan with a B, why don't you go dab some Camembert on a lovely slice of pumpernickel? Mitch thinks. "You'd be surprised how long," he mumbles.

"You mean it was less than ten?"

Mitch's fist would fit nicely between Brendan's dimples.

For the next two hours, Mitch finds himself trapped in the living room in various conversations that include topics like granite countertops, mutual funds, and time-shares. He doesn't feel like staying very late, so at 10:00 he catches Sharelle's eye and motions to the front door. She gives him a confused frown and walks to the kitchen. He follows her there, and she's pouring herself a glass of iced tea.

"I guess we're not going," he says, and she shrugs.

"Just a bit longer, okay?" she says and walks back to the living room without waiting for an answer.

Mitch takes a bottle of oatmeal stout from the fridge and walks to the garage to hang out with the smokers. He makes himself invisible by sitting slightly back from the rest of the circle. Around 10:30, Sharelle peeks her head in and motions that it's time to go.

Sharelle drives. He could have driven, but it's not worth getting into.

"You ever heard of second-hand smoke?" she says.

"No. Never."

"How many beers did you have?"

"Twenty-three. Thanks for the trust."

"How long were you in there?" she asks.

"Only a little while. I got tired of the living room. Why'd you act confused when I motioned that I wanted to go?" he asks.

"When?"

"Before I talked to you in the kitchen. Actually, there were a number of good opportunities to leave earlier. All through the night."

"All through the night?" she says.

"So, were you pretending not to understand?"

"Yeah, Mitch. I wanted to act stupid and confused. Because that's how I roll."

"You knew we were both tired and didn't want to be up too late."

"We agreed to be gone by eleven. I didn't realize it was your bedtime. What are you, five years old?" she says.

"Fuck's your problem?"

Sharelle blinks as she stares at the road, her head cocked slightly towards him.

"Excuse me?" she says.

"You heard what I said."

"Since when do we call each other names?"

"I didn't call you a fucking name. I asked you what your problem was," Mitch says.

"Absolutely nothing. Everything's awesome. Couldn't be better."

"That's fucking great."

"FUCKING FUCKING FUCKING FUCK." Her front teeth bite her bottom lip as she hurls each word into the windshield. Mitch leans his elbow against the side window and rests his temple on his fist. He feels queasy. They drive the rest of the way in silence.

When they walk into their front hallway, Mitch says, "I'm going to stay up and watch the news."

"Because you're so tired and don't want to be up late," she says, walking to the bedroom.

"We could use a bit of time and space tonight. Big day tomorrow," he says.

"As you wish," she says. She stops at the bedroom door. "Thanks for a terrific night," she trills in a false sing-song voice, staring at the door.

"No, thank you. It was completely awe-inspiring." He walks to the living room and turns on the TV. He feels a pang of shame for his sarcasm and hostility. *Fuck's your problem?* He imagines her teeth biting her lip as she throws her disdain at the windshield. To quell his expanding regret, he focuses on that frown at the party: Eyebrows lowered at him, lips pursed. *I didn't realize it was your bedtime. Thanks. A terrific night. Terrific.* He lets her words feed his bitterness until it balloons into something large enough to overpower the urge to go to her in the bedroom.

He turns off the TV, unfolds an old British Airways blanket from inside the ottoman, and pulls it over his shoulders. Then he lies down on the couch.

I didn't realize it was your bedtime. What are you, five years old? No, Sharelle, I'm not five years old, he thinks. I'm not a kid. I get it, and I'm hurting just as much as you are.

As he's dozing off, he hears the bedroom door creak open. He sits up and listens to her footsteps in the darkness and decides to walk to the kitchen and meet her halfway. As Mitch removes the blanket to get off the couch, a light turns on and the bathroom door closes. He lies back down and hears the surging spit of the shower head.

How did we get from there to here?

What are you? Five years old?

"We were both wound up about today. I apologize for ignoring that you wanted to leave the party early," Sharelle says the next morning, without taking her eyes from the newspaper.

"Accepted," he calls out from the kitchen counter. "I acted like a child with the beer and hiding in the garage. I apologize too." He takes his bowl of Cheerios and sits at the table across from her.

"Accepted. 'Accepted,'" she mimics. "Sheesh, we sound so mechanical."

Mitch lifts the bowl and tips the leftover milk into his mouth, nudging the remaining pieces of cereal into his mouth with his upper lip.

"I know. Everything about our lives seems mechanical and clinical these days. Toast?" he says.

"Not supposed to eat or drink for eight hours before. I can't."

"Right. Sorry."

Last night seems unimportant, probably because today is egg retrieval. The simplest description of it is that Sharelle's eggs will be harvested, each one injected with Mitch's sperm in a Petri dish, and then prepared for incubation. The complexity and coldness of the clinical jargon is not lost on Mitchell. This in vitro lexicon wouldn't sound out of place on a chicken farm: eggs, harvesting, embryos, incubation, fertilization.

But it is the reality. If Mitch and Sharelle ever hope to create their own child, it won't happen as result of their bodies and souls coming together: where they sink into each other and he is welcomed into her essence completely, where the convergence of love and pleasure begets new love and life.

That possibility has vanished. So today they will harvest. That is how it will be.

They will be harvested, and they will wait.

APRIL 17

Mitch begins his hospital-room speed march earlier this time, about ten feet before he gets to the door, in order to have maximum momentum and velocity when he enters the room. When he gets to Opa's bedside, he waits for his eyes to jerk open at him. He counts to ten, then twenty, then thirty. Nothing. He puts a tentative fingertip on Opa's arm.

What if he doesn't respond?

Opa stirs and his eyes flutter open. Then they close again.

It is overcast inside Opa's hospital room—like being inside a tent on a muggy day. Mitch watches Opa sleep, the lips parting slightly and the cheeks twitching with the intake of each breath. The bushiness of Opa's eyebrows makes Mitch smile. This is what Santa Claus looks like without his red hat and beard. Bushy white eyebrows. Yes, Old Saint Nick.

The clock numbers start with 9, so that's really late. You want to hear Santa come down the chimney. Mommy and Daddy said he'd come about midnight, but that's so late for five-year-olds. You left milk and cookies and Cheerios for the reindeer. There's a noise downstairs. Santa's here! Crawl out of bed and walk to Trevor's room.

"Trevor, I hear Santa," you say. Tap him on the shoulder.

"Go back to bed. There's no Santa."

"I hear him."

"Santa is make-believe."

"He's here. I'm going to say hi to him."

"Good night. He's pretend. Like the yeti."

"What's a yeti?"

"Good night."

Downstairs on your tiptoes. Sneaky walking into the living room to the chimney. Milk and cookies are still there. You see the kitchen light on and hear mean whispers. Walk down the hall. Open the door and peek inside. Chair upside-down. Grown-up red juice spilled. Broken glass.

Mommy sitting in the corner with hands over her face like peekaboo. Daddy standing over her and pointing a finger in her face. Hissing: F-words and S-words you're not supposed to say. Open the door all the way. Walk over to him. Pull on his pant leg. He jumps a little bit and sees you. He folds his hands like praying time.

"Oh, Mitchell, you're up," he says.

"Why are you sitting in the corner, Mommy? Do you have a timeout?"

"Mitchell, why aren't you sleeping?" He talks gentle and pats your head. "Mommy has a pretend timeout. Mommy and Daddy are just playing and doing funny things. We do that on Christmas Eve."

"Opa says we shouldn't say swears and bad things, even if we don't mean them," you say.

"Your grandfather is right. I forgot. You don't need to tell Grandpa about our pretend game, okay?"

Mommy pulls her hands away from her face. Her eyes are puffy. She gets up and winks at you and has a funny smile. Daddy walks to the sink. He splashes water on his face. Mommy comes to you and sits on her knees.

"Why did you wake up, Honey?"

"I thought I heard Santa. Mommy, I'm thirsty."

"Come over to the sink, little buddy. I'll give you some water," Daddy says. He comes over and takes your hand and walks you to the sink. He pours a cup of water half full.

"Time to go back to bed, Mitchell. When you wake up, it'll be Christmas," Mommy says.

"Is Santa still coming?"

Now Daddy sits on his knees next to you. "Santa is coming. I promise he'll be here like every year. Now go back to bed. Be a big boy."

"Come on, Mitchell. I'll put you to bed and snuggle with you," Mommy says.

"Can Daddy come too?"

"You go with your mother now, buddy. No telling Grandpa, right? Big guys keep secrets." You move your head up and down. You suck your thumb and Mommy carries you on her shoulder. You put your head in her neck. She takes you upstairs to bed. She sits on her knees again on your bed and brushes your hair with her hand. Close your eyes.

"Good night, Mitchell."

"Goodnight, Mommy."

"Mommy loves you and will always take care of you." You make your head go up and down again slowly on your pillow, and she moves her thumb on your wrist. "Mommy will be here in the morning. She'll be your angel. Always here. Sleep tight, Mitchell."

She's your angel. Always.

Opa's eyelids flutter again, and Mitch strokes his forearm. "Good morning, Sunshine," Mitch says.

"Hey, Big...Boy." Opa's voice is hushed and raspy.

"Power napping for an all-night kegger?"

"Cat nap."

"How you feeling?" Mitch runs a hand along the bony spine of Opa's forearm.

"Rough."

"I'm sorry."

"Me too." Opa closes his eyes. "Sucks," he says, drawing the word out slowly. Then he opens his left eye and adds, "As they say."

"As it were."

"Yeah."

"Are you uncomfortable, Opa?"

"My comfort...is not...important."

"Should I ask them to give you more pain medication?"

"No."

"Another pillow?"

"No. Nothing. Just you."

"You don't need me, Opa. You just need your second wind."

"It's you...that doesn't...need me...anymore."

"I'll always need you."

"Why?"

"Because I do."

"No. Why?" His right eye opens now.

"Because I need you here to tell me it's okay," Mitch says. "That everything will be okay in the end." Mitch and his thoughts bleed imagery: I need you to put a dropje into my hand and let it scorch my cheeks with saltiness, let my eyes stream with water from the salt. I want my giant grandfather back. Shake my hand up and down in an arc so hard that the torque snaps my arm in half. Then rip that broken arm from its socket with your shaking. Make me laugh so deeply I can't breathe. Squash me with your hug, boom your laughter so loud it crushes my eardrums. Don't drive away in your truck and leave me chasing after you, my fingertips clawing at the tailgate so that I can be with you a little longer. Stay here and hold my hand.

"Everything...will be ok...Big Boy," Opa says with a hushed sigh from deep within. He lightly massages his own wrist where his watch should be.

"I'm not ready to say goodbye," Mitch says. Deep, hollow pockets underline Opa's eyes, which seem to pulsate. Opa clasps Mitch's hands in his and holds them. Mitch gnaws on the inside of his cheek.

"You have people...who love you here."

"That's true."

"That woman you married...would drop everything for you."

"Yeah, I guess."

Opa gives a feeble squeeze of Mitch's hands and grimaces with the effort. "Make her grateful. Every day."

"That's what you did with Oma, didn't you?"

"I tried."

I won't disappoint you," Mitch says.

"Plant your feet...on the ground. Claw. Scratch. Fight...for it, Mitch."

"I'm not going anywhere. I promise."

"Dig a hole...in your living room and...stick those size 12 boats of yours into the...hole and fill it in with cement...You make this life work. It's a gift."

"Okay, Opa," Mitch says to the window.

Opa pulls away his left hand and lays it on Mitch's cheek, directing his head back so he's looking at him again. Then he lays the hand back onto Mitch's. "Cement, Mitchell."

"Cement," Mitch says. Opa closes his eyes, and Mitch gently rests Opa's hands on top of each other on his chest. "Has Trevor been around?"

Opa's eyes flash open. "No, tell him to. Please." Opa's left arm strains upwards, and his thumb hooks the lapel of Mitch's shirt. "Tell him, okay?" The arm falls back to Opa's side. "Soon."

"Okay. It's definitely not personal. He's very busy, but he'll come soon. I swear."

"It feels like I might...be changing addresses soon."

"No, you're not going anywhere. The Canucks haven't won the Stanley Cup yet. Plus, we've got a lot more to chat about."

"Like your bed wetting," Opa says. Mitch winds back for a fake punch, and Opa lifts his right hand with a feeble blocking motion. "Finally, you've got me...where you want me, eh? Took forty-six years."

"Get a good sleep. We're getting up at five for Crenshaw."

"I'll need an extra thermos...of coffee."

"You only drink unleaded. What would be the point?"

"Indeed. See you...at five-thirty then."

"Slacker."

"Soppy Shorts."

Mitch starts to walk to the door, but he turns around and returns. "I know men don't do this," he says and cups his hands behind Opa's head. He kisses him on the forehead.

Opa's eyes stay closed and he smiles. "Only the biggest men do," he says.

"Good night, Grandfather."

"Night."

APRIL 18

The embryo replacement is this morning. The most precarious step in the process is the shortest and simplest: The doctor takes a catheter from the lab, inserts it through Sharelle's cervix and into her uterus, transfers the embryos, and then vaginally inserts a progesterone capsule to support the lining of the uterus. Sharelle lies on the table for a few minutes, listening to some soft music under low light. Then very slowly and carefully she gets dressed.

The doctor who does the replacement appears to be in her mid-thirties.

Is she tired?

Is she inexperienced?

Do her hands have the DT shakes?

Does she check that she has the right embryos?

Is she unfocused on her work because of an impending divorce?

Is she infertile herself and jealous of those who aren't and randomly sabotages others' cycles at the most critical juncture in order to enact her revenge so she can feel just a little bit better for a few minutes before she goes home and feels remorse and successfully performs the procedure the next day on another patient thereby allaying any suspicion caused by a spike in failure rates on procedures she's performed?

Piercing through all these paranoid clouds of doubt is this certainty: The only way genesis will happen for Mitchell and Sharelle is if every phase of this man-made circumvention of nature has gone off perfectly, and if it continues to do so. Of course, getting to this replacement stage is not guaranteed for many women, due to factors such as chromosomal abnormalities, degraded embryonic viability, or naturally-elevated levels of pituitary FSH production. They should be grateful that they could get even this far.

Now, the success of this embryo replacement stage depends on the doctor's avoidance of uterine contractility that could lead to unexpected expulsion.

Or it may hinge on whether the embryos become entangled in cervical mucus.

Or the embryos may just end up misplaced in the uterus due to cervical stenosis.

Or utero-cervical angulation.

Or a generalized distortion of the cervical canal.

If this cycle fails, however, the most likely explanation will be much easier for Sharelle and Mitchell to comprehend.

No one will have any fucking idea what went wrong.

APRIL 23

Opa is gone. He died on the morning of their embryo replacement. Mitch had his phone turned off during their procedure and missed the call. It happened quickly, and Mitch didn't get to say goodbye. The previous afternoon, he had the chance. He didn't take it. You only get one chance. By his side, no interruptions, Opa's full attention: The opportunity was there. He failed to seize it. It was the perfect time. It wasn't supposed to end like this. Why did he go? Mitch just needed one more minute. How do you miss that chance to say it? That afternoon before. To tell someone something simple that means everything. That afternoon before the night before the morning. He didn't tell him. What was Mitch's hurry? No kids to take to soccer practice. No pediatrician appointments. Keep strong feelings inside. Deep breaths. That previous afternoon. The last afternoon. Just a kiss. He kissed him. A kiss without the words. The previous, prior afternoon before the end. The preceding afternoon. *Pre-* is a prefix meaning before, *cede* is a root meaning *to lead.* The afternoon came before the morning. It led to the morning. A kiss preceded nothing. Didn't lead to the words, simple words: Goodbye. You are my breath, my oxygen.

At the viewing earlier, Mitch half-expected the sweet smell of tobacco as he filed through the line and approached the casket. Instead of Opa, he found a gaunt, waxy face jutting out of a casing of bones inside nearly the full length of the cherry-wood box—a polished-up caricature out of a vaudeville show. An enormous marionette ready to be outfitted with its horizontal control bar and strings. He wants to close the lid. Stop staring at him, everybody. He's gone. Mitch feels hollow and dry, like somebody slit him down the middle and ladled out his guts.

He's sitting in a pew with Sharelle, Trevor, Megan, Mom, and her brother Joop. Trevor has planned the whole funeral service because it was felt he was artistic and good with words, what with having a PhD (ABD) in English and all. The church is full. Standing room only, in fact. Many words are spoken about Opa's interest in civic politics and his volunteer work at the hospital. No one mentions his sense of humour or the fun he liked to have or his stories and games, or the way he made you feel like you were the only person on earth that mattered. Mitch wishes someone had asked him to speak. He's good with words too.

Afterwards, they drive to the cemetery and the preacher gives a short meditation about the grave being both the most awful and the most joyous place in the universe. He reads the "Yea, though I walk through the valley of the shadow of death" passage, and then everyone takes turns pouring a handful of dirt on the coffin. It is planned that the final act will be Trevor and Mitch each pouring their dirt. They walk up. Trevor dumps his handful on in one shot, but Mitch lets his run through his fingers onto the coffin. He feels like he's betraying Opa because he can't make any tears come. He takes a brand-new roll of dropjes from his pocket and sets it on the coffin. He turns and walks back to the others with Trevor behind.

Finally, Mom walks up and places a single yellow rose on the coffin to say the final goodbye.

They stand by the grave for a few minutes, and then people start to disperse. Trevor gives Sharelle and Mitch an awkward hug. Megan's hug is firm and lingering. The four stand next to each other for a few more seconds and then Trevor shuffles off, hands in his pockets. Megan reaches around and rubs Mitch's back, smiles at him, and then follows Trevor to their car. Sharelle links her right arm with Mitch's left, as he stares at the mounds of dirt on the coffin. "I'm here, okay? I'm right beside you," she says. "Can I walk with you through this?'

Mitch bends down and kisses her arm. "Yes. Always."

After the burial, they are in a church basement where refreshments and cake are served and people are saying things like, "He has been called home," and "What a servant he was." Sharelle helps by serving tea. Mitch makes his rounds, saying hi to distant relatives and tolerating the small talk. He wants to be alone.

Opa won't be striding into the yard anymore. His shoelbak disks will remain stacked inside their compartment, and the dates on his calendar will be clear. Mitch knew this day was coming, but he still thinks that if he drives over to the little house by the creek, Opa will greet him on the porch and give him a root beer. "Allo, Mitchell," he'll say. "Have a beer. On me."

Yes, Mitch wants to be alone. Sharelle gets that, and Opa would too. As Mitch wanders through the basement, he wishes he were invisible. He wants all these people to eat their shitty, synthetic cake and leave him alone.

Here comes Jake Aldenberg from Opa's veterans group. Opa introduced them once, and Mitch has run into him several times in town. Jake is a friendly man—that particular version of friendly that involves exuberant hand-shaking and asking you how you are but excludes any form of sustained listening or full-hearted empathy. A true interrupter-in-waiting.

"Mitch, my condolences. This is a joyous day in a sense, isn't it?" he says, shaking Mitch's hand and then clasping his other hand around it.

"The joy is palpable," Mitch says. *Hilarity and whimsy abound.*

"He's free of all that pain and suffering."

"Okay."

"Your Opa talked about you a lot."

"Thank you." Mitch pastes on a fake half-smile.

"What you up to these days? You got any kids yet?" Jake gives an exaggerated overbite and lifts his shoulders back and forth with his fists clenched, throwing out a couple right jabs—like a boxer warming up in the ring.

"Nope."

"When you gonna get cracking with that?"

"I don't know."

"Time's a wasting, son. You're gonna get left in the dust. Come on into the club, Mitch. The water's fine."

"We're infertile, Jake." *Fuck you if that makes you uncomfortable.* "So we'd love to join the club, but that's looking less and less possible every month. Okay? There you have it."

"Sorry, Mitch. I...uh...Good luck with all that." Jake says to Mitch's feet. Then he retreats to the men's room across from them.

None of you really knew him.

Leave me alone.

APRIL 30

Trevor and Mitch are standing in front of Opa's garage. Mom has asked them to help clean it out. She and her brother Joop and his three daughters will go through everything in the house. Opa kept an immaculate garage, so their job is simply to inventory everything and organize it for removal. The garage has the light musty smell of weed killer. A rake clings to the wall, its forks caked in dried earth, the grooves in its shaft worn smooth. There is a half-full bag of cement and a shiny green electric lawnmower in the corner (bought on "the Craig List" he told Mitch last year). Its cord is wrapped meticulously around the handles and a pair of unused gardening gloves sits on top as if to keep the cord in place. Trevor holds a clipboard and writes as Mitch walks through and calls out items: hacksaw, concrete drill, extension cord, chest freezer. The tools with handles all have their home on a piece of corkboard on the wall, their outlines traced in black permanent marker. Opa was very precise. Mitch calls out each one, and then he sees the shoelbak table.

Very bad things.

"One shoelbak table," he announces.

"How do you spell that?" Trevor asks.

You're the PhD candidate. "S-H-O-E-L-B-A-K."

"Let's wrap this thing up."

"Let's."

Mitch wonders what happened to Trevor's sense of humour. What happened to the fourteen-year-old Trevor who would bring Mitch along to the orchards at the beginning of the summer, leveraging his excellent reputation as a productive cherry picker by insisting that his younger brother be hired along with him, saying, "We're a package deal," and having the amused and impressed boss hand them their ladders and pails for the season?

"So you want to 'wrap this thing up,' do you?" Mitch asks.

"I'd like to get this list done. You?"

"I wouldn't want you to get carpal tunnel syndrome recording the remnants of Opa's life," Mitch says, clenching the wrist and flexing the fingers of his right hand. Trevor sniffs.

Here they stand with a clipboard in Opa's garage, listing his things. Mitch wonders how well this list accounts for Opa's life. Do extension cords and hacksaws summarize him? Is this inventory the story of who Opa was, the legacy he passes on? How about this box here with the old green vest with plaid lining that's stuffed loosely over a collection of accumulated chaos—an old bumper sticker from his war veterans' group, extra shoelbak disks, Ziploc bags of screws and nails, Allen keys, and plastic outlet covers? Is his life defined by such jetsam? Trevor doesn't seem to have a problem recording the minutiae of Opa's life. To him it's only a list. For Mitch, a life is not a list. Is this what it all comes down to in the end?

In the corner against a small bookshelf is Opa's favourite fibreglass fishing rod—stiff enough to handle anything, pliable enough to feel the fight of the fish for the sport of it. And on the top shelf behind it: a notebook. Mitch has forgotten about how Opa kept track of who went on each fishing trip and what they caught. He opens it and finds about fifty entries. For each one, Opa has written the date, who was there, and how many fish were caught. They start in 1978:

July 17, 1978. Me, Tony, 14 rainbows.

Trevor glances at them over Mitch's shoulder. "Cool. Kind of anal, but cool," he says.

"Yup. I want to find my first trip." Mitch flips through them and finds it. *June 28, 1981. Me, Trevor, Mitchell. 21 rainbows, 1 squeaker.*

Mitch remembers that Opa phoned the house the night before. "Is there a grandson there by the name of Mitchell Van Laren?" he said when Mitch answered the phone.

"Hi, Opa."

"Do you have warm clothes, Mitchell? Long underwear and wool socks?"

"Yup. I think so. I'd have to ask Mom. Why?"

"Am I to understand that you turned twelve this year?"

"Yeah. You know that, Opa. You were at my party," Mitch said.

"As you know, I start taking you boys fishing when you turn thirteen. However, your brother insists that you're ready and that he wants you to come. Beginning tomorrow, you will become a fisherman. That is that."

"I can come? Okay! I'll be ready, Opa!" Mitch said. Mom made Trevor go with Opa once a year. What he had once enjoyed, Trevor now said he hated.

The next morning, Opa drove over with his boat and motor at five a.m. and woke them with promises of three-pound rainbow trout and hot chocolate. Mom got up too and cooked the three of them oatmeal while Opa fixed sandwiches piled with roast beef, tomatoes, and mayo. They hopped into the truck by 5:30, fully loaded with their gear. Mom stood on the porch and waved as they backed out of the driveway.

They were out of town in two minutes flat and flew onto empty Highway 46 as it steadily snaked into the mountains for an hour, then turned left onto a gravel highway called Bear Verge Road that rattled their organs for twenty minutes with its washboard surface created by the ruts, and finally crawled for seven kilometers of potholes on the lake-access road—a road passable only by pick-up or four-wheel drive, Opa smugly reminded them.

They got to the lake and soon the boat was gliding through glassy mountain water. Crenshaw was big and shaped like a figure eight, with two roughly thousand-acre sections of water joined by a narrow inlet. Opa called the sections *Alpha* and *Omega.*

"We only fish in Alpha. Always Alpha," he said.

"Why never Omega?" Mitch asked.

"Because our lines will get stuck in the rhubarb," Trevor said.

"Rhubarb?" I asked.

"The seaweed. Opa calls it rhubarb," said Trevor.

"That's right," said Opa. "Omega is full of seaweed. Alpha is where we fish."

"But I see some boats fishing in Omega," Mitch said.

"Foolish. That means more trout for us in Alpha," Opa said.

"Actually, almost all the boats are in Omeg—"

"Mitchell, we will never fish in Omega. Ever. This is how it will be." Opa sounded fierce.

"Okay. I was only wondering why," Mitch said.

"I know, Mitchell," Opa said. He pinched the brim of Mitch's baseball cap and gently twisted it back and forth. Then he reached down and showed him how to tie the fly to the end of the sinking line, wrapping the end of the leader around the line a few times and then tucking it through the loop.

"Most people cast with a flyline, Mitchell," he said. "That's a parlour trick. We troll." He showed Mitch how to release his line, set the hook, and play the trout. Then he told him about The Limit—how they were legally allowed to keep seven fish each.

They threw out their lines and started trolling, the outboard motor puttering against the stillness of a wall of fir trees along the lake's edge. A damp chill from the morning air was reason enough for Opa to open his big silver thermos full of decaf coffee ("Like it or not, we drink coffee when we fish"). They had just begun sipping when the first strike of the day sent Trevor's reel screaming. A fierce rainbow trout in this deep, cold mountain lake was fighting magnificently and then flopping and somersaulting on the floor of the boat, dancing in paradox to Trevor's stoic and mechanical posture. Mitch's head was buzzing: icy water, dancing trout, giant trees. Being with Opa. Being a big guy.

Opa fished too, but he focused on steering the boat and running the clunky outboard motor. It was a beast, an old McCulloch, which must have weighed a hundred pounds. It ran for a while and then conked out. Opa played with the choke and grabbed the cord to restart, grasping the front face of the motor and pulling straight back with the other hand, his forearm muscles rippling. There were a few sputters, and soon the engine was flooded with gas. Opa stopped after a few pulls and rested.

"Doesn't that thing drive you crazy, Opa?" Mitch asked.

"Deep breaths is the trick," he said. "It is important to keep our strong feelings and anger to ourselves. Otherwise, we make others suffer for our lack of discipline. You can endure a lot by breathing deep."

He sat and looked out over the lake, his back rising and falling with each deep breath. After a minute or so, he began pulling again and playing with the choke until the motor finally restarted. "I can never count on this crazy thing. Someday, I'm going to pick it up and throw it in the lake," he muttered. Opa couldn't say his *th*'s, even after fifty years in Canada. *Dis crazy ding.*

Mitch sipped on his bitter coffee and tried to think about the names he'd memorized of lakes in the province that began with the different letters of the alphabet. He had gotten to *H* for Hathaway Lake when the tip of his fishing rod twitched twice and then erupted in a jerking motion.

"Opa, I got something here." Mitch's voice seemed deeper, his shoulders wider.

"Take your time, Mitchell. Don't force it. We have to play him for a while, so he gets tired." Mitch followed Opa's every word. He wanted this one.

The fish got closer to the boat, and it thrashed its tail on the top of the water before submerging again.

"It's time, Mitchell. Bring him in close, and we'll net him."

Mitch obeyed and soon a flash of gold appeared under the surface, and Opa scooped up the fish with the net and pulled it onto the floor of the boat. The fish had a long snout and forked tail, and Mitch knew that this was no trout. Its long mouth held no teeth.

"Mitchell, you've caught your first squeaker. A lot of people call them 'squawfish,' but that's offensive to our native people. It's better to just call them 'squeakers.'" I haven't seen one in a while because they usually don't bite on this kind of fly," Opa said. He ripped the hook from the fish's mouth and threaded it from the net. Then he stood facing the boys and vice-gripped the foot-long fish at waist level in his massive hands.

"You don't have to kill him," Trevor said from the bow.

"Yes, Trevor, I'm afraid I do. He doesn't belong here." Sitting sideways on the middle bench, Mitchell turned and stared at his deep-red face and the throbbing veins in his forehead. Opa's lips pressed hard together and clenched inwards, the lowering of his eyebrows making a furrowed triangle above the bridge of his nose. "He's small, but he'll destroy this lake. He'll choke out every pure thing."

"You can let him live. Just throw him back," Trevor said, fists tight in his lap.

"No."

"It won't make any difference." Trevor stopped, gulping for a breath. "To anything."

"It'll make a difference to the trout fry he devours."

"Please don't do it?" Trevor leaned forward and extended his arms, palms up. "Let the Department of Fisheries take care of things."

"It'll be too late, Trevor," Opa said in a calm voice. "I'm going to do this. And you're going to sit on your bench and keep fishing, okay?"

"You don't like doing this, *do* you?" Trevor said. He stood, with his bottom lip bulging.

"I absolutely *do not* like doing this! Please sit down."

Mitchell jerked in his seat at the sudden ferocity in Opa's voice.

Opa never gets mad.

"What are you going to do with it, Opa?" Mitchell asked in a half whisper.

Trevor sat back again. "He's going to bash its brains out on the edge of the hull," he said softly. "He did it last year too."

"I'm going to make this lake a little cleaner than it was five minutes ago."

"Why?" Mitchell asked.

"This fish is a cancer. It tries to destroy everything because of its selfishness." Mitchell winced at "cancer."

Don't be angry, Opa. Let's fish together.

Opa raised the fish to eye level, a slight tremble in his legs. "Mitch, you boys don't need to watch. Everything will be okay." Mitchell felt a pang of nausea and closed his eyes.

"Then please don't do it this way, Opa," he heard Trevor say. Mitchell opened his eyes and saw Trevor climb forward, pull the knife from the sheath hanging on Opa's belt, and hand it to him. "Please?"

Opa studied Trevor's face and then itched his forehead in the crook of an elbow. He gave a long breath through his nose and took the knife, and then he lowered the fish onto the bench seat and bent over it. His hand held it firm, and with one stroke the blade sliced through the spine and lopped the head off along the gill cover. He tossed the head overboard and then, bloody sinew dangling from the opening, he tossed the carcass into the water. He rinsed the carnage off his hands and the knife in the icy water, sat down, and kept his eyes to the stern. The deep purple hue of his neck was fading. "I'm sorry, Trevor." The fingers of his right hand reached down and absently rubbed the aluminum nameplate riveted to the front of his chain-handled lunch box. *Clarence*, it read.

"Why didn't you want him to?" Mitchell whispered to Trevor. Trevor closed his eyes and turned around to face the bow. Repulsed and electrified, Mitchell sat and tried to swallow.

Opa sheathed his knife.

They continued to fish.

The Limit that day came at 4:00. Trevor pulled in the twenty-first trout, and Opa announced, "Our work here is done. Time to go home." He told them to pull in their lines. Once they were in and the rods stored safely, it was time to clean the fish and put them in freezer bags. Opa showed Mitch how to make a slit along the soft underbelly of the trout and then use his fingers to remove the guts and sinew. A black sludge coated the underside of the spine, so he had to run his thumb along it and rinse with water. Off came the head and then the fish was put into a freezer bag and then inside a black garbage bag. Opa kept a roll of them with the life jackets. Trevor cleaned fifteen and Mitch cleaned six while Opa slowly motored the boat to shore. They threw the heads and guts into the water as they went. When they were done, Mitch sat with his right hand over the edge and let his fingertips ripple and undulate through the surface of the water.

Once on land, they transferred the gear to the truck and put the fish in a cooler. Mitch was tired and sleepy from being outside in the sun all day. "That was a lot of work cleaning up. Couldn't we have done it all when we got home?" he asked.

Opa wrapped a long steel chain around the outboard motor to secure it to the spare tire in the truck bed so the outboard wouldn't get damaged on the rough road. He tied the last link to the rest of the chain with a shiny new padlock and sat down on the tailgate next to Mitch while Trevor finished stowing gear. "Life is messy, and there's no reward without hard work. The world is broken, and we endure times of tribulation. Someday, there will be wholeness again. A new earth. Right here."

Trevor said, "Clean-up time. The Great Tribulation." He added, "Sucks" under his breath and cast a nervous glance at Opa.

"Tribby Time," Mitch said, and Opa seemed to wince at his informality but didn't say anything.

Opa drove the first seven kilometers on the lake access road, with Trevor on the passenger side and Mitch in the middle. When they got to the gravel highway of Bear Verge Road, he pulled over and switched places with Trevor. After allowing Trevor to drive for only about two minutes, Opa told him to pull over.

"Already, Opa? Can't I drive another couple clicks?"

"It's Mitch's turn. Nope, sorry."

"I can't drive, Opa. Mom will have a massive cardiac episode," Mitch said, wriggling with excitement.

"We need to train you, Mitchell. In case Trevor and I are incapacitated and unable to operate the vehicle. It's a safety issue, really," Opa said and gave Trevor a slap on the shoulder. Trevor flinched.

Once they reached a straight stretch, Trevor pulled to the side of the road. He climbed out and grudgingly walked around to the passenger seat, the other two sliding one place to the left—Opa in the middle and Mitch behind the wheel. Opa explained how to start the truck with the clutch down, shift into first gear, slowly release the clutch while pressing on the gas, and manipulate the three-on-the-tree gear shift. Straining forward to see over the dashboard, Mitch listened carefully and tried to think of an acronym to remember the steps: *Clutch, Brake, Key, Gas, Release. C-B-K-G-R. Can Bears Kill Green Rottweilers?*

With his butt perched on the front edge of the seat, Mitch pressed his feet firmly on the clutch and brake, started the engine, and moved his right foot to the gas pedal while lifting his left off the clutch. Opa chuckled as the surging RPMs were snuffed by Mitch's eager clutch foot lurching the truck forward into a stall. Trevor sat with the universal cringing symbol—left arm across stomach, right hand shielding the eyes. Then after a dozen attempts, Mitch successfully started the truck again and got it moving in first gear.

"Well played, Big Boy. You're a natural," Opa said.

Mitch began to roll down his window to put his arm on the doorframe, like he'd seen Opa do sometimes. As he turned the stubborn window roller, the truck's engine gave a lusty roar for second gear.

"Never mind the window. She wants another gear, driver." Mitch pressed down the clutch, maneuvered the gear shift into second, and then forgot to keep his speed up. The truck stalled, shuddering.

"For frick's sake," Trevor said.

"You probably drove perfectly the first time, right?" Mitch said, throwing him an eye dart.

"I'll take over any time you're ready to quit," Trevor said.

"He's doing fine. Just a little while longer," said Opa.

For the next mile, they jolted along as Mitch relentlessly bunny-hopped and stalled the truck. Finally, Opa decided to give his grinding clutch a rest. He helped Mitch pull the truck over to the side. Mitch turned off the ignition and started to open the door. Opa extended his right hand. Mitch handed him the keys, and Opa took them with his left hand and kept the right one extended. Mitch clued in and shook it. "You drove, Mitchell. And you fished. This is an important day for you. But here's something much more important, and don't you ever forget it," he said and leaned in closer. "Never tell your mother about me letting you boys drive, or your Opa will suffer through a time of tremendous tribulation." Then he winked and flipped a dropje into each of the boys' palms.

Mitch puts the notebook back on the shelf. Then he picks up a deflated orange soccer ball on the shelf underneath it.

"I haven't seen this in a long time," he says. "The official Dutch original."

"I thought this was lost. I loved this! Opa and I kicked that back and forth a few thousand times," Trevor says. "It was kinda our thing, ya know?"

"It wasn't your thing. No. He bought it for me."

"You're letting romantic nostalgia cloud your recollections," Trevor says and reaches for the ball.

Mitch tucks the ball under his arm. "I'm not romanticizing anything. You've got everything else you want. Let me have the ball."

"Really, he did give it to me."

"He played it with you sometimes, but he gave it to me. You've got things confused with that orange shirt you wore."

"What did you mean that I've got everything else I want?"

"Forget it," Mitch sighs.

"We'll figure this out later. Go ahead and keep it under your arm like a monkey spanker."

"Oh, okay, let's 'wrap things up.'"

"It is a wrap. I'll just add my soccer ball to the list. The rest of this crap is too insignificant to bother with," Trevor says, clicking the pen loudly.

"Insignificant."

"Insignificant. Yes."

You're more insignificant to me than you've ever been.

Trevor and Mitch don't talk again until later in the afternoon when they're grilling burgers for supper. Some of the aunts and uncles are over, sipping Earl Grey tea and catching up on the accomplishments while sidestepping the failures of one another's children. Trevor is running the grill, and he's laid the burgers in three rows of four. He insists on always being the griller; he calls it a "science and an art." The symmetry is flawless.

Trevor closes the lid and a bubble of gum slowly expands from his lips, the pink orb building in diameter. It pops unexpectedly, startling him, and he peels the wet membrane off of his upper lip and chin. He takes a piece of white wax paper from the spent burger stack and puts the gum inside it. Then he folds the paper in half three times.

"You sure you asked everybody how many burgers they want? These are almost done, and I'm not putting fresh ones on," Trevor asks.

"Yes, that would be apocalyptic to have to do that. I told you the right amount." The burgers hiss and squeal. "I wonder how many fishermen would keep a notebook like Opa's," Mitch says.

"He was odd. Couldn't figure him out. Didn't know him that well anyway. Not that he cared," Trevor says.

"That is totally not true," Mitch says. "He was really interested in you."

"Nope. I was like the...ugly stepchild. Step-grandchild. You were his buddy."

"Seriously? That is so not how it was."

"You didn't see it because you and he had your own little club going," he says.

"Club? Give me a break."

"A club is precisely what it was." Trevor holds the *s* for an epoch. *Pre-cisssse-ly*. "I never had a chance."

Talk about self-pity, Mitch thinks. What a victim. "I don't know what else I can say. You have it totally wrong," he says.

"Anyway," Trevor says. "He wasn't so perfect."

"He was about as close as you can get." Mitch opens the lid and peeks inside.

"Don't worry, the burgers are fine. 'Close to perfect': that's such a naïve thing to say."

"Did you say *nave*?" Mitch closes the lid.

"I said naïve, and you know it."

"Why do you want the ball so much if you weren't in this so-called club?"

"Romantic nostalgia. Except my facts are correct."

"This is really not our decision. Should be Mom's. She'll remember who he gave the ball to."

"We're grown men. We're not bugging Mom with this right now." There's that decisive tone Mitch hates so much. This is how we're going to do it, and it's the only way.

"You always know exactly what the correct thing to do is, don't you?" Mitch says.

"What?" Trevor sputters.

"Nothing."

"I keep talking about doing the correct thing?" Trevor says.

"No. You're just always right." Mitch stares at the lid. He can tell from the thickness of the emitted smoke that the burgers are starting to burn.

"Really." He leans on one hand on a handle of the grill, feet crossed.

"You're batting a thousand. I don't even try," Mitch says.

"So. you sit back and wait. Let everybody else make decisions and then shoot them down."

"Shoot them down?" Mitch enunciates the Os in *shoot*.

"That's right."

"When do I ever shoot you down?"

"Constantly."

"I never say shit about you."

"You don't have to say anything," Trevor says.

"So you're mad about what I don't say." "The little looks you give Sharelle when I'm talking. Smart ass smirks."

"Absolutely no clue what you're talking about," Mitch says.

"No, absolutely no clue. Like about my PhD."

"You mean about your ABD?" Mitch says.

"There you go!"

"What?"

"The way you said that: 'ABD.' Like it's a big joke."

You mean your Big But? Mitch can't help but smirk.

"You have no idea how hard academic life is!" Trevor spits.

"You keep reminding me, and everybody else."

"You know what? Forget it." Trevor puts his other hand behind his back.

"Let's," Mitch says.

"And forget about some bullshit soccer ball. Who cares?"

"Obviously *you* do. A lot."

"I've already forgotten about it," Trevor says and gives a double thumbs-up.

"Somehow, I have a feeling you'll be mentioning it again soon," Mitch says and mimics the thumbs gesture.

Trevor puts his hands behind his back and faces away from Mitch and the grill, up into the western hills. Mitch peeks down and sees dense smoke stream from the grill. He does nothing to stop it. "I want that ball because I loved Opa, okay? I loved him a lot," Trevor says.

"I did too," Mitch says. *Wow, how unusually expressive*. "Look, if it's that important to you, keep the ball."

Trevor slowly spins to face Mitch. “That’s cool. Let’s think about it for a bit, though.”

“It’s not exactly an issue we need to strike a committee to examine. It’s a ball. Just take it. I left it in the laundry room.”

“Fine. Thanks.”

“Oh, and one more thing,” Mitch says, and raps his knuckles on the grill lid. “You’re on fire.” Trevor hurls the lid off of the grill, and billowing clouds of smoke pour out. The burgers are carbon pucks.

Burnt burgers. Four rows of three. Three rows of four.

Three rounds of failure: this is what failure looks like in your world.

MAY 1

The blood test will be tomorrow. So will the Phone Call. Mitch knows (they both know) that there's nothing you can do to prepare yourself. You learn to not allow your mind to peek over the edge into a different horizon. You just end up leaving a piece of yourself there that you won't get back. Distract yourself. Do something with other people, so you know that life has other dimensions that will continue with or without a child. That's what he read in a magazine article once, anyway. Frankly, he's tired of being told how they should think about or process any of it. Unless you've experienced having your dreams volleyed back and forth like a tennis ball—utterly out of your control and unseen by almost everyone who knows you, all within the span of a month—it's best to speak lightly.

It's a Saturday morning, and Sharelle and Mitch are on their way to her sister Heather's house for a family lunch. Norman and Audrey are coming over too. Ravi and Heather never seem to make enough food, so a stop for a donut and coffee at Coffee Break is in order. As Mitch opens his car door, Sharelle says, "I am super hungry. Like ravenous." Mitch closes the door again.

"Like you could eat the ass off a dead skunk?"

She laughs. "Maybe even."

"I'm sure it's nothing. People get hungry, right?" he says and darts his eyes quickly back and forth with a very slight nuance of mischief in his grin.

Super hungry. Super. Hungry.

Sharelle opens her door, turns to it, and peers back over her shoulder at him. "Had a big breakfast too," she says. She seems to exit the car extra carefully.

Super hungry. Ravenous. Don't let yourself go there. No expectations.

Mitch gets out, walks to the front of the car, and takes her hand. "Let's see if they have any skunk's ass on special." They walk to the entrance, Sharelle a half-step slower than normal. When they get inside the shop, the line extends almost to the door. As they stand at the back deciding if it's worth it, Mitch hears a little boy's voice from behind the low wall beside him.

"Mommy, I want to collect more robots from the dollar store. I want blue and red and yellow and purple and green."

"Uh-huh." A boy and his mother are sitting at a table. About five years old, he is sipping on chocolate milk and playing with a shiny, white toy robot. The mother is wearing a pair of acid-wash jeans and a skin-tight yellow T-shirt that says, "COUGAR: Approach with Caution." Her eyeballs bulge as they scan back and forth across the pages of a newspaper. The want ads.

"And Mommy, I want to get all the robots in the whole world."

Her voice is husky. "Damien, please stop talking. I can't concentrate!"

"Mommy," he says. Rustle of the newspaper as she turns a page. "Mommy, Mommy." Rustle. "Mommy!"

"Damien, honestly, give Mommy a minute. She's searching for something important."

"Mommy, you know what?"

She gives a lingering sigh. "What is it, Honey?"

"My robot doesn't work."

"That's because you kept messing with it and didn't turn it off, and now the batteries are dead again." She growls under her breath, takes the robot from his hand, flips the power switch back and forth, and then puts the robot down on the table. Then her voice softens, "Sweetheart, you need to turn it off when you're not using it."

Mitch turns to Sharelle, and her head is tilted to the side, looking over at the table. She leans into Mitch's ear and her bottom lip grazes his ear lobe. Electricity shoots from the base of his skull into his torso and groin.

"We have any batteries?" she whispers.

"The garage door opener," he says. "I'll be right back." He goes back to the van and soon returns with two AA batteries.

Sharelle takes them and walks over to the table. "He sure is a cutie. You mind if I give him these batteries?" she asks the mom.

"Thanks. Yes, he can be a cutie. I mean, you are a cutie, right Damien? You're mommy's sweet boy," Cougar says and lays down her newspaper.

"Can I have the batteries, Mommy?" the boy says.

"We don't take things from strangers," Cougar says. "But we'd better make an exception for this nice lady. You must be a mom." Sharelle is silent. "I can tell."

"What makes you say that?" Sharelle asks.

"You have that way about you. You're used to giving things up for others."

"I'll leave them here if you want," Sharelle says and sets the batteries on the table.

"Thanks!" the boy says.

"You're welcome," Sharelle says to Damien.

"That's very kind. I told his stepdad to get him rechargeables. But times are tough for everybody I guess."

"Yes, they are tough," Sharelle says.

"We mamas gotta stick together, don't we?" Cougar says and nods at Sharelle.

"Gotta stick together," Sharelle says and rejoins Mitch.

"This line hasn't moved for ten freaking minutes. What a shit show." Mitch hears a wheezing voice behind them. They both turn. A man with curly grey hair is standing in line. He's holding the hand of a little girl in a pink dress with blue ribbons in her hair. Frizzy edges of his hair shoot out from under his *Bob's Crane Service* cap. His face is leathery and sallow. With precision, he balances an unlit cigarette on the tips of his lips.

Sharelle puts a hand on her hip and glares at him. "You mind watching your language? There are kids here." She motions her head at his daughter. Mitch pats the small of her back. *Take it easy.*

"This place just drives me nuts, ya know? Epic cluster, man." He wheezes under his breath and coughs. Mitch turns around again and stares at the fluorescent red words on the menu board until they start to blur and double, and then he is nine years old.

"What a total cluster! Nobody's going for the puck," Dad says, staring at the TV. "Canucks are all bunched up at the blueline."

"Yeah," you say. "Which ones are the Canucks again?"

He laughs. "White guys, Mitch." He puts his arm around you. You rest an elbow on his shoulder. Buddies. Watching hockey with Dad.

"Aren't you two cozy," Mom says from her armchair. "I could use some of that action." She gets up, puts her *Reader's Digest* down on the coffee table, and drops on Dad's lap. She sits sideways, her legs running across your lap. "By the way, Mitch, your father's a genius."

"Yes, he is," Dad says.

"Your Dad is going to be the King of Landscaping."

"Yup, partner came through," Dad says.

"What's landscaping?" you ask.

"Yards and gardens. Making people's lives better," he says.

"Is it like lawn mowing?"

"No. Not that. No. So much more," he says.

"You can mow my lawn anytime," Mom says. "I mean, well..."

They're laughing, and Mom is so red. Dad kisses her on the mouth. Gross.

"Seamus will do all the technical stuff. I'll do the schmoozing," he says, between kisses.

"In that case, you can schmooze me any time," she says.

"Take notes, Mitch. How to be a ladies' man."

"I thought women always married men who were like their fathers," you say.

"Not this woman," Mom says. "Your father and Opa couldn't be more different."

"That's for sure," you say.

"Meaning?" Dad says and turns his neck to you.

"Just that Opa and you are different."

"They're both blue collar," Mom says.

"I'm blue collar? What do you mean?" Dad says. "I'm a mover and shaker. How is that blue collar?"

"I just mean you're self-educated."

"Education again, huh?" He grips her by the hips and lifts her off.

It's starting. You get up, grab a comic book from the table, and walk out to the porch. The hand-painted sign on a post says, "Home Sweet Home." You sit down in a lawn chair. Read. Enter the story. It's okay. Enter in. Read. The comic book pages ripple in the warm wind.

Soon, you've read five pages. Can't remember any of it. Begin again.

Dad walks out the door and sits on the bottom porch step, head in hands. He turns around, sees you. Flash of yellow teeth, then a whisper like sandpaper. Always that whisper when he's angry. "What you sitting there for Mitchell, huh?"

"Nothing."

He pulls a cigarette from his shirt pocket, lights it, takes a deep drag, inspects you up and down.

Smoke shoots out his nostrils. Dragon. “You like provoking.”

“No, I just like reading.” Show him the book.

“Push my button and retreat to the porch. Eavesdropped, didn’t you?”

“Just reading. Heard nothing.”

“How you know there’s anything to hear?”

“You said ‘eavesdropping.’”

“You a smart-ass lawyer?”

“Not smart.”

“No, you’re not. You’re lucky I have a controlled temper. My father would shellac me for contradicting him like that.” He takes another deep drag, leans against the post. Drifting blue smoke. Hazy words, *Home is where the heart is home is where the heart is home is where the heart is home is where the heart is.* Two nouns, two verbs, one conjunction, one definite article. Learned that in grammar book. *Is where the heart is where the heart is where the heart is where the heart is Home sweet home sweet home sweet home sweet home sweet home sweet home sweet home sweet home sweet home sweet.*

Dad inhales, stares, smirks. “Where’s Trevor?”

“Delivers papers Wednesdays.”

“So here you sit. Bored, right?”

“No, just like reading.”

“You read a lot.”

“Really like it. Very gratifying.”

“You think you’re a genius.”

“No, not smart.”

“Ever heard of exercise? I was a great athlete.” He leans away from the post, cigarette between thumb and index finger, takes a quick last drag, throws the butt into a flower bed. “Last time I watch a hockey game with you. Ever.” He walks back inside.

Never say he's different than Opa. That sets him off. Go to the shed and grab your bike. *I made fun of him. I didn't mean to. He's a great man.* Coast down Main Street, wheels clicking on each syllable of *Home sweet home sweet home sweet home sweet home sweet home sweet home sweet home sweet home sweet home sweet home sweet home sweet home sweet home sweet home.*

"You know what you want?" Sharelle says.

"Almost." Mitch decides on his order. Then he glances around the restaurant, and that's when he sees him. He's been to Coffee Break a few times on weekends, but this is the first time he's ever noticed him working here. Four feet tall. Finger stubs, red hair, skin of milk. He's wearing standard-issue franchise garb—shiny black shoes, polyester pants, pin-striped shirt, visor.

Even after all these years, Mitch knows that it's Larson.

Mitch watches him, noticing that he is still always in motion, always doing something. Larson's main job seems to be securing the loose trays. He scans the restaurant and when he finds one, he adds it to the stack resting on a table on the condiment bar. He slips his arms under the stack, takes it to the kitchen, and then returns and refills utensil bins.

While he transfers some forks into a bin, the manager and the drive-thru kid are standing by a nearby till. Leaning against a wall with his feet crossed, the kid stands in supreme confidence with his headset over his ears and little merit badges pinned to his uniform. The manager grabs the back of her hair in a pigtail and rolls an elastic band around it while they talk.

Larson stops scanning for trays and goes over to tell the manager something. As he walks away, she turns to the kid and rolls her eyes. The drive-thru kid makes his lower lip bulge outwards with his tongue in some sort of mockery. They share a little giggle. Larson doesn't seem to notice any of this and keeps mechanically working—somber and dreary. At one point, he looks right at Mitch and then continues scouring the restaurant for trays, apparently not recognizing him.

Has nothing changed for Larson in all this time? Mitch thinks. Is this all there is for him? Twenty-eight years later, towing his chaotic body around town, willing his left hand to grow fingers and grasp hold of something, what has he gotten a hold of? Just trays and knives and spoons? I should have waited for you at the corner. I failed you. *Someday, you'll need someone to walk with you.* I failed you, Opa.

"Why are you staring at that guy? You know him?" Sharelle points her thumb towards Larson.

"No."

"You're not even looking where I'm pointing."

"The tray guy. No, don't know him."

"You have a weird expression like you know—"

"Nuh uh. We're up," Mitch says as they reach the front of the line. The manager calls them over to her till. Mitch stands at a right angle to her, his back facing Larson at the utensil tray. Sharelle steps to the counter.

"Welcome to Coffee Break. May I help you?" She gives a big flash of teeth. Mitch's eardrums pulse with hostility.

Aren't you a big deal with your mocha-colored tie and your self-satisfied supremacy over a disabled employee?

"Yes, you may. One large coffee. One caramel crunch donut," he says. He stresses the *k* sounds in caramel crunch. He wants her cells to absorb the beta rays of his antagonism. Sharelle casts him a confused frown.

"I'm very sorry, but we don't have caramel crunch." Her name tag says *Wendy*.

"How about Strawberry rhubarb?" Mitch wants to follow it with *Wendy* but doesn't.

"Uh, no sir."

"Why don't you tell me what kinds you *do* have?" This time, he adds "Wendy" under his breath.

"All the kinds of?"

"Yes, all the kinds." He listens to a stammered recitation of eighteen varieties.

"Banana cream," Mitch says. "Would you like any muffins at all?" she asks.

"Did I ask for muffins?" It slips out, and he instantly blushes at his rudeness and his eyes shift to the menu board.

"No thank you," Sharelle says. "Sorry about...that," she adds. Wendy is smiling through her teeth now. It must take tremendous effort. "Am I allowed to order something too?" Sharelle says, squinting at Mitch.

"Oh, sorry. What would you like?" Mitch says.

"My usual." This is a test of his chivalry and knowledge of her. He's already failed the first half.

"Vanilla latté. Lemon scone," Mitch says decisively and holds his breath.

"Americano. Blueberry scone. Let's go decaf this time," Sharelle says.

"Right. Sorry," Mitch says. *Yes, decaf.*

"Are you dining in today?" Wendy asks.

"No, we will dine in our vehicle today, thanks." Mitch says. She fills their order and wishes them a great day. As they turn to leave the shop, there's a metallic clatter from the kitchen and Mitch catches a last glimpse of Larson hunched over a spilled cylinder of spoons. Wendy turns around to help pick them up.

I am sorry, Larson.

They arrive at Heather and her husband Ravi's place. It's a three-storey townhouse that's been "gentrified"—the lower-class undesirables and the great unwashed are apparently not welcome and the neighbourhood has been converted to middle-class townhouses where young families can have eternal playdates and compare stroller chassis.

When they get to the door, the oldest son Drew lets them in and they walk into the kitchen. Everyone is sitting there, including the four kids.

"Thought you'd never get here," Ravi says.

"Big line at Coffee Break," Mitch says. *Uh oh.*

"You stopped for coffee first?" Audrey says.

"What's wrong with my coffee?" Heather says.

"Nothing. Nothing at all. Just our little Saturday ritual," says Sharelle.

"I remember those footloose days of disposable income. Lattés and spa treatments," Heather says. "When it was all about me."

Norman gives a slow and deep snuffle, his arms folded across his chest.

"Sorry we're late," Mitch says. He pulls a chair back for Sharelle and then sits down beside her. They begin eating.

Soon, Norman and Audrey are asking their standard grandparent questions about school and sports. The kids politely answer the questions. The oldest, Drew, describes his after-school math academy and Audrey nods approvingly. Then all are regaled with tales of Katrina (the second oldest) and her ballet recitals ("She's going to the provincials, you know," says Ravi). Gabriel, the next in line, is apparently a wonderful painter, and he has recently finished a special evening course taught by a famous local artist.

"Gabriel is learning about impressionism," Heather says.

"Isn't he ten?" Mitch says. Sharelle swats his knee under the table.

"Tell us about impressivism, Gabe," Norman says.

"Impressionism. They just introduced it, Dad," Heather says. "I tell you, he's learned more in one week than he'd learn in a year in art class at school. Those teachers waste half the time helping all the special needs kids with—" She stops, glances at Mitch and begins to intently study her arugula salad. *You spoiled, sanctimonious fool.*

Drew, Katrina, and Gabriel sit with magnificent posture, napkins spread neatly over their laps and utensils held with subtle precision. They have learned how to converse with adults and to mirror their parents' unending portrayal of familial bliss: one that says, "We are kind; we are confident; and we are oh-so-respectful to all adults and never have bad thoughts towards anyone. And my, how we love having every aspect of our existence regulated and hovered over. See how we smile till our cheeks ache? Note how our dimples pulse with joy and happiness." It is a scene that would, in its polished and orchestrated preciousness, make even Norman Rockwell throw up in his mouth.

And then there's Vincent. Wonderful, interrupting, non-compliant Vincent. He is marvellously untamed by Ravi and Heather's micro-managed and detail-oriented parenting program—their baby sign language, religiously charted toilet-training and nap schedules, complex behavioural sticker system. No, Vincent has not bought into the program. He is four years old, and he doesn't give a shit. Mitch sees this as something to be encouraged. Vincent is sitting across from him and as the conversation continues, the boy finishes his plate and begins to lightly tap the butt of his fork on the table. After the first couple taps, Mitch catches his eye and gives him an approving smile. Three more taps, louder still.

"Vincent, quit it," Heather says.

Tap, tap, tap. Ravi is sitting beside him and leans over to whisper something in his ear. Vincent stops and takes a sip of milk. Then he starts again. *Tap, tap, tap, tap.*

"Vincent Charles, stop tapping," Heather says and then smiles nervously at Audrey, giving her an awkward wink. Audrey's lips are puckering.

"Vincent Charles, keep tapping," Vincent says. *Tap, tap, tap, tap.*

More hushed whispers from Ravi. As Vincent listens, he lifts his head, purses his lips, and raises his eyebrows in mock toddler arrogance. Sharelle splutters a chuckle into her sleeve. Mitch coughs with a hand over his mouth to hide his rapidly expanding joy, while Heather's eyes dart from Mitch to Sharelle and then narrow at Vincent.

"Hey, Vinny. Do you want to come sit with me?" Sharelle says and pats the empty chair beside her. "I can do that airplane thing with the fork."

"Yeah, my mouth is the airport, right?" Vincent says. He puts down his fork and starts to get out of his chair.

"No, you stay in your seat," Heather says. "He needs to learn how to eat like a big boy, don't you Vincent?" She turns to Sharelle. "And we do prefer *Vincent*."

"I just thought—" Sharelle says.

"We've done this before, Sharelle. He needs to get into the routine," Heather says.

"It's working like a charm," Sharelle whispers to Mitch.

"Sorry?" Heather says.

"Nothing. It's all good. I was trying to help," Sharelle says, waving a sausage in the air that she's impaled on her fork.

Vincent picks up his fork again and continues. *Tap, tap, tap, tap*. Louder now. *Tap, tap, tap, tap*. Vincent takes his knife in the other hand and begins tapping it. He looks at Mitch, who smiles at him. *Tap, tap, tap, tap, tap, tap*.

"Stop this right now, Vincent," Heather says again.

Yet another pleading whisper from Ravi.

Vincent begins to tap the utensils in a rhythm now.

Knife...fork...knife...fork...

Knife...fork...knife...fork...knife...fork. Then faster. Knife, fork, knife, fork, knife, fork, knife, fork.

"Vincent! That is more than enough," Heather says in a loud whisper.

Two seconds of silence, then the double beat starts. Knife, knife, fork, fork, knife, knife, fork, fork. Ravi grabs Vincent's left hand. Fork, fork, fork, fork, fork, fork. Muted whispers from Ravi with forks throughout. Fork, fork, fork. Ravi covers both tiny hands, and Vincent tries to squirm loose.

"Stop, or it's a timeout," Heather says.

"Uh oh, watch it, Vincent. It's the dreaded timeout," Norman says.

"So, Mitch, how's your school year going?" Heather says in desperation.

"Wish we had timeouts when I was a boy," Norman says. "Instead it was the belt. We listened though."

"Vincent listens too. He's just...tired," Ravi says.

"I'd be tired too, if I had as many toys as he has," Audrey says.

"Kids prefer the box more than the toy itself, I figure," Norman says. Vincent has pulled one hand away. Knife, knife, knife, knife.

"School is fine," Mitch says. Knife, knife, knife, knife, knife, knife, knife.

"That's it!" Heather says. She pastes on a smile and says, "Boys will be boys" to Audrey as she walks over to Vincent. She grabs him under the armpits to remove him. Vincent grips the arms of his chair like a clamp. Drew is meticulously slicing a sausage into pieces. Katrina and Gabriel are frozen, the latter's fingers smoothing the tablecloth in a circular motion.

Audrey says, "Hey, Vincent, do you want to sit with grandma?"

"No!" Vincent says.

"Let go. You're going to timeout," Heather says.

"*You're* going to timeout, Heather!" Vincent says.

Sharelle sticks her mouth in the crook of her elbow and releases a deep belly laugh, her upper body shaking violently. That sets Mitch off. There's no possible way he can contain the pressure anymore, and he puts both hands over his face and splutters muffled bursts of laughter. Tears start to leak through, which he wipes with his palms.

Audrey gets up and walks over to Vincent. "Vincent, come with Grandma and we'll have a little talk."

"Mom, please, let us deal with this," Heather says.

"Mom, thanks, but we can handle it," Ravi says with rising intonation on *handle*.

"Vincent, Grandma won't want you to come over to her house if you act like this," Audrey says and starts to pry his little fingers off the chair. His other hand releases its grip on the armrest, makes a fist, and lands with a hard slap on her mouth. Then there is utter silence, except for the living room clock that ticks in time to Audrey's slow-motion movements of lifting her chin, opening and closing her mouth in a steady motion like she is gasping for oxygen, then dropping her left hand from the chair, bringing her right hand up to her mouth, and turning to Heather. Her mouth continues its open-and-shut quest for air.

"Well, I'll be a son of bitumen. That little bugger," Norman says. In the next instant, Ravi has Vincent whisked from the room. Heather takes a napkin and begins dabbing at her mother's mouth, despite the absence of blood.

"Dad, can you pass the coleslaw?" Sharelle says cheerily, trying to maintain a sympathetic expression. Mitch hasn't seen her this happy in a long time.

"He's tired. Pre-Kindergarten is a tough adjustment," Heather says.

And she dabs.

Lunch finishes with polite conversation around the table. As Mitch and Sharelle walk by the laundry room on the way out, Ravi is holding the door shut, so Vincent will stay in timeout. His little voice cries, "I don't like you, Daddy!"

"Now Vincent, you don't mean that," Ravi says and stretches his lips wide at them in a fake, almost conspiratorial, smile. "Somebody needs a nap," he adds.

"*You* need a nap. And I'm not gonna play with you ever again!" Vincent yells, and his little fists bang on the door, his muffled shrieks rising and falling. The tug-of-war continues, the door opening a couple inches and then slamming shut again. Ravi is flushed from exertion.

"Strong little guy, eh? Good luck, Ravi," Mitch says.

"Yes, he is strong. Very strong," Ravi says.

"Vinny is awesome," Sharelle says.

"I know."

"No, I mean that. Vinny is fantastic."

"I do know that. But tell that to his mother," Ravi says and waves as they leave.

The second they have driven out of the cul-de-sac, Sharelle and Mitch exchange corner-of-the-eye glances and smile broadly. There is no heartache or unspoken venom condensing in the air, no *fucking fucks* hurled at the windshield. There is simply Sharelle and Mitchell smiling their way across town in a Honda Civic with no Cheerios ground into the carpet or plastic rattles rolling under the seats. Together—they are in this life together—they make their way back to their basement suite, the modest little home they have built in which they are conceiving their story, and Mitch knows that for these next few minutes that is enough. They are good enough.

He is good enough.

MAY 2

They've both called in sick. Sharelle went in for her blood test, and Mitch got caught up on some grading for school. When she gets home late in the morning, they pass some time by sitting on the living room couch and watching CNN. School lockdowns, capsized ferries, flash floods, and defaulted national debts pour onto the screen from across the globe. At one point, a crowd of Middle Eastern men are lifting a makeshift stretcher over their shoulders, a lifeless figure's bloody arms dangling over the edges. They hurl their shrieking rage into the sky.

They stare at the TV and wait. A tiny red sidebar in the corner of the screen says 11:59 EST. Mitch looks at Sharelle, who keeps her eyes on the TV, and he puts his hand on her knee and stands up.

"Should I call?" he asks. Silence. "I'm going to call."

He takes his phone from his shirt pocket and walks over to a chair by the window. Sharelle remains on the couch and puts her head between her knees. Mitch examines the keypad.

This is how it's going to go, he tells himself. I will now dial the number, and the nurse will answer after one ring. She will say, "Oh Mitchell, so glad you called. These are the phone calls I love, the ones that keep me going because I normally see so much heartbreak. Mitchell, Sharelle couldn't be more pregnant, and I can tell by the hCG numbers that there's no doubt! I would bet on twins! Really. It's over, Mitchell. It really is over. You two are an inspiration to all childless couples that sometimes you need to hang in there and trust that everything will be okay."

That's how it'll go. Mitch dials the number from memory and hits the green "Call" button. Nothing. *Check the number. It was right, so try again.* Still nothing. *I'd better double-check the phone number in our address book.* It's in the drawer in the TV console. *This is not how it's supposed to go.*

Mitch walks over to the drawer. It won't open, so he pulls harder. It budges a couple inches, and he sees a pile of papers that are stuffed inside. He jams his fingertips inside and pulls the ends of the papers from the top corner, pressing them down and pulling the drawer open with the other hand. Then he starts digging through the mess of paperwork. He glances at Sharelle. She now has her elbows on her knees with hands clasped, index fingers pinching the fold above her upper lip. She's observing his fingers fumbling through all the paperwork in the drawer.

Fumble, fumble, fumble. Mitchell Van Laren fumbling his way through his fumbling life: fumbling with locker combinations and beer mugs and syringes. Stop it.

He finds the address book and walks back to the window. He sits down and checks the number. The last digit was wrong.

It's gonna be okay.

He dials. "Zenith Centre for Reproductive Health. This is Amy. How may I help you?"

"Hi, this is Mitch Van Laren calling about the pregnancy results for my wife Sharelle?"

"One moment please." Zamfir's pan flute plays. Breathy, supple. Mitch remembers Mom playing her Zamfir eight-track over and over.

We can do this. We're building a story together. It's our turn. It's all part of a bigger journey and we don't know the whole picture yet and—

"Hi, Mitchell. This is Miranda, one of the IVF nurses." Miranda's accent is warm and rhythmic. Australia.

She sounds so friendly and happy. I knew it. Thank you, God. I knew it.

"I have Sharelle's blood test results from this morning. So, I'm afraid that the results don't indicate the elevated levels of hCG that we would normally want to see, so it appears to be negative for pregnancy. I'm sorry." Mitch starts to think of questions to ask, but he already knows the answers. Miranda continues. "Certainly it is sometimes possible to get a false negative, but all indications are that the cycle has failed." She gives him some details about follow-up appointments and discontinuing Prometrium. Mitch feels a cold draft.

The cycle has failed.

Failed. Fail. Failure.

"Thank you. For everything you've all done," he hears himself say.

Oh God, Mitch thinks, don't make me turn around. You tell her, Miranda. You come over and stare deep into my wife's eyes and tell her the cycle has failed. Let me go to sleep and wake up and reset. I can't see another part of her that's died. I don't want to watch her sunken eyes deepen another shade, the creases between her eyes and ears gain another line. Please, don't make me. What will she say when I turn and look at her?

What are you, five years old?

"You're welcome. Again, I'm sorry. Everyone here at Zenith gives their regards."

Mitch puts the phone in his pocket and turns around, and Sharelle is bent over with her head between her knees again like before, as if she hasn't heard a thing, but he knows she has because her back is shaking. He walks over and sits down and holds her on the couch, combing strands of her hair through his fingers. "Why is this happening to us?" The words squeak out from the tightness of her throat.

"I don't know. But I'm here. I don't know." He holds her and listens to himself talk softly about keeping up hope and counting all the good things in their lives. The doctors said they were prime candidates, remember? They'll get through this. He goes to the kitchen and pours two glasses of Merlot, and they soon finish the bottle in silence, his right hand pouring each glass while the left holds her stiffly. He tucks Sharelle into bed and tells her that everything will be all right, and she should have a rest. She gives him her thinnest smile and the crook of his arm cradles the back of her neck, as he lies on the top of the bedspread next to her. "I don't know," he whispers to her again.

Why is this happening to us?

Mitch strokes a strand of Sharelle's hair and plummets fast to that place he doesn't want to go.

How much longer can we be a scaffold for each other? Creaking in the buffeting wind, bearing the other's shifting weight and the brunt of cursing disappointment. We're getting tired, Sharelle. We've been the shoulder so many times—my beautiful girl, my broken Sharelle. So many times.

MAY 6

On the following Monday morning, Mitch is alone in the staff room. Before school, they had a follow-up appointment with Dr. Williamson who agreed they should try one more cycle. They'll try an extra procedure called Assisted Hatching. The eggs will be harvested, fertilized, and then their outer membranes will be thinned with a chemical to make it easier for the embryos to attach to the uterine wall. It will be their absolute last chance. They're going to take time off first to give Sharelle's system a rest and to save more money.

Mitch hears the crunch of gravel in the parking lot outside the window as teachers and aides gradually arrive. It's been quiet in here this morning. Jenna, the Learning Assistance teacher fresh out of college (Learning Assistance is always capitalized, she's told him), came in a few minutes ago. Jenna posts inspirational messages on Facebook at an astounding rate—"Failure is life's way of reminding us we're not in charge" and other such nuggets of wisdom. She likes to eat breakfast in here each morning. As she chomps on her Corn Flakes, she tells Mitch that it seems he is coping really well with the whole losing-the-baby thing since it's only been eight months.

"I would have been a wreck," she says.

"Would you have? What exactly does a wreck look like?" Mitch says.

"I just...wouldn't have been able to function," she says, and then quickly disappears to her classroom.

Get back to me once you understand what real loss is, Jenna. Some life experience will help.

Trenton, the librarian, comes in and reminds Mitch about some overdue books and asks if he could keep the kids more quiet when they do research. Mitch asks himself if the Dewey Decimal System would fit sideways up Trenton's ass. He says okay he'll do a better job of keeping them in line and sends him on his way. Mitch goes to his mailbox and finds a pink slip from a parent. He hates pink slips. Some parent has a beef about too much homework or not enough homework or unjust treatment. Or more likely it's from Lyra. *It's Lee-ra, not Lie-ra.* Her daughter is "exceptional" and Lyra gives him suggestions every so often on how he can challenge her more. He always affirms her comments and assures her that he is trying different things to challenge her gifted daughter, but he's really not. The note is a reminder of a student council meeting tomorrow.

Mitch used to get thank-you notes from parents. "You've really drawn out Francine this year" or "Thank you for finding the best in Samuel." He used to care. He used to think that what he did made a difference.

He grabs some papers from the copy room he ran off on Friday and forgot about. The pages are all hole-punched on the wrong side. *Son of a bitch.* He climbs the stairwell, and when he gets to the top he can hear their high-pitched buzz already, and for a second he thinks it's coming from another room, but he knows it isn't. He approaches the door. It's really loud. Lyra and another parent are volunteering today in the library, across from his room. They're standing in the hallway, looking towards the classroom, and they whisper something to each other when they see him, which he replies to with a sheepish grin that's supposed to say, "Kids will be kids." He opens the door and forces himself to do his usual rendition of Monty Python's "Ministry of Silly Walks." No one notices.

It must have been a full moon last night. There's something in the air. They're unsettled and wild-eyed. Agitated like bees. He sits down at his desk and asks for quiet. The volume drops slightly, and a few kids glance at him, but the talking continues. He asks them to open their English notebooks, and a couple of kids start to. The rest do as they please. It's never been this bad. It's like a paralytic dream where he can't speak or move.

That's okay. Go ahead and talk amongst yourselves. I'm the professional educator, but you know best. Let me know when you're ready to learn, K? Like, LOL.

The first lesson is supposed to be on note-taking and paraphrasing. A pain in the ass to teach. He decides he'll give a quick, sketchy intro and then assign a bunch of pages in the text. His mind is not in the game. He'll tell them not to ask him questions for ten minutes, to struggle through it. Some will examine their books for five seconds and then give up and wait the full ten minutes until he's ready for questions. Learned helplessness. He could choke them.

Mitch rises and stands at the lectern. He likes lecterns—something to stand behind. The classroom volume is back to maximum again.

Why can't I stand here and get some common respect?

He turns and peers at the clock on the wall behind him. That might get them to be quiet. "Okay, let's get started." It's getting louder. Half of them are sitting on their desks. He feels a tingling in his temples, heat on his face. From the back, Cecilia lets out a shrieking laugh that sends ice cubes down his back. Randall, the boy beside her, is trying to poke her stomach with a pencil. In the centre of the room, Candida has her head down like she's sleeping. Donald opens his textbook and slams it shut next to her ear, and she springs up and tries to kick him but bangs her shin on the side bar of his desk. She puts her head down again, this time in pain. Mitch thinks she's crying.

"Mr. Van Laren!" Cecilia calls from the back. "Randall's poking me!"

"Randall, that's enough," Mitch scolds but is enveloped by the clamour.

"Mr. Van Laren!" she yells again.

"Mr. Van Laren!" Rheanne's voice pipes up from the front right side and Mitch turns to her. She tries to say something, but her voice is drowned out too.

"Mr. Van Laren! Mr. Van Laren!" Cecilia again. She gives another piercing cackle of laughter. The feeling is worse now, like he's getting smacked in the head.

"Van Laren!" a boy's voice says in the back. Mitch tries to determine who it is. Probably Luke.

"Luke! Was that—" he begins.

"Mr. Van Laren!" Rheanne says above the din.

"Hey, Mitchell!" It's the same boy's voice. He says it right as Lyra pokes her head in the door and pans across the room. She is smirking. Her daughter is sitting calmly at her desk with hands folded. Lyra shakes her head at Mitch and closes the door.

He stares at the brass doorknob, and it seems to grow and ebb, throbbing like a beating heart, and now he is watching himself. He grabs the front legs of an empty desk in the corner of the room by the window. The pencil crayons on top fall, clatter against the wall, and then do somersaults onto the carpet. The desk weighs nothing and he whips it around like a pendulum and flings it across the front of the room—the entire width—and it flies with a slow rotation into the wall near the door. The drywall caves in, and white powder flies out of the crevice. Some of the kids jump from their chairs. Rheanne has fallen to the floor and is crab-walking backwards on her hands and feet. Retreating. There is unbelievable silence. No one is talking anymore. A fine mist of drywall dust is falling to the floor.

Mitch's voice is almost a whisper. "Do I have your attention now?" Silence. He sweeps his eyes across the room, not sheepishly but not proud either. He walks over to the desk that's sitting with two legs inside a large crevice in the wall and two legs in the room, like it's meant to be that way: a study carrel for an ADD student. He crouches down, looks inside the wall, and then cocks his head at the students. "A little spackle should touch that right up," he says. Then the door flies open and Esther the principal is there with Lyra right behind her.

"What in the...what is going on here?" Esther says.

Mitch walks between the rows to the door and all eyes are on him. At least it's quiet. He steps into the hall with her. "I got a little upset."

"A little upset." The fingertips of her right hand are pressed on her forehead, and her eyes are studying various parts of his face.

"Do you want me to clean it up?" Mitch asks.

She peers back into the classroom.

"No. You should go home. Do you need anything from the room?"

"No."

"Stop in the office and make a statement of everything that happened, and then you need to go home right away. Don't talk to anyone. Go to my office and wait for me there."

He shuffles towards the stairwell and sees behind him that students and teachers have spilled into the hall to see what is going on. I need you, he thinks, as his foot hits the first step. He leans on the railing and descends, losing more of himself with each step.

I need you. Opa. Why aren't you here to tell me it's okay? See what a loser I am. Look how I've fucked it all away.

When Mitch gets to the office downstairs, he borrows a pen and a piece of lined paper from Marianne the secretary, who doesn't have a clue what's going on. He sits down in a brown plastic chair usually reserved for misbehaving students, and he puts his name in the top right-hand margin. He thinks of a title. "Incident" comes to mind and he focuses on the clock to estimate what time the "incident" happened and writes 9:02 a.m. on the left side on the second line. He starts to think about the specifics of the event and then finds himself getting up and pushing the chair back under the table. He gently places the sheet into the recycle bin and slides the pen into his back pocket.

Then Mitch walks. Out the office door and straight to the front glass doors. He stops and pushes the big square handicapped button and the doors slowly swing inward, and then he is outside in the sunlight. He turns around see if anyone is following him. No one but a couple of grade six kids, who were probably on their way to the gym. He moves quickly now to the parking lot. He knows that he should wait in the office, but that's the last thing he wants. He gets to his car, drives carefully through the lot and then swings west down Bennett, over the bridge, and out of town.

Drive north. Don't stop. Keep driving.

Thin bolts of light are struggling through the clouds as Mitch passes the vineyards and drives along the lake. Out on the far side, a small fishing boat is trolling past Fernando Island. There's hardly any traffic for a Monday morning. Does Sharelle already know? Did the school call her at the travel agency? He should be the one to tell her what happened. He'd better call her. He pulls off the road by the boat launch at Bell's Cove and turns on the radio. An old power ballad from the 80's: "Don't Know What You Got." He shuts it off. He's not in the mood. He can't call her either.

He gets out and sits on the bumper at 9:30 on a Monday morning and tries to get the tears to form. He hasn't cried since childhood. His shoulders tremble, and his bottom lip quivers. He feels condensation forming on his lenses and wipes them with the back of his thumbs, but he finds no moisture. He takes a few deep, shuddering breaths, and he sits and pans across the lake. All is still as a mirror.

Mitch stands up and searches for some flat rocks to skip. They're all too round. He sees one the size of a playing card embedded in the clay. He pries it out and flips it over in his hand. The underside of the rock is rounded. Useless. He drops it and keeps searching, and finally he finds a reasonably flat but very big rock. He winds up and lets it go, but one of the edges catches on his thumb when he releases it and the rock flutters onto the edge of the shore and rolls into the water with a tiny splash.

An old man in a small motorboat comes from around a corner and putters to shore. Mitch walks over, grabs the boat's bow, and pulls it farther up on shore for him. The man nods at him.

"Any luck?" Mitch asks.

"Trolled all day. Nothing." The man climbs over the bow and onto shore. "Came up empty."

"You gotta fish harder, I guess," Mitch says and forces a smile.

"Fishing as hard as I can. Makes no difference," he says.

"You try wet flies or sticking with the heavy hardware?"

"I always use a Kitimat with some flashers. Sounds like you know fishing," the man says as he starts unloading gear. Mitch helps him lift his boat onto a pickup that's parked adjacently.

"A little. Haven't gone in a long time," Mitch says.

"A waste of time today. A bust. Tried to remind myself that it's just good to be out on the lake," he says.

"That's what my grandpa used to say," Mitch says. "But I think that's kind of—"

"Bullshit. Kind of bullshit," he says and smiles at Mitch.

"No. Well, I don't know." Together, they carry the outboard to the truck, and the man tosses his other equipment under the boat into the truck bed.

"It's a mystery all right," he says and turns back to his truck. Then he climbs in and drives off.

That's your answer? Mitch thinks. It's a mystery? That's not enough for me. Why am I here? Why am I falling into oblivion, lungs full of amniotic fluid I can't expel, fluid jammed farther down my throat by every rejection and failure and loss, making it impossible to scream? Why was I taken from the womb and stamped with this twisted DNA ladder and then left to flail and wail with no sound? Can't make a sound. No sound. Nothing to pass on, nothing to care for, nothing to teach, nothing to love, nothing to beam with pride over, nothing to give the chance to make it right, to do it right, to get it right. I wanted to get it right. A mystery is not good enough. Not anymore. Don't drive away. Don't leave me here.

Mitch gets back in the car and keeps driving. He opens the driver side window, and the whoosh of the rushing wind fills his ears. It feels pleasantly distracting. Movement and sound. Rushing air. He rolls the window all the way down and sticks his arm out to feel the warm airstream. If he could, he would close his eyes and try not to feel anything other than the moving air. Warmth. Forward motion.

Mitch is transported back to a rented convertible on the Honoapiilani Highway from the airport towards their honeymoon condo. Sharelle's face stands in profile against the sun. She lets out a yawn and a ray of sunlight peeks through the gap in her mouth. Her yellow hair wavers in the backwards airstream. Some dangling strands are caught on her left ear, and he lifts them over and then runs the fingertips of his right hand along her cheekbone.

"You must be a new husband. Very hands-on," she says.

"And that's a problem because...why?" he says. She scrunches up the side of her face in a wink. "You can't wink, can you?"

"Why don't you watch the road?" she says.

"It's gotta be mostly eye and a little flash of cheek. Not so much face."

"No, it's all face. And you bought this wink yesterday, so you might as well live with it."

"I love your wink, actually."

"That's better." She rests her head against his shoulder.

"We are on a honeymoon!" Mitch says.

"You and me," she says. He smiles. Sharelle closes her eyes, and they drive for several minutes in silence.

"So, how many kids you want to have?" Mitch asks.

Sharelle's eyes jolt open. "Wow, ever heard of conversational foreplay?"

"You mean, like a segue or prefacing remark?"

"Something like that."

"Okay, fine. Mrs. S. Van Laren, at this time I would like to formally request that we now transition our conversation to the topic of child-bearing," he says.

"There you go. As I've stated thirty times already, I think I'd like to pump out a couple kids anyway. You're more of a Waltons kind of guy, right?" She sits up and drums her hands on his right leg.

"I think four to five would be good."

"How very Amish of you."

"I guess it will depend on how it goes."

"How it goes is that I'll turn into a whale for nine months, be violently sick and uncomfortable, and then try to deliver a watermelon through my vag. Cursing your name between contractions, of course." She laughs and clasps her hands behind her head.

"Okay, maybe three to four."

"And apparently you want me to repeat the above steps two to three times. You don't want one boy and one girl? Isn't that the suburban family dream?"

"You mean a boy named Noah and a girl named Madison?"

"Yes, and they each have their own bedroom with gender-appropriate wallpaper and a 'Periodic Table of the Elements' jigsaw puzzle? You know, to leapfrog them over the other kids?" She slaps the back of her hand into the palm of the other.

"Totally. And they have a tutor in kindergarten to help build pre-algebra skills. They also subconsciously listen to French-language CDs during their naps?"

"No, no. Latin."

"Right." They both laugh.

"What you haven't mentioned is the creation of these two to four children," Sharelle says, putting her feet on the dashboard.

"But that involves indecent acts."

"Yes, indeed it does. I'm as troubled by that idea as you are. Do you think you're still up for that sort of indiscretion?"

"Well, I could try to fight my way through the shame, but it wouldn't be easy. And I'd have to remove your corset first, which is a project in itself."

"Yes, and then you'd have to warm my puritanical loins." She slowly draws her knees apart. "You know how cold they get."

"Oh my." He swallows. "Yes, frigid."

"Or maybe I'll take you right here and now," she says matter-of-factly.

"Whoa. Calm yourself."

"You watch yourself, or I'll make you pull this thing over. Grind you into dust."

"Must you be so carnal?"

"Whatsa matter, big boy? You can't handle me. I knew it."

"Really."

"Really." She leans into his face, her lips brushing his cheek and settling in his ear. "Little buddy is afraid of girls," she taunts, in a moaning whisper. "He can't handle a real woman. Should we take you home and put you down for a nap, fella?"

A sign says, "Napili Pineapple Plantation next right." Mitch turns right onto the road. "What's the deal?" Sharelle asks. He says nothing and turns left onto a side road, then left onto another that ends in a gravel clearing bordered by a grove of papaya trees. A large metal container stands in the middle of the clearing, and Mitch parks between it and the trees. "And we're parking here because..." she says.

He puts his finger to his lips. Seat back. Grabbing her low-rise jean cutoffs by the belt loops. Pulling her onto his lap. Sliding fingers through strands of hair where her spine starts. Soft puffs of air into her ear. Breathing quickens. Wind flits across the top of leaves. Tongues push and slip and circumscribe. Hands slide down her torso and up under the white halter top. Skin taut. Capillaries full. Humid. Maui.

"You're right. I can barely handle you," he whispers. Sigh. Halting breath.

"You can handle me. Oh, you can do anything you want," she says between raspy gasps. "Handle me, Mitchell." A whispered "forever" in her ear. Denim sliding along goose-bumped skin, then satin. Engorge. Black leather seats. Interlocked fingers. Are you in this with me forever? No matter what? Forever?

Yes, I am, Mitch. Yes. Yes. Yes. Yes. Yes. Yes. Yeah. Yeah. Yeahhhh. Yeahhhhhhhh.

Hungry. Up and down and through. Slide. Free fall.

Pineapples. Papaya. Pacific breeze.

Seared. Consumed.

Forever.

The sign ahead on the right brings him back: "You are leaving the Amara Valley." Mitch is leaving the valley. He opens the glove box to find a map. There's nothing in there but the owner's manual, insurance papers, and an old expired passport: *Van Laren, Sharelle Annette. 16 DEC 71.*

Sharelle Annette. She who endures probing fingers and stainless steel specula and injections that force her body to produce eggs at a rate twenty times what's normal—a human pincushion who shares his name, who yearns to have a child with him. She who, time after time after time, has walked hand in hand with him to the clinic for egg retrieval, carrying her old Adidas gym bag with consent forms and toiletries and the soothing CDs she's allowed to bring to calm her nerves during the "harvesting." How many times he has walked with this same patient, *16 DEC 71*, to this same Promised Land and watched her be ushered into the washroom where she puts on the light-blue gown and hair cap and steels herself for another round and then unlocks the door telling herself this time it'll work and is led into the treatment room by a soothing nurse who pats her hand and rubs her back, while Mitch sits in a chair in a nearby room masturbating with a time-dependent frenzy, his hand sliding up and down his tingling fount, focusing on the sensation to distract him from the reality of this degrading substitute for lovemaking, while she waits on the table for her eggs to be harvested and then fertilized with the sperm he has generated through his primitive rubbing, and Mitchell who, job done and seed delivered, then walks over to the room and stands beside her and whispers rehearsed words of comfort and encouragement again and again as the eggs are suctioned from her exhausted uterus and every detail of them studied and rated under the microscope of the waiting technician—will they be graded a *C* or even *B* again, or will they be an *A* grade this time, making their probable death after fertilization and replacement one rung further up on the ladder of grief? Does he want a child as much as she does? she must think. She has gone forward and done it again and again, through the pain and tears and Phone Calls and injections and fertile sisters and four-child family pyramids in glossy photos and babies all around her, babies playing and laughing and crawling and teething and drooling and suckling and smiling everywhere, on TV in the playground the passing stroller the next car at the traffic light in the grocery line at the bank. She's done it all anyway, to build this story together through her pain, Sharelle, who so badly wants to get it right and make it right, and Mitchell, masturbating Mitchell, is standing in the way, Mitchell fumbling to screw the lid onto the specimen jar and pass it through the hole in the wall to the lab tech, the endorphins still humming inside his spinal fluid. Does she know that this is not who he is? That if there were any way he could make it about more than spraying his DNA through the wall, that if he could take every single shard of her broken spirit and stab it into his flesh, he would? Does she know—in the deepest, vastest way possible, that he is fully invested in this story? That it's the only life he wants to build, that as long as *Sharelle Annette Van Laren 16 DEC 71* has breath in her nostrils, he wants to be the conduit through which the oxygen passes? That Mitchell Van Laren, the one she's chosen for her deliverance, is not giving up? On her, on them?

He can't leave the valley.

He has nowhere to go, and he can't keep driving north. There is more to fix than he can begin to conceive. Sharelle. Her parents. His students. Staff. But it will have to start with Sharelle. She knows what pressure he's—they've—been through. He thinks she'll understand, but he wants to be able to explain it to her. He hopes no one else has told her.

There's no choice but to try again. He needs to work harder. He makes a U-turn and heads back. He wants to do something for Sharelle. He wants her to know he cares about her. That she's important to him and they can get through anything. He'll make a special meal for her tonight and explain what happened. They'll figure it out. She'll understand the strain. Sharelle loves chicken skewers on the grill. That's what he'll make.

Mitch stops at a grocery store in Sapperton and buys what he needs. Then he heads back into town. He has another stop to make. Sharelle's been talking about a display cabinet that she really likes at Walstrom's Furniture. He's kept telling her to wait until it goes on sale. It never has. He's going to surprise her. He buys it for the full $600 and loads it into the Civic and straps down the hatch with a bungee cord. He drives home, unloads the box with the unassembled pieces, and lays it on the living room floor.

He preps the chicken skewers and wraps them in foil. He puts them in the fridge and cleans up the mess. Then he checks the cordless phone and finds eight missed messages. They are looking for him. They're worried about him too; he knows that. He doesn't want to hear the messages. He thinks about his options. There are few. Realistically, there is one. Go back to school and tell them about all the stress he's been under and that it has all become too much. Pay to fix the wall and make a formal apology to all the kids and their parents and ask forgiveness. That's what he'll do.

Sharelle will be getting home from work in a few hours. He wants to have the display cabinet set up, and he wants to be cooking food when he tells her. Then he won't have to look her right in the eye. It won't seem like such a big deal if he says he had a little breakdown in class today, while he's basting pieces of chicken in peanut sauce. It's all about the delivery. Maybe she will understand. Maybe she will hug him and say she's sorry everything came to a head like this. *We're in this together, Mitchell. We're going to make it. We've got what it takes.* And then she will see him with new eyes, reborn in the knowledge that he is the One. The only one she needs.

The phone rings. He tries to ignore it and start assembling the cabinet. It's solid. Dark oak. There are no words in the assembly instructions. Only complex pictures with ambiguous arrows and a maddening assortment of screw sizes. Mitch is not a visual learner, and he needs language, of which there is none.

After nearly three hours of matching diagrams to parts and his hand aching and palm blistered from the hexagonal Allen key's edges, he's finally done. The last step says to bolt the unit into the wall at the top with two long screws and a strap. A safety precaution for children. He moves the stud finder along the wall. The electrical hazard signal keeps beeping. He does this several times and the signal keeps beeping at different spots. Forget it. He can always do it later. If they need to.

Mitch puts away the tools and vacuums the sawdust. Then he stands at the other end of the living room and regards the cabinet. He should probably put some things in it. It has different nooks at varying angles. He sets up a few framed pictures from their trips that they've been meaning to find a place for. He fills the rest of the nooks with books about popular music and travel. *Top 100 Rock Albums, Lonely Planet Eastern Europe*. Then he showers.

He meets Sharelle at the door at 4:30 and gives her a kiss on the cheek while she's bent down taking off her shoes. She lets off one of her long, exhausted sighs. The travel business is tough. Everybody books trips online now. She rises again and gives him a peck on his forehead. Good. She hasn't heard.

He stares at her until she catches his eye, and he tries his little mischievous grin.

"What have you been up to?" She bites her lower lip.

"Nothing," he says, holding the last syllable for a couple extra seconds. Mitch moves his eyes back and forth from Sharelle to the living room. Like a metronome. She walks into the living room while unbuttoning her coat, and he follows her and watches her expression.

"That's great. Did you do that today?"

"Yup."

"When did you have time?"

"I made time. See, I put up some pictures. Remember this one from Lithuania? Remember the nude beach? How I dropped everything and pranced? When you took the picture, you made that sign look like it was covering my bum." She doesn't laugh at the word *bum* like she once did.

"Thanks. It's really terrific." He opens his arms to give her a hug, but she doesn't see it and brushes past him and goes to the closet to hang her jacket. This is probably a good time. He can't wait until supper.

"Something bad happened today," Mitch says.

"Oh." She starts unclipping a barrette from her hair.

"It was a very unfortunate event." She leaves the barrette and puts her hands in her back pockets. He fidgets with his hands and she stares at them.

"Ten-point scale?" she asks. They used to rate their days from one to ten when they were first married. A rating of one was Winning the Lottery. Ten was a Nuclear Winter.

"8.5," Mitch says.

"Not a nine?"

"Okay, yeah. Nine."

Sharelle finishes pulling out the barrette. She clicks it shut, walks over to the stairs, and puts a foot on the bottom step. She turns and locks eyes with him. Her voice is low and even.

"No, Mitchell. Your principal called me. It's pretty much a ten."

October 1979

Mitch's social studies homework that day in grade five was to interview one or both of his parents about an important world event that had happened in their lifetime and record their reflections on its impact. It sounded kind of cool, Mitch thought. Dad knew a ton about history and was always spouting off historical events. "Could've been a history teacher once, if I had the opportunity," he had said. But he wasn't to be bothered after dinner. Still, maybe it was something they could do together.

Mitchell tentatively walked into the living room where Mom was reading in her armchair and Dad was in his recliner watching hockey highlights. "Hey, Dad. Can you help me with something?" he hushed.

Dad continued to stare at the TV. "Is the house on fire?"

"No."

"Is Trevor running amok with an axe outside?"

"No. He's doing homework."

"Then I can't think of another reason why you'd disturb my 6-7 time."

"Something I can help with, Mitchell?" Mom said.

"I need to ask my parents about an important world event during your lifetime and interview you about it."

Dad swivelled his chair towards Mitch, and then his eyes rose to the ceiling in thought. "And who'll be listening to it?"

"My teacher and entire social studies class."

Dad clicked off the TV and sat back in the chair. "Sounds right up my alley. Of course, I've got time for you, son. Good to see they're giving you useful homework. Okay, I've got a fascinating event for you." Dad sounded interested, even excited.

"Really? Maybe we could work together on it. I'll meet you at the kitchen table, okay Dad?"

"I'll grab you guys a couple of Cokes for energy," Mom said.

"You got it. Be right there," Dad said and walked over to a pull-out drawer inside the coffee table. Mitch walked upstairs to his room, found his tape recorder and a new cassette tape, and walked back downstairs to the kitchen.

As Mitch unwrapped the cassette and loaded it into the machine, he heard Dad enter the room and then a newspaper slapped down on the table on top of Mitch's hands. He startled for a second and then pulled his chair back and laid the paper flat on the desk—a copy of the Vancouver Sun from November 1978. On the cover was an aerial picture showing the splayed bodies of men, women, and children lying face-down on the ground. Mitch swallowed some excess saliva in his throat and moistened his dried-out lips. He focused on the image of a small child, probably an infant, lying with one arm across its mother's back. Then his eyes travelled down to the caption: "Suicide in the Jungle: Hundreds Dead." Mitch pushed the paper forward on the table.

"Quite something, eh?" Dad said.

"It's from two years ago."

"Yup. Did you hear about it in school? Or do they only talk about labour rights and Karl Marx?"

"We heard about it."

"French Guiana is a long way off, but it could happen anywhere. Could happen here," Dad said. Then he sat down beside Mitch, pulled the paper between them, and smoothed it out.

"It was Guyana. Jonestown was in Guyana," Mitch said.

"You're getting it mixed up with French Guiana."

"Um, no. There's three. Left to right—Guyana, Suriname, French Guiana. But it doesn't matter really?" Mitch said it as a question, in order not to appear contradictory.

"Left to right, eh Mitch. How about calling it east to west, like it should be?"

"Actually, that would be west to—" Mitch stops. "The paper's right here. See, it says, 'Guyana.'"

Dad pulled his chair back, turned it to face Mitch, put his foot on the side of Mitch's seat and leaned close into him. Mitch leaned to the left and looked back sideways at Dad. "How much did it cost, Mitchell?"

"How much did what cost?"

"Your MENSA membership? Is it a one-time fee or do you have monthly payments?"

"I just learned about it in our South America unit in social socials class. That's all."

"Oh, you learned it in your 'unit'? Is there a unit on respecting the experience and knowledge of your parents?" He susurrated on 'parents.' I don't believe in corporal punishment, Mitch, because of my father. But I swear. The way you push my buttons. Sometime you'll go too far. It won't be pretty."

Mitchell felt a cold sensation in his back and he was now leaned over almost 45 degrees. "No, but they should teach a unit like that. You're right, Dad. I shouldn't correct you like that."

"I like the sound of that: 'You're right, Dad.' I don't hear it often enough. Say it again."

"You're right, Dad."

"Wow, was it as unbearable to say as you thought it would be? And by the way, trivia does not equal intelligence."

"Okay."

They both almost simultaneously leaned over to the right again, and Mitch smoothed out the paper this time. "You saved this for almost two years," he said.

"Yes, I saved it."

"Why did you save it, Dad?"

"Because it's fascinating. Don't you think?" His voice was cheery.

"It's horrific. Why did they listen to Jim Jones? Why didn't they leave?"

"He was creating something special in the wilderness. A new way of living. Freedom, honour, greatness. There's freedom in discipline, believe it or not. But he went a little nuts."

"He definitely disciplined them. A little nuts is right."

"He loved them. He was like a father. There's no stopping a father who wants to be with his family. Even one as bat-shit crazy as Jim Jones."

"Ah, such love!" Mitch said, trying to lighten things.

Dad put an elbow on the table and leaned his cheek on his fist. He smiled at Mitch, but his eyes were vacant and faraway. "Kind of beautiful, in a way," Dad said, turning and caressing the picture with his fingertips. "They either gave themselves completely to his vision, or life wasn't worth it. Mediocrity wasn't an option. Only greatness. But it was still insanity."

"So they couldn't leave. He wouldn't have let them," Mitch said, hushing his voice for no discernible reason.

"No, he wouldn't have. Makes you imagine what might have been." His fingers traced the outline of an adult body on the photo.

Mitch decided to ease the mood. "Kool-Aid, Kool-Aid, tastes great. Gotta go to the bathroom. Whoops, too late," he sang, just as Mom walked in the room. He faked a laugh.

"Mitchell Alexander!" Mom said. "Toilet humour again. Boy, what a fine catch you'll make as a husband someday." She put her hands on her hips in mock sternness.

"But I'm so cute, right Mommy?" Mitch said and Mom dropped a hand and tweaked his cheek. "Yes, that you are." She examined the paper, and her other hand dropped. "Tony, why are you showing him this? That's not for a child."

"Mitch isn't a child anymore. He's an intellectual apparently, at least as far as obscure South American countries go," Dad said.

"It's not appropriate for him." She started to pick up the paper, but Dad dropped an arm over it.

"Mitch needs to see that life is hard. It's not all lollipops and Trivial Pursuit."

"I actually don't think I want to do Jonestown. Sorry," Mitch said.

Dad took his left hand and slipped it under his cheek beside the right, creating a sleeping gesture. "That a fact? What do you actually want to do?" he asked, mimicking a child's voice.

"Could I interview you about the moon landing?"

"The moon landing. Perfect. Epic human dramas happening right here on the ground, and Mitchell wants to learn about men in spacesuits," said Dad.

"It's Mitch's project, so he should do what he wants," Mom said.

"Since when does Mitch know what he wants? Or what's good for him?" Dad said.

"It's an astonishing achievement, and it happened the year I was born," said Mitch.

"Moonbeams and lunar golf, right Mitch? Neil Armstrong with a five-iron, huh? Fine, ask your mom about the 'astonishing' moon landing," he said, then slapped his hands on the table and jumped up. He grabbed the newspaper with one hand, the top pages crinkling in his grasp. "See if I help you with your homework next time," he hissed in Mitch's ear. Then he folded it in half, tucked it under his arm, and headed to the door. "There you go, Jean. The stage is set for you to swoop in and be the good cop. Again. Have fun." He took two slow-motion leaps across the room to simulate a moonwalk and left.

See if I help you with your homework next time. There you go, Jean.

Greatness.

INCUBATION

AUGUST

It's been almost four months since The Incident in April, during which Mitch has been on short-term disability. The school wanted some time to assess the situation, and the summer break would allow the dust to settle. Esther sent him an email about the paid leave and asked him to submit a detailed statement of the episode. Her email was professional as always, using phrases like "resolution of this situation" and "levels of professional conduct." Then he met with the school board. He will be on extended probationary status and can come back a week from tomorrow for the start of the new school year.

He will have to work to re-establish trust after The Incident. Other than that, he's not sure if anything will change. He'll show up in the staff room at 7:50. He'll put on the coffee and read the paper for a few minutes. Teachers will filter in, and soon there will be the usual banter about cutting corners on curriculum or hogging the photocopier. He'll put in his little contributions but mostly sit and listen.

He'll teach the same way: He'll use mostly "project-based learning," which is a fancy way of saying that he'll assign large projects, sometimes individual and sometimes group. He'll begin with a group project on periods of world literature. The kids will spend their class time researching and preparing. Then they'll present their projects, which is a good way to eat away big chunks of time. The presentations will have to be at least seven minutes long, or he'll take points off. Still, kids like Kenny Hodgson will show up with nothing to present and then take the zero because they don't care about their grades. Mitch doesn't care about the grades either, since giving a zero is a lot easier than grading some grammatically hopeless, half-plagiarized gibberish by some kid whose idea of great literature is a vampire trilogy.

In October, there will be parent-teacher conferences. The mom and dad will come into the room to meet with Mitch. He will fumble through the meeting and search for things to say. He will be grateful if one of the parents is a real talker and fills in the space with idle chat. The mom will listen intently and ask questions about how her child is doing. The dad will sit silently with a thinly disguised sneer as Mitch talks about "applying oneself" and "acceptable classroom behaviour." The sneer will say, "You're a pathetic little teacher with soft hands who works with kids and doesn't know what real work is like or what life in the real world is." He will hate that father and dread his judgment. Mitch will try to sound as un-teacherly as possible and throw in a few slang words to sound like he is a man's man. He will say, "Jeremy's gotta kick it into second gear" and "Kristin needs a fire lit under her butt," but the father will know that he is only trying to sound virile. At the end, he will remind them to call or email if they have any concerns. Then he will assemble a smile through his gritted teeth and shake their hands as they leave. He will then check them off his list. This year will be the same as all the others. Like every fall, he'll be right back to square one.

Sitting here at his desk, Mitchell studies his unit plans for the year and the learning outcomes that have to somehow be met through them—how every student must be able to understand writing conventions, and compare ideas among texts, and present ideas effectively—and the verbs in the updated-yet-again curriculum plan start to murmur senselessly in his mind and leak meaning, and he can no longer distinguish among them: *responding, analyzing, paraphrasing, summarizing, contrasting, engaging*. Devoid of their sense, the words sit on the page like unrisen cakes, their deflated letters thrown onto the page like spatter, and Mitch realizes that something has to change. He can't do this anymore.

Sharelle and Mitch are mere roommates now. They don't talk about anything other than the minutiae required to co-exist in a household. Sharelle has lots of friends she can talk to anyway. They're always over, hanging out with her in the living room. They talk in an intimate way, their knees almost touching as they nod and unblinkingly gaze into each other's eyes in empathy. Sharelle has given Mitch an ultimatum: he will get some help sorting through things. Mercifully, she's left the alternative unsaid. All this works out well anyway because the school has required him to attend an assertiveness course. "Healthy Paths to Emotional Expression," it's called. Sounds like a bunch of psycho-babble bullshit, he thinks.

Sharelle has also brought up the idea of marital counseling, but they've agreed that they need to catch their breath first and simplify. As a couple, they've spent enough time with professionals and doctors lately. The idea of another appointment with another clinician's introduction of, "Hi, my name is Dr. This and That, and my role will be to help you move forward with such and such" feels like too much to bear. Sharelle said, "I need a break from another new, well-researched idea about how to fix us." The dust needs to settle for a while.

There hasn't been the slightest possibility of sex. At night, they both read under their separate lamps. Sharelle turns her light off first, rolls over, and cocoons herself in the sheets. Mitch doesn't even bother trying to initiate anything. He daydreams all the time, generic women's faces and bodies popping in and out of the frame of his mind—pursed and moistened lips with darting tongues, pencil-eraser nipples, asses round as melons, hourglass hips. There was a soap commercial the other night that showed a woman jogging in tight black shorts. Her breaths were rhythmic sighs, her skin shimmering with sweat. Mitch rewound it on his PVR and watched it five times, his breathing getting shallower with each viewing. They were just shorts; she was just jogging. He feels like a fourteen-year-old.

Mitch walks into the lobby of the community centre, where "Healthy Paths" is starting this afternoon. Sharelle has gone to her parents' place for the weekend. She needs a break. She's telling Norman and Audrey that Mitch needs to stay home and prepare for the school year. He goes to the registration table and picks up a file folder with his name on it. A few people are milling, but he doesn't feel like talking to anybody. He walks a few feet away and stands against a wall near a water fountain. While opening the folder and perusing the handouts, he hears, "Hey, it's Mitchell, right? Mitchell Van Laren." Standing before him is Kylii. Beautiful, terrifying Kylii.

Mitch has seen her in town occasionally since high school. He's wanted to talk to her but could never think of a good opener. Somehow, asking her, "Do you remember distilling potassium permanganate?" doesn't quite cut it. So he's gone to his default setting, which is to avoid eye contact and hope she doesn't see him. So far, it's worked. But right now, the default is no longer an option. He is face-to-face with Kylii Tikkanen; she has correctly identified him as Mitchell Van Laren, and he needs a response.

Kylii is so magnificent that Mitch is worried his legs will buckle and he'll fall to his knees. He gently puts one hand against the wall. She is the same Scandinavian demigoddess with satiny black hair, which now drops down to her shoulders. Automatically, his eyes do a quick scan downwards. She's wearing a pink tank top underneath a thin, unzipped white sweater. The two sides of the sweater are parted from her cleavage like drapes, and he can see where the mounds of her breasts start to rise. She has tight black jeans that hang low on her waist, revealing a hint of her hip bones. Mitch squints at her to make it seem he can't quite place her, but then he focuses so much on the importance of giving this impression that he fails to realize that his eyes have moved down to her breasts. A wave of purple heat floods his face.

He forces himself to look in her eyes but with a distant aspect to it—to give the impression that he's trying to recall her name, to place her in his enormous memory bank of women. Am I staring too intensely? he wonders. "Kyle—Kylii. Tik-a-nen," he manages to say in a reasonably ordinary voice. He tries to soften his glare, but now he's squinting again. He focuses on the bridge between her eyes and hopes he doesn't appear cross-eyed.

"Actually it's Kylii Doerksen now. Nice to see you, Mitchell," she says and smiles.

"It is. I mean, it is good for me to be seeing you. To see you." He reaches in and gives her an awkward shoulder hug. Clinique Happy fills his nostrils. Sharelle wears the same perfume. He just hasn't noticed in a while.

"So, who have you been doing?" Mitch asks.

"What?" She still laughs the same way. The deep intake and blissful gasps out. He doesn't realize his mistake at first but laugh anyways.

"Who have you—What have you been up to?" He wonders if his face will be permanently purple.

"Working. Keeping busy. Keeping trouble at bay."

"How's your husband? Steve, right?" *Is it weird that I know his name?*

"Steven. We're sort of in a separation situation right now. Long story."

"Sorry about...hearing...that. We all hit patches of hard times. Rough patches. Of...times." It's like he's watching himself talk. He can't even hear it.

"This isn't a patch. More like a free fall." She strokes her empty ring finger with her left thumb. She lets go and puts her right hand in her sweater pocket.

"Did you get married?" she asks.

"Sharelle is my wife. Met her at university. She's from the East." He hesitates and then says, "We're having a tough go of it ourselves lately."

"You taking a class here?" she asks.

"Yeah, a communications class. For work and stuff."

"Is the teacher's name Gina?"

"I think so."

"Then I'm in the same one. For work and stuff." She smiles, playing with her right earring.

They walk to their classroom in silence. There are twelve chairs with their individual names on them. Mitch finds his and sits down. Kylii is three seats to the left. Most of the chairs are filled including the two between them, so he can relax and study his folder again. Soon, everyone is seated and Gina introduces herself and explains the topics they'll cover. She tells them that this class isn't merely for people who are meek and submissive. Assertiveness is about "healthy ways to express your emotions." There are all kinds of people here, including those who are overly aggressive.

Like the lady beside him. Margaret. She has frizzy red hair with grey roots, and she wears a denim smock. During a lull when Gina goes to the office to run off a couple forgotten handouts, Margaret turns to Mitch and says, "Surprised to see some men here."

"Really? I thought there'd be more," he says.

"Why would there? Men are really out of their element with this stuff."

"Are we?"

"I've been in a number of relationships. As soon as you get into emotional territory, the guy is done."

"Maybe you've met the wrong guys," Mitch says.

"How would you know?"

"I know some guys who probably get it."

"I spent four years in college and three years in grad school dating lots of guys, and I never met one who had any emotional intelligence whatsoever," she says.

"I'm sorry. For what it's worth, they do exist," he says and gives an encouraging smile. She sighs, murmurs something to herself, and starts thumbing through her phone.

Gina returns and leads them in the chanting of a mantra: "Namaste. The self in me honours the self in you."

"Namaste. The self in me honours the self in you," the class incants. "Namaste. The self..."

After this, they're split into two groups and asked to read some scenarios and talk about how they'd respond to them: If you ordered a steak at a restaurant, and it was slightly overdone, would you send it back? When you're upset with your spouse or partner, how do you tell him/her? Kylii is in the other group. The time trudges on, and Mitch stays silent.

At the end of class, they have to say something positive to another classmate in front of everybody. The point is to practice receiving and giving compliments with confidence and poise. Mitch is asked to say something nice about Margaret. He tries not to appear like he's searching for words. He turns to her and says, "Margaret, you have a real strength of character, and you definitely know what you want."

"Thank you, Murphy," Margaret says.

"Mitchell," he says. She doesn't correct herself and starts studying her fingernails. Mitch reaches down and tightens a shoelace.

The activity continues, and then it's Kylii's turn.

"Kylii, please give Mitchell a compliment," Gina says.

Kylii turns and faces away from him across the circle.

I didn't realize she was shy.

"I feel comfortable and safe around you, Michelle. You're a real people person," she says.

She said Michelle instead of Mitchell. Must be really nervous.

"Thank you, Kylii," he says at the same time that a woman across the room says it. There are some titters. "Sorry, I thought she said 'Mitchell,'" he says and bows his head, shielding his eyes in mock, real anguish.

After class, everyone packs up and he thanks Gina for a good first class. He asks her if it's okay if he misses the next session because he has a "Meet the Teacher" event at school.

"Mitchell, let's try that again," she says.

"Pardon?"

"This time, I want you to look me square in the eye. Keep your chin at a 90-degree angle to your body and tell me that you won't be here next week. Don't ask. You are a person with agency and entitlements." In the corner of his eye, he sees Kylii leave the room.

"I'll be gone next week for a school event," he says, almost in a whisper.

"Better. We'll work on your volume and enunciation soon enough," she says. As he walks to his chair to get his folder, she says, "There are some things we can't change. Who you are and how you feel is in your DNA, Mitchell. What you can change is how you think about it."

He is dismissed, so he grabs his folder and walks into the lobby. Kylii is there, getting a drink from the water fountain. She's bent over leaning into the fountain with her left hand pinning her hair back away from the stream. She finishes drinking, wipes her mouth with a thumb, and turns and sees him. "Cutting class already, eh?" she says.

"Can't help it. A teacher's thing I gotta go to. At the school. At school."

"What school do you teach at?"

"Kingsley Middle."

"So, are you like the teachers we had in school?"

"I'm not much of a teacher. Pretty mediocre."

"I doubt that. I'm sure you're a great teacher. But that English teacher we had. Now that's mediocre. What was his name?"

"You mean Powell McAllister?"

"That's it!"

"I called him Portly Powell."

Kylii inhales deeply and emits a glorious wheezing laugh and leans down to hold her knees, continuing to look at Mitch. "Portly Powell?" Another intake of air and then blissful gasping emissions. "That's freaking awesome!" She reaches out her hand to give him a fist-pump, and he inexplicably extends a high-five instead, his hand patting her closed fist. Then he pulls the hand back, mortified, and Kylii's laughter runs its course. "I can't believe he kept his job. I wonder if he's still around," she says, upright again.

"I don't know. Maybe he's dead," Mitch says. His facial temperature has receded to a low simmer. He can breathe again. He's talking to Kylii Tikkanen, even making her laugh. He can do this.

"I was thinking more like retired, but okay," she says, lifting her eyebrows.

Mitch can't think of anything to say and tries to put his left hand in his front pocket, but he already has his wallet and keys in there because his right pocket has a big hole and he has no back pockets, so there's barely enough room. He forces his fingertips into the pocket, probing for some room to maneuver, and has to settle for sliding them in only up to the first knuckle. He feels like he could squirm right out of his clothes. Thankfully, Kylii opens her file folder and fingers one of her handouts. "I guess you'll be missing next week's session on 'active listening.' A shame."

"I'll get by somehow," Mitch says.

"I'll fill you in on what you missed."

"That would be appreciated. I'd appreciate...that."

"Maybe Portly Powell, if he's not dead, can come in as a guest speaker and talk about what makes a good leader." She folds her upper lip over the lower.

"You remember that?"

"That was so...brutal. I lost all respect for him after that. That must've hurt."

"Yeah, well. Things happen in high school," he says.

"Still..."

"Yeah, it hurt. But I survived. Still here."

"So you are. Good to see you, Mitchell. I'll take great notes for you."

"Thanks," he says.

She turns and starts walking out, and then she stops and looks back at him. "Oh, and for what it's worth, I do feel safe around you, Mitchell," she says.

There is a tingling sensation in his legs. Kylii is almost at the door when Mitch takes a big chance. "Stay away from potassium permanganate," he says in Mrs. Trethewey's nasally voice.

She turns to him with a blank expression and says, "Um, okay," and then she's gone.

Mitch feels the crimson tide pooling in his face again, and he takes a long, cold drink from the same fountainhead over which Kylii Tikkanen has just hovered her lips.

July 1974

Mitch sat in a big lawn chair by the campfire, watching his dad fold a dish towel in half over a thin yellow rope that was tied between a tree and the picnic table. It was the first and last time camping with him.

"Your grandpa says I should spend more time with you guys, so here we are."

"Why didn't Trevor come?"

"He's got a poofy little piano recital." He pulled his chair beside Mitch and sat, and they watched the fire. It was quiet, the sun was going down, and it was past Mitch's bedtime.

Super fun!

Mitch's dad had a video camera around his neck. "Nothing better than this, eh Mitch?" He took the camera out of the bag and pointed it at the trees, then at the faraway seashore, then at Mitch for a few seconds, then back to the ocean. Click. He shut it off and put it back in the case. "Someday, Mitch, I'd love to build a cabin in a place like this. Live simply."

"What about Mommy and Trevor and me?"

"You could come visit."

"Daddy, can you teach me how to catch fishes?"

"Hard thing to learn. I never have much time. Gotta work."

"Okay."

"I'd build a cabin down there. C'mon, I'll show you." He rose and walked to the campsite edge, hands in pockets. Mitch climbed from the chair, caught up to him, and grabbed his arm. His dad kept his hands in his pockets and looked out over the trees—soldiers marching all the way to the ocean. Halfway across the forest was a small lake, shiny in the sun. "Right there's the spot. I'd build it by that lake."

"You're good at building things, Daddy." Mitch wanted to live on that lake with him and be a man like him. They walked back to the fire together and sat down.

"I'd escape and be free."

"Daddy, you want to see my owey knee? I scraped it on the sidewalk and Mommy gave me a Band-Aid." Mitch pulled up his pant leg. "See? I took it off last night by myself."

"That's not bad. She gave you a Band-Aid for that?"

"It was a bad one. So bad." Mitch gently poked his knee.

"Sometimes a guy needs to suck it up, Mitch. It's okay to get hurt. Your mom coddles you."

"She's a great cuddler. Yeah."

"No, she coddles you. Treats you like a baby."

"She says I'll always be her baby boy. Trevor is her big boy."

"What does your mom say about me?" He leaned forward, eyes cold. Mitch felt scared. *Mommy must make him so mad.*

"She says you're nice."

Mitch's dad leaned back in his chair. "So many super things I could do. Great things."

"Super Daddy to the rescue!"

"Your mom thinks money grows out of our butts." He pulled out his buckskin leather wallet—the one with the large orange stitches that Mitch had given him the previous Christmas—and stuck his mouth into it. "Echo, echo," he hollered into it.

Mitch giggled. "That's funny, Daddy. And money doesn't grow out of our bums."

"Then you tell her that. She's bleeding us a nickel at a time."

Mitch didn't want to talk anymore and sat quietly watching the fire spit and crackle. They sat for a long time, the stars as shiny against the darkness as the tiny bulbs on his Lite-Brite set.

Then it was time to crawl into the tent, and Mitch's dad told a scary story about a park ranger becoming a wolfman at night. Mitch didn't want to sleep.

You might get nightmares and Mommy's not here. Hide in the sleeping bag.

"This is what big boys do, Mitchell."

You and Daddy in a tent. You're a really big boy.

"Good night. Go to sleep now."

"Daddy, do I make you mad sometimes?"

"I get mad when people keep their ears closed."

"Do I have open ears?"

"You listen better than the others."

"I'll never close them. I promise."

"Good night, Mitch."

"Good night, Daddy."

In the middle of the night, the wind made howling noises and Mitch was afraid. The tent was shaking and the side closest to him lifting up, the canvas billowing and shuddering. He reached for his dad. He wasn't there.

Mitch turned the flashlight on and sat up, and his dad was standing at the other side of the tent with his fingers down on one corner and toes on the opposite. Like a bridge. The tent poles made a creaking sound. His face was red and he was sweating.

"Dad."

"Go back to sleep!"

"I'm scared."

"I said to go back to sleep!" He banged his hand on the tent floor, yelling at the wind. "Piece of shit tent!"

His dad leapt to Mitch's side of the tent and used the same position to try to flatten the flailing canvas. The side he'd just left lifted up and rumbled. His dad jumped back again to the other side. Soon he was flitting from one side to the other, the edges lifting and thrashing the second he left.

"Fucking piece of shit! I'll show you, bitch!"

Mitch turned off the flashlight and pulled the sleeping bag over his head, then put his hands over his ears and took deep breaths.

You're a turtle. Count to 100. Come out and look. He's still a bridge. Climb back in and count to 300. The wind goes whoosh. You want to go home. Stop being mean daddy

AUGUST

When Mitch gets home from his class, he sees that the bedroom door is closed. Sharelle must be working on her laptop. He goes to the living room and sits down to watch TV. As usual, the remote's missing, and he checks the usual places: between the cushions and behind the pillows. Then he crouches down on all fours and feels under the couch for it. His hand slides along the carpet and then it runs along the smooth surface of something flat. It feels like a book. He nudges it out with a fingertip, picks it up, and sits on the floor. He studies the cover: "Can't Wait to Meet You: A Book to be Read in Utero." On the cover is a picture of a clay animation. A woman with flowing auburn hair and a bright canary-yellow gown is gazing down at her swollen belly. She's holding a handful of balloons in her hand. He opens the book and reads one of the middle pages:

> *Little One, so glad you're on the way.*
> *Can't wait for your very first birthday!*
> *There's so much that you will get to see.*
> *But first, I'll meet you and you'll meet me.*

Mitch flips back to the title page where Sharelle has written, "To my darling Lynnette." Before she became an "expired fetus," they had named their unborn girl Lynnette. The name means waterfall. "Lynnette, I promise to be the best mommy I can be. Like the name of this book says, I can't wait to meet you! Love, Your Mommy." Mitch feels tiny tremors inside his fingers. He closes the book and traces around the meandering outline of the largest balloon with his left index finger. It's a pink orb, swollen in blotches at the edges from the artist's pressed fingertips on clay.

He closes his eyes.

He and Sharelle are newlyweds at the head table. He's reaching down to his right and holding her left hand, putting her ring between his thumb and middle finger. He turns it back and forth, letting the overhead light glint off the diamond from different angles. Then he gives it a full rotation around the finger and leaves it facing straight upwards. He peers into her eyes and watches her pupils get bigger with the slowly dimming lights. Her irises disappear in the growing darkness, and he turns to the big screen at the other end of the room. There's a close-up of a pink pair of socks. Heather has put a slideshow together, and footage from an 8 mm video is being shown.

The camera zooms back and shows Sharelle sitting cross-legged on a throw rug. She is about four years old, and she has a baby doll laid out in front of her. She's putting the little socks on it, her concentration fierce. There's a plastic fake bottle of milk for the baby beside her. She finishes with the socks and grabs the bottle, jamming it a little too roughly into its mouth. Everybody in the reception hall laughs as she tries to remove it, but it's stuck. She yanks on it, and then the camera's put on the floor. Her mother comes into view, and a communal intake of breath travels through the hall: Samantha. It'd be seven years before cancer cells stole her left breast. Eight years before they stole her. She is Sharelle—the same soft ringlets of hair spiral down to her shoulders. With exaggerated concern, she puts her hands on her hips like Sharelle does, bent at the wrists and fingers extended. Then she reaches down and gently rotates the bottle until it slips from the doll's mouth. She hands it back to Sharelle and gives her a kiss on top of her head. So gentle. There's a murmur of pleasure in the hall. Mitch looks over at Audrey. She's puckering.

Opening his eyes and sitting on the floor with the book flat on his palms like he's holding a begging bowl, Mitch pictures pink socks on babies. He imagines the softness of Samantha's voice. He recalls some of the words he's overheard Audrey say over the years. The demands:

When will you start calling me Mom, Sharelle?

Your father's chosen his love, and now you must love his choice.

The judgements:

Career or family. One of them has to give.

Back in our day, women had only one degree in mind—the MRS.

Are you eating the right foods, Sharelle? So much processed stuff in your diet.

And the cruelties:

If you stop obsessing about getting pregnant, then it will happen. Psychosomatic is all.

I bet you'd do it differently if you could, Sharelle.

Oh, to turn back time, eh Sharelle?

Not the mother type, my dear. Not the mother type.

Mitch imagines Sharelle sitting on this couch with a baby slurping on her breast. Audrey's forced to sit beside her and watch. She sees Sharelle's joy and contentment. The baby stops, lifts its head, and sneezes in Audrey's face. Audrey takes a tissue and dries her nose and mouth. When the baby's done feeding, Sharelle holds it in front of Audrey, and it coos. Sharelle praises it and devours it with kisses, and then she holds it on her shoulder with its arms dangling over. It closes its eyes and rests its head against her neck. Audrey's lips are twisting back and forth. Her jaw is clicking with a steady twisting tempo from left to right:

Click. Click. Click. Click.

It's twisting faster. Click, Click, Click, Click.

Allegro now. ClickClickClickClick.

Mitch wants to watch her try to hold their baby in feigned interest. Its squirming legs kick her ears. Its tiny fists lash out at her and reject her attempted hugs. A fountain of gurgling drool springs forward and flows into her mouth.

May that drool pour down her throat and choke her. May she gasp and cough to expel that fluid. May that child turn its back to Audrey and nestle back into the soft pocket of its mother's neck.

Oh, to turn back time, eh Sharelle?

Turn it back. Turn your back.

May she drown in our child's drool.

Mitch doesn't want to watch TV. From the bedroom, he hears the sound of the shredder he bought at a liquidation sale. Sharelle hates clutter, and she's paranoid about identity theft, so she shreds everything. He rises from the floor and walks into the bedroom. Sharelle is sitting in an office chair at the desk in the corner. There's a thick, green hanging file lying on the desk. The quick, high-pitched whine of the shredder becomes a slow, deep whirr as she feeds a paper into its mouth.

"What are you shredding?" Mitch says above the returning whine.

"Odds and ends."

"Such as?" he asks, as she picks up another paper. He walks up to the desk and lifts the cover of the folder, studying the top page. He flips through several more pages with his fingertips. "Clinic records!"

"Yes."

"Stop! How much of this have you shredded?"

"A few pages. What's the big deal?"

"These are a record of our cycles!"

"The clinic has copies too." She keeps her eyes on the shredder.

"Why wouldn't you ask me?"

"You mean for permission? My bad," she says in a mock lilt.

"Turn it off."

"They're taking up space."

"Turn it off now!" Mitch barks.

Sharelle takes another paper from the folder, reaches down, and starts shredding it. Her movement is so robotic. His chin is trembling. He walks to the wall, unplugs the shredder, and flings the cord against the wall. Sharelle reaches forward, grabs the cord, and plugs it in. She picks up another paper and prepares to feed it. Mitch unplugs the cord again and holds its prongs in his hand. She puts a fist around the cord underneath his hand, and scowls into him. The centres of her eyes are like sunflowers, the yellow irises flaring outwards from the black holes like sunrays.

"I'm shredding some old memories," she says. "Old hits from the past. You're quitting anyway."

"I am not quitting. I'm working at it just as hard as you are."

"That's why we're living on one and a half incomes right now. Because you're working so hard."

"Why don't you shred my short-term disability checks then? Have at it."

"It beats taking apart a classroom and jeopardizing our future." She raises her eyes to the ceiling like she's distracted—nonchalant.

"I'm so sorry about showing emotion. I'll go comatose from now on."

"You know how much shit I'd like to throw around the room? But I don't. That's called self-discipline. Adulthood."

One notch above a whisper, Mitch says, "In that case, go ahead and shred. If that's what you want to do, shred them all."

"Huh?"

"I'll help you." He drops the cord, yanks the lid off the shredder, and grabs a handful of shredded paper. The thin accordion strips are stiff in his hand. He holds them out to Sharelle. "Run these through again."

"I don't want to."

"You want to erase our history, so go for it. Run them through. Do it a hundred more times until there's a pile of powder." She keeps staring at him. "Then take the pile outside and light it on fire."

"Quit it." She releases the cord from her hand.

He pictures her lighting the powder on fire, the particles sparking like fireflies as they travel up into the night—shooting stars on a black canvas.

"There's a lighter on the mantle. Go for it," he says.

"You're being a baby!" She pulls the strips from his hand and tosses them back into the shredder's canister. Her hand comes down to her hip—wrist bent, fingers extended. "What were you thinking about while you were throwing your tantrum at school, Mitchell? What popped into your head?"

"Nothing. I wasn't thinking."

"Perfect. Thank you. A lack of thought is just what we needed," she says.

Mitch bends down and sits on his knees in front of her. He puts his hands on either side of her seat. "I want you to stop shredding. Please?"

"I *need* to shred them."

"And I *need* you not to shred them," Mitch says.

"Why?" she roars, throwing up her arms in a V.

"Because when this is all over, I want to be able to look back and see what we came through."

Sharelle's arm moves to her lap. "Let me spare you the effort. 'Forty-one-year-old Caucasian female subject presents bilateral fallopian hydrosalpinx. Surgical interventions have proven insufficient.'"

"And the forty-six-year-old male? 'Subject presents impaired spermatozoan motility. Recent varicocelectomy performed with only slight increase in motility,'" Mitch says.

"So, the share of responsibility would appear to be eighty percent female subject, twenty percent male."

"The ratio of responsibility is fifty-fifty," Mitch says.

"To the layman, then, the male and female subjects are officially screwed." Sharelle holds the vowel for an eternity: scroooood. It sends a dull ache through his stomach.

"No they're not, because the subjects are exploring all the options."

"Why are they? It's killing them: their bank account, their happiness, all of it."

"Because they've made it this far. And they're not giving up." Mitch lifts his hands off her chair and leans back onto his calves. "She wants this so badly, above everything else. Everything," he says. He whispers the word *everything.*

"Having a baby is what women do."

"So, a baby will make her a woman?"

"Something like that. You don't know the first thing about it," Sharelle says.

"I want it as bad as you do. But it doesn't define us. Our worth." He leans forward and tries to put an arm on her shoulder, which she shakes away.

"So, you 'want to be able to look back and see what we came through.' That's fantastic, Mitchell. Nostalgia," she says. She narrows her eyes at him and clenches her jaw. Heartburn stings Mitch's chest. He stands and, maintaining eye contact, he backs to the bed and sits. She swivels her chair to follow the movement, staring at him with the tip of her thumb in her mouth. It feels like a showdown. He relents first by staring across at the shredder. It's quiet for a while.

"Why do you do that?" Mitch says.

"Do what?"

"Look at me the way you just did. Like I'm an insect."

"I don't know how else to look. I hurt. All the time."

"I hurt, too. So, tell me more about it. I want to know." Mitchell's cheeks are flushed. He locks eyes with her again.

Sharelle gets up and puts the lid back on the shredder. "Why don't you have a rest?" she says, not unkindly. She leaves the desk lamp on and shuts off the main light. Then she walks out and pulls the door closed. The latch doesn't fully click, and the door creaks open an inch.

Mitch is alone sitting on this king-sized bed with its dark oak frame, its headboard carved with elaborate leaves and spiraling tree branches. He moves his eyes over the room's taupe walls, which are grainy in the soft glare of the lamp. A thin line of light peeks in from the hallway. He turns and observes the vertical beam it casts on the blown-up photo on the wall above the headboard. It's a side view of him and Sharelle lying on their stomachs in the grass at the Cliffs of Moher in Ireland. Their heads are peering over the edge of a precipice. The beam of light cuts across him at the ankles.

Mitch lies on his side and stares at the brown and green checker patterns in the bedspread. Earth tones. He's alone on this same bed where she used to perch on top of him with an elbow on either side and cup his head in her hands, running her tongue along his and then lifting her head as his lips explored the base of her chin. Pressing his shoulder blades with her fingertips and gyrating her hips to their private rhythmic melody as they glided together through that soft, candlelit other-world—the world that once existed before intimacy devolved into circled dates on the monthly calendar. He pulls the bedspread into bunches and holds it as he once held her.

Don't walk away from me, he thinks. Remember how you used to make me shake with laughter, Sharelle? Remember how I held your hand in front of my friends and they teased me? I smirked at them and told them they were jealous, that they could never get someone like you. I said you were way out of my league, and that I had to hold onto your hand so you didn't slip away.

You've slipped away—disappeared with the turn of a doorknob. Don't leave me falling, my hand reaching up for yours and my legs kicking like a newborn. I need you to reach down and find me. I need you to dilate, Sharelle.

Don't slip away forever. Forever don't slip away.

Forever.

AUGUST

Trevor and Megan have sold their house and are renting Opa's from Mom and Joop. It was the most sensible thing, Trevor said, when you consider the housing market and the inheritance tax implications and all that. Mitch figures he knows what he's talking about, and Mom wanted to stay in her own house.

Mitch has gotten together with Trevor a few times this summer: the latter's attempts to be a listening ear. They've mostly sat drinking beers on the porch, Trevor giving Mitch that look—the one that says, "What's wrong with you? Why can't you do the right thing?"

Trevor and Megan have asked Mitch and Sharelle over today. Sunday afternoons are usually their "Family Time" where they play games with Rachel or go for a hike, but they're making an exception. A "little check-up," Trevor calls it. Sharelle chose to stay home and get caught up on a backlog from work.

On Mitch's recommendation, Norman is there as well to give some ideas about updating the kitchen. "We want to stay under $5000, though," Trevor has said. "Money's a little tight."

Just before the four of them sit down at the kitchen table, Norman excuses himself to use the bathroom.

"You ever met Norman?" Mitch asks.

"Don't you call him Dad?" Megan says.

"I call him Norman. You ever met?"

"At your wedding, right?" Megan says.

"Yes, right."

"He seems like a good guy," Trevor says.

"He can be a good guy. He says what he thinks. You have to be careful or he'll dominate the conversation."

"I don't let people dominate my conversations," says Trevor.

Just stop. Stop.

Norman comes back and gives them a nod. He ignores Megan and talks directly to Trevor: "Good to see you again, Trevor. What you been up to?"

"Usual stuff. Teaching at the college. Research. Writing."

"Trevor will be Dr. Van Laren in the near future," Mitch says.

"Well, golly, we're in the presence of greatness," Norman says.

"I wouldn't go that far," Trevor says.

"I got a nephew working on his master's in culture studies. He's a thesis away from joining a thousand others in the fast food industry. But that's only a master's. He's no doctor like you," Norman says. Trevor forces out a polite smile. Mitch has never seen him squirm like this before.

Ouch, Trevor. You'd better get control of this conversation. It's getting away from you.

"Let's talk kitchen cabinets," says Megan.

After five minutes of listening to cabinetry brainstorming ("I like the idea of a glazed finish." "Yes, and what about birch veneers or maybe thermofoil vinyl?" "Oh, I don't know. It's such an important decision. What if we go with laminate and choose the wrong one? We'll be screwed."), Mitch excuses himself and walks outside to the back porch. Standing there, he can hear the water from the creek moving again. It's a trickle, but enough to be considered a creek. It smells like rain today—like a wet towel on the clothesline. The summer heat is relenting and now it showers once in a while, and soon the tourists will leave. Green is starting to return to the valley. He takes in a deep breath in his nostrils and sits down on the railing.

Mitch thinks about how many evenings Opa spent sitting on this very porch, listening to the creek and rotating his wedding band around his finger. Round and round, clockwise and counterclockwise. Alone on this porch, he must have ached to have Oma back. What was that like to build a life with someone—a life full of shared joys, heartbreaks, triumphs, and regrets—and then lose that person?

The dreams that Opa and Oma had for their family—for their son and daughter sitting wide-eyed as they gazed out the side window of their Studebaker in this new, enormous country free of war and the internal limits imposed by history—must have been limitless too. To watch those memories and dreams disappear and to be left behind as the sole repository of them must have been excruciating.

Deep breaths is the trick, Mitchell. You can endure a lot by breathing deep.

Mitch walks inside, hoping that the discussion is done. From the sounds of it, Megan and Norman seem to be engaged in an exclusive conversation replete with various measurements and types of color casts. Megan sketches a diagram while Norman talks, and then she asks some follow-up questions and segues into rubbed bronze drawer handles.

"I think I've offered all the insight I can," Trevor says. "Come on, Mitch, let's head to the porch.

With Megan and Norman huddled over some sketches on the kitchen table and Rachel playing on the living room floor, Trevor and Mitch go to the front porch and sit down with a beer. Their lawn chairs are side-by-side and two feet apart—the way they prefer.

"You happy with the house?" Mitch asks.

"Yup. Lot of shit to update, though. The whole kitchen needs upgrades. He kind of let it go."

"He was a bachelor. Did you expect lace curtains?"

"I thought he'd put more into it."

"Well, now you can make it your own. Must be nice."

"Yeah."

Mitch takes a big slurp of his Guinness and has to cough, and some beer spills onto his white T-shirt, the free one he got at the Walk-A-Thon fundraiser for the Valley Fertility Fund that he and Sharelle did last year.

"Let me get you some spray stuff for your shirt," Trevor says.

"Don't worry about it," Mitch says. "Doesn't matter." He takes another sip.

"Things are pretty shitty right now, huh?" Trevor says.

"Things are shitty."

"I'm sure you'll turn a corner soon. A new school year. A fresh start."

"Turn that frown upside-down." Mitch says.

"I'm only trying to show...compassionate regard," Trevor says.

"You are. I'm sorry." Mitch takes another big swig.

This is as good a time as any. Not going to keep tiptoeing. Ask him.

"So, I want to ask you something. Don't be all dramatic. Just listen," Mitch says.

"Sure."

"Where do you think Dad ran off to?"

"Wouldn't know. Asshole Hall of Fame, most likely."

"You must have some good memories of him, though."

"A million. He was a semi-finalist for the Nobel Peace Prize."

"Come on, you're older than me so you must remember something good."

"He never hit me. But he had a chip the size of Greenland on his shoulder. And Opa cut him no slack at all."

"Nope. Hated him," Mitch says.

"Opa black-listed him from the get-go. The math says it all: Mom and Dad got married six months before I was born. It doesn't take multivariable calculus to figure that out."

Mitch says, "Oh, so you were a preemie. I knew it! That explains your developmental delays, particularly in terms of...uh...elevation."

"Your height did wonders for you. Was Sharelle the first girl you kissed, Mitch?"

"I did plenty."

"Yeah, you and your Cheryl Ladd poster, within the candle-lit solitude of your bedroom." Trevor vigorously rubs his palms together.

"That's not fair! It was Farrah Fawcett," Mitch says, in a conciliatory tone. "What's weird is that Opa used to go fishing with him all the time."

"Opa would go fishing with Charles Manson. All he wanted was to be on the lake. More than that, maybe he wanted to somehow…connect… or understand Dad."

"Or keep him close by."

Mitch nods. "Where do you think Dad went?" he says.

"I don't know, man." Trevor dips a finger into his mug of Guinness and scoops up some foam. He licks it off his finger with a slurp.

Like Opa used to.

Opa puts his finger into the glass of advocaat and licks it. He loves that stuff: an egg, sugar, and brandy pudding. Seventeen percent alcohol. Only for adults. You just poured it for him. He's over for dinner and chatty—asking about school, laughing at Trevor's riddles, sitting beside you and poking you with his fork prongs.

"You playing any sports, Trevor?" he asks while you're giggling.

"Soccer's just starting."

"Great! Let me know your schedule when you get it. I see you're wearing the colors too. Well done!"

Trevor looks down at his orange World Cup Soccer shirt. "Thanks," he says.

"You know what those letters on the patch stand for, right? KNVB?" Opa says.

"Koninklijke Nederlandse Voetbalbond," Trevor says.

"You bet your gouda-loving backside. And the translation please, Mitch, for 200 points?"

"Royal Dutch Soccer," you say.

"What's this 'soccer' you're talking about? It's football," Opa says. "You want me to take you behind the barn with the big wooden spoon?"

"Maybe you should take your spoon and eat your soup with it," Mom says.

"Let's *all* focus on our soup for a while," says Dad, sitting on Trevor's right.

"How about fine arts, Trevor? You taking music lessons?" Opa picks up his spoon.

"This and that," says Trevor, blowing on a spoon of chicken noodle soup.

"This and that, Mitch. A little of this," Opa says and pokes your armpit, which makes you squeeze your arm tight with the spoon clamped inside. He yanks it out and reaches across the table and pokes it in Trevor's stomach. "A little of that." Trevor grabs his giant hand: a pretend life-and-death struggle for the spoon.

"Dad, stop it. Let them eat."

"Sorry, Jeany. They look so delicious!"

"Opa, don't eat me!" Trevor yells.

"My dad would have never tolerated this at the table," Dad says.

"Trevor, in the war I became a cannibal. People taste like chicken," Opa says to you, sitting back in his chair. "Mitch probably tastes like Cornish game hen."

"You taste like KFC," you say.

"Take your best shot, Big Boy." Opa puts down the spoon and grabs his fork.

"Dad, honestly! We're eating. You guys are impossible. Can't let you sit together."

"One time, we were screwing around at the table and my dad dipped his spoon in a cup of hot tea and poured it on my arm. Stung like a hornet. I guess I learned a lesson, but I still won't drink tea to this day," Dad says.

"Opa's bullying me." Opa's prongs poke into your ribs and you bend over laughing, then he has your head in a pretend chokehold, gives you a Dutch rub with the heel of his palm, friction burns on scalp. Cackling and wheezing for air. Paralyzed.

"The Dutch will never win a World Cup," Trevor says, plunging in for another spoonful and then blowing on it at close range. "Last year was the closest they'll ever come." He lifts his chin at Opa. "I'm just wearing the shirt because I feel sorry for them."

"You're next, Mr. This and That," Opa says. He stands and raises the fork above his head, and then leans across the table. Trevor jolts backwards and the soup flies from his spoon onto the front of Dad's shirt.

Dad jumps to his feet, throwing his arms out and staring down at his shirt. Then he makes a growling noise.

"Whoa, I'm sorry, Tony. My fault completely," Opa says, lifting his eyebrows at him and sitting down. "Just got carried away."

"It's okay. Completely," Dad murmurs, sitting down again.

"A bit jumpy, aren't we, Tony?" Opa says.

"Are we?" Dad says and glares at him. Then he bends and licks the biggest of the wet spots.

"The manners! My goodness, do you guys have any idea what it's like to live with a bunch of boys? We need another girl around here for balance," Mom says.

"I bet Trevor has lots of lady friends. Bring one over sometime, Trevor. For dinner. For balance," Opa says. "Can't rely on Mitch. He's too young. Still afraid of girls." He leans into your face and wiggles his eyebrows.

"I can hold my own in that department," you say.

Opa starts to reach his arm around your neck for a headlock, but Mom won't have it. "Opa needs a timeout. Don't think I won't, Dad," she says.

"Okay, easy does it Jeany. I'll act my age."

"You mean you'll act like a dinosaur, Opa?" Trevor says and laughs.

"Opasaurus. Characterized by long body and small tuft of fur on top," you say. While everyone else laughs, Dad runs both hands over the front of his shirt.

"That does it!" Opa's prongs jab between your shoulder blades. "How's the franchise coming, Tony?" Opa says overtop of your cackling. "Lawn mowing, right?"

"No, it's not lawn mowing. It's landscaping. And it's not coming. At all. Silent partner backed out. Chicken shit."

Opa stops jabbing. "I've told you not to talk like that around my grandsons."

Dad glares for a second. "Sorry," he mumbles.

"Sorry to hear about the lawn mowing thing going belly-up."

"Landscaping," Trevor says.

"Sorry, landscaping."

"I'm sure you're devastated," Dad says.

"Somebody's got a bee in their bonnet," Opa says.

"How about just passing the trout fillets, Clarence."

"Some are pretty small, Tony. Sure, they were legal?"

"Minimum size is twelve inches. They're legal."

"Not those little ones. I'm not eating fingerlings. Look at the tiny bones everywhere. Ridiculous," says Opa.

"Small ones taste best," Dad says.

"You afraid the big fish are too much for you?"

"I'm afraid of nothing."

"Don't eat chicks before they're chickens, right Opa?" you say.

"Once again, Mitch, you and I have an understanding. Speaking of chicks..." Opa puts a fork prong on your arm and starts sawing with his knife. You turn the fork on his leg, giggling, and then make a rug burn on his arm. He yelps while Dad scowls.

"I caught those bitching fish legally, Clarence. They're fine."

"Extinguished these beautiful creatures before their time. And I told you to watch your language with these boys here."

"A little dramatic of you. You'd keep the odd undersize."

"No, I'd never. I respect the created world."

"Hard time believing you wouldn't."

"Believe it."

"Guys, can we just eat?" Mom says, her head stooped over her plate.

"Nothing small about anything I do," Dad says.

Opa slaps his utensils down on the table, folds his arms, and leans forward. "You won't destroy one this small when I'm fishing with you. Not on my watch," he says.

"Calm down, Clarence. Sheesh."

"It'll be the first and last time."

"Seriously, calm yourself."

"I'm calm. Just stating a fact." Opa lifts the fork again and runs his thumb along the prongs while he watches Dad picking out trout bones. Then he puts each prong underneath his thumbnail one-by-one. Flick. Flick. Flick. Flick. "It's not like you majored in fishery management in college."

"Dad never went to college," you say. Dad looks up at you from the fish bone he is flexing between his thumb and index finger, and he tosses it onto his plate.

Flick. Flick. Flick. Flick.

Trevor plinks down his beer mug on the deck. "I don't think it's best to ask Mom about any of this either," he says.

"What is the big deal with—"

"Really. Don't ask Mom about it," he says in a low growl.

"Why do you keep saying that?"

"She doesn't like talking about it. Besides, he barely messed with you. You were the golden goose."

"What are you talking about?"

"I was the rodeo clown. Mom rode the bull, and you sat in the stands, eating popcorn," Trevor says.

"Popcorn."

"Yes. While you were chewing, I bore the brunt of his whining bullshit."

"Was the popcorn salted and buttered?"

"Sure, yeah, 'cause that's important to what I'm saying."

"Let me know when you're ready to be fair," Mitch says. They sit in silence for about a minute. "You were never home when he started in on me."

"Wow, what an amazing coincidence."

"And he didn't put you in the hospital."

"So you say, but that sounds like a weird accident. He never touched us."

"No, never. He just knocked me off the kitchen island."

"Yes. Out of nowhere," Trevor says.

"It was out of somewhere. I've explained it to you."

"Not very clearly. The story doesn't add up."

"Suit yourself. In any event, I wonder where he is now."

"Who cares?"

"You've never wondered?" Mitch asks.

"Nope. I don't wonder where the Unibomber is either."

"I don't really want to talk to him again. I'd like to know where he took off to," Mitch says.

"Sitting on his ass in Mexico. I don't know."

"You don't just take off. There are reasons. Didn't Mom fill out a missing person's report?"

"I don't know the minutiae of everything that happened. I'm sure she did. She's smart."

"I can't believe how impossible it is to talk to you about this."

"I got stuff to do, Mitch. You done with the questions?"

"This is important to me. Stuff to do?

"Yes, stuff like maybe I'll throw some desks into the wall and..." He stops and runs his hand through his hair.

Mitch slams both hands on the arms of the lawn chair, leans forward, and cocks his head at Trevor. "How about if I throw you into a bloody wall?"

"I shouldn't have said that. It was inappropriate."

"Inappropriate. That's totally the word I wanted to use!"

"I said I was sorry."

"No you didn't, actually!"

"Mitch, let's calm down."

"You are so fucking hostile. I don't get it." Mitch springs from his chair. "Go do your stuff. Thanks for the beer." He bends over and picks up his mug, then walks into the kitchen. Megan has her back to him, her hands in a sinkful of dishes.

"Hey Megan, I appreciate you having me over. I gotta go," Mitch says putting his mug on the granite surface of their newly installed kitchen island and then leaning on it with his right hand.

Megan pulls out her hands and grabs a dishtowel, and then turns and walks to him as she dries her hands on it. She stops in front of Mitch and tosses the towel on the island. Then she puts her arms around his neck, pulls him into her, and hugs him. As he brings his arms up to return her hug, his right hand knocks the mug onto the floor and he hears it smash. He tries to pull away to get it.

"Leave it," Megan says. "It's only a mug." She holds him for a few more seconds and then she pulls back, takes his right hand with her right, rubs it a few times with her left hand, and gives it a pat.

"Mitchell, he does care about you. We care about you."

"I know, Megan. I know that you do."

"I mean it. He does care. He doesn't know how to show...things."

He forces a little smile and slowly pulls his hand out. "Where do you keep your dust pan?" he asks.

"I'll get it, Mitch. Seriously, leave it."

"I want to clean up my mess. Let me do it. Please," he says. She points to a closet, and he grabs a broom and dustpan. The core of the mug is still intact but has a crack running from top to bottom. The handle is broken off and the rim has two big chunks chipped off. He throws the big pieces in the dustpan, and then gets on his knees and sweeps up the splinters.

Accountability.

He empties the dustpan in the garbage can and puts it and the broom away. Megan watches him the whole time.

"It's a totally lame mug, Mitchell. You actually did us a favour," she says.

"I'll replace it. I promise."

"Don't worry about it. Honestly. I think we'll manage, Mitchell. Somehow." She winks. "Come back soon. I've got about a dozen more I'd like to get rid of."

"You're just...tremendous. I'm glad Trevor married up," Mitch says.

"Wow, 'tremendous.' When they were dishing out hyperbole, you went back for seconds."

"Thanks again, Megan."

Mitch goes down the steps and walks barefoot on the grass, watching the ground so he doesn't step on any Chinese chestnuts—their long prickles can puncture and burn the skin like scorpions. He notices how big the pine tree is that he planted in Kindergarten. It's almost as high as the power lines and will need a trim sometime. Rachel is playing on the swing that Opa built for the grandkids. Mitch watches her for a while and then gets up and walks over and gives her a push. "Higher, Uncle Mitch, higher. I'm a birdie. I'm like a birdie."

“Yes you are, Rachel. Just like one.” He pushes her gently again, and she squeals and looks over her shoulder at him and grins her toothy grin. She rises and falls, her silky blond ringlets rustling with the draft of each arc.

Accountability.

In a few weeks, Mitch will stand in front of a new group of students and start again. He will grasp the edge of the lectern with his hands and lean forward, and he will explain that even adults make mistakes. “We all do things we’re not proud of,” he will say. “Everyone has flaws. I am no better.”

Things have to change. He needs a new life.

AUGUST

Left. Right. Left. Right. Mitch sits upright in the chair, his eyes tracking the green light. Left. Right. Left. Right. Back and forth. Monotony. Follow the light.

He's spending ninety minutes with Narland Bremseth. "Healthy Paths" has been okay, but after the last class he was talking to Gina about his general sense of anger. ("Irrational episodes of deep internal combustion," he told her. "Oh, you mean you're angry a lot?" "Uh, yeah.") She's referred him to Dr. Narland Bremseth—some sort of guru for the perpetually agitated. Mitch can't help but marvel at the clichéd dimensions of it all: a middle-aged guy going to anger management alas.

I've reached a new high.

Mitch has agreed to see Bremseth, partly because his office is in Thronehill, a solid eighty kilometers away. He doesn't need any kids or parents seeing him walking into an "anger specialist's" office. That would get tongues wagging: *There goes the schoolteacher. Poor guy. He must've blown a gasket.* He'll do one session to try it out. His insurance will pay part of it.

So here he sits in Bremseth's office. Mitch spent the first couple minutes trying not to grin at Bremseth's first name. *Seriously, Narland? Ouch.* The inability to get that name out of his mind, coupled with the excruciatingly humorous reality of Narland's crooked nose ("Hockey puck," he explained at the outset with a whiff of defensiveness) and pointed chin (God's genetic tomfoolery, it seems) has caused Mitch to bite quite severely on his thumbnail in a life-and-death struggle not to laugh. He wouldn't want to make Narland angry.

For the first hour, they talked about Mitch: his background, how he deals with emotions, what he remembers about growing up. There have been a lot of awkward silences. Narly talked about "big and little *T* traumas": bullying, episodes of feeling worthless, infertility "events," Dad. Then Narly suggested that they spend the last thirty minutes doing a bit of work and asked if it was okay if they did some trauma therapy called EMDR. He explained how it worked: You recalled a traumatic event and rated its emotional effect at that moment on a scale from one to ten. Then you stared at a black bar with a tiny green light bulb on each end. The bar was perched on a tripod and the bulbs took turns illuminating, every two seconds. Your eyes had to follow the lit bulb back and forth. The tracking movement was supposed to help the brain form new pathways to help process events. If all went as planned, your rating would go down after tracking the light for a few minutes. Narland uses it with victims of rape, abuse, and war. So Mitch sits in an office chair, the bar in front of him and Narland to the side. He lifts his butt and pulls on a plastic handle to raise the seat. When he sits down again, the chair sinks back to its original position and he thumps down in the chair.

"Minor technical issue," he says. "I should get that fixed. No matter. Mitch, I want you to choose an event."

"Are you able to narrow that down a tad?"

"The event should be something you found upsetting or traumatic. A big or little *T*," Narland explains.

"I see. Okay, let's see what we've got in the old memory bank," Mitch says. He starts to think intently about it and ends up with this: *I'm sitting in a broken office chair staring at tiny green lights, and Narland is watching my every expression, and now I'm supposed to come up with a little or big T. Pop-psych bullshit. I'm in therapy with ol' Narland and his chinny-chin-chin. Ol' Narly took a puck to the nose.*

Mitch pictures the therapist skating towards a defenceman at the blue line, who lets off a quick slapshot and here it comes, but Narland has his stickblade tilted at too high of an angle on the ice and the puck deflects off it and plunks him on the nose, and he drops to the ice, nose in his hands and his skinny legs flailing in shock and him spinning round and round in grimaced agony.

Mitch puts his thumbnail back in his mouth and bites hard. "Have you selected an event?" Narland asks.

"Oh yes, indeed," Mitch says around his thumbnail and then his cheeks swell with mirth, and he gives a cough to let out a little laugh.

"It appears to be an amusing event, which isn't really the idea."

"Yes, you're right. Sorry," Mitch says and glances over at Narland, who has a pinky finger inserted in his nose and Mitch looks quickly away and then lets out a robust, full-bellied laugh.

"My goodness, it must've been a doozy of a memory," Narland says and politely laughs. "But we really need to refocus and evoke something more in tune with our purposes here."

"Absolutely right, Doctor. I'll focus on more evoking. My apologies," Mitch says and tries to concentrate. He closes his eyes. "You're talking childhood stuff, right?"

"Not necessarily, but from what we've already discussed, that might be appropriate." Mitch massages his forehead with his fingertips. "You mustn't try too hard, Mitchell. Just let the memory come. Little or big *T*s, okay?"

"Might be a little one," Mitch says.

"Fine. You remember what those were, don't you?" Your grotesque features and lack of bedside manner, for instance? Mitch thinks. He grins and coughs out another giggle. "Focus, Mitchell."

I'd love to focus, Narland, but I need you to stop studying my every feature.

Mitch is getting annoyed, for which he is grateful because it makes him stop smiling and giggling.

How much time is left? This sucks. This chair sucks. My knees are up by my freaking chin. Speaking of chins.

Narland's face in his mind again. Cough and titter. Sniff of irritation from Narland.

$100 an hour to have you be annoyed at me for having a few laughs? But really, this chair sucks. I look like Opa did in Oma's armchair. Was he as tall as I remember? My giant Opa.

Opa is walking down the porch stairs, through the yard, around the corner, and out of sight. You're standing at the window, watching him go.

"You were real buddy-buddy with your grandpa, huh Mitch," Dad says.

"Opa."

"Huh?" He walks from the table towards you. From the corner of your left eye, you see an orange flash and footsteps trailing out the room. Mom is frozen in the middle of covering some food, a stretch of plastic tight against the metal teeth of the box's edge.

"He's my Opa, not just my grandpa."

Mitch opens his eyes. "Have you chosen a memory, Mitchell?" Bremseth asks.

"Yes."

"How do you rate its emotional effect on you?"

"Six."

"That's a somewhat low-rating event, but it's okay as a departure point. All right, let's begin." The bar lights up, and Mitch follows the light back and forth. Left. Right. Bremseth's breaths are the only sound. Left. Right. Left. Right. Left. Right.

"Don't you correct me! You seemed to really like him grinding my gears about the small fish." He's standing over you. Your bladder feels loose. Clench so you don't pee.

Left. Right. Left. Right. Left. Right.

"What does grinding my—"

"Do you think it's funny that I didn't go to college, Mitchell? Sorry, let me rephrase. Does it provide you with whimsical mirth that I didn't attend a post-secondary institution?"

"No." You hear a door close upstairs.

"Because I didn't have the chance and had to work, that makes you better than me?"

"No."

Mom puts the box on the counter and clasps her hands. "He didn't do anything wrong, Tony. You're misreading things."

"You and Grandpa. Regular old pals, eh? Come on, let's go look at your books." He puts his fingertips on your back and guides you into the living room. Then he nudges your head to within a foot of the bookcase.

Chronicles of Narnia, A Wrinkle in Time, Journey to the Centre of the Earth, Lord of the Rings. So many prepositions in the titles. Fantasy genre isn't real, just good versus evil, good wins in the end, it's a fantasy. Fantastic. Fantasy.

"Here, peruse some books, Mitch. You love them so much."

Left. Right. Left. Right. Left. Right. Left. Right. Left. Right. Left. Right.

"Such wonderful literature. And your mind is so open to them. It's just lovely. There's just one problem. Your ears are sealed tight. Bunged right up."

"Tony, leave him alone!"

"Or maybe they're too small."

"He's learned his lesson. Let him go!"

He whispers slowly, "You mind your business, Jean. I'm teaching him some manners."

"You've taught him enough!"

"Someone has to parent. You're good cop, I'm bad cop. Now you listen to me, little chick. Maybe if your ears are bigger, you'll listen to my needs and not have to embarrass me again."

"I wasn't trying to, Dad."

"Pull down on your ear lobes, Mitch. Let's stretch those babies and open 'em wide."

You pinch your lobes, pull down, and feel the pressure.

"I want you to really pull."

You pull harder and feel the pain shoot through the edges of the lobes.

Journey to the Centre. To the Centre, the core, the essence, the epitome. Take me on a journey, Opa. Take me away to the centre.

Left. Right. Left. Right. Left. Right. Left. Right. Left. Right. Left. Right.

"I'm pulling as hard as I can."

"Let's forget the steady downward motion and try really reefing on those suckers."

Yank down on your ears. Feel a burning in the lobes.

"Not just once. Keep doing it."

Yank. Yank. Yank. Yank. "My ears hurt, Dad. Please let me stop."

"His ears hurt, Tony. Stop, please. Please, please, please, please, please, please." Seven pleases. Ticking grandfather clock strikes seven. One hour till bedtime.

Left. Right. Left. Right. Seven times. Left. Right. Left. Right. Left. Right. Left. Right. Left. Right. Left. Right.

"Reef hard, Mitch. Feel that burn? That's the sensation of growing up."

Yank ten more times.

"That's the spirit, my boy."

The thought flutters into your mind. You know what will make him stop. You drop your hands to your sides, turn around, and look at him. "I'm going to tell Opa about this," you say.

His eyes close for a second. "No, you won't. And he wouldn't listen, anyway. Your grandpa's an old fool."

"No he's not."

He leans into your face and says, "He doesn't know shit about shit. And, on a side note, if you ever disrespect me again like you did, I won't let you see him again." His tone rises, like he's talking kindly to a toddler.

"That's not true, Mitchell. Tony, please stop this."

Dad jolts upright and nudges you to the side. He reaches his hand into the second shelf and sends half of the row of books flying with one sweep of his arm. "Jean, please don't interrupt me. And please shut your ugly fat hole."

He leans into your face again. "Guess what else, Mitchell?" he says, almost in a whisper. He takes a step back and folds his arms with a satisfied smile. "Your grandpa is dying." He says the last word like a triumph, like he's breaking wonderful news.

"Mitchell, don't listen!" Mom says.

"Hey Jean, please shut up. That's strike two."

"Opa will live forever," you say.

"Wrong again, Mitch. Liver cancer, boy! He's got an eighteen percent chance of surviving. Eighteen! How do you like those odds, eh? Ouch." He shoots a glance at Mom, expecting a comment. Silence.

"Opa's not sick. He's strong. He put me in a headlock at lunch."

"It's inevitable, 'Big Boy.' His cells are dividing, and he'll be toast before you know it. And then who'll be your buddy? The librarian? Your grandpa's a loser. Losers need company. That's why he hangs out with you."

"Opa loves me."

"No, he doesn't. He feels sorry for you. But...he'll take a dirt nap sometime soon. And then your little Loser Soiree will be over." He stretches his arms above his head and yawns loudly.

You hear the words surge from your bowels: "YOU'RE a loser!" Dad leans back into your face. His chin drops to his chest, eyes cutting a swathe forward.

Left. Right. Left. Right. Left. Right. Left. Right. Left. Right. Left. Right.

"What did you say?" A strange, even lower whisper.

"*You* are the loser! Only *you*!" He grabs your shoulders, but you squirm from his grasp and run into the kitchen towards the island. His eyes are wide, face purple. You look back as he lunges at you, but Mom's shoulder knocks him into the fridge. He bounces off it and keeps coming. You screech as you run around the island away from him.

"I'm telling Opa everything! Everything you've ever said or done!"

He stops chasing you, and now you're on opposite ends of the island from each other. His hands are squeezing the edge of the island.

He knows you're serious. He's scared of Opa. He won't hurt you now. You've got Opa on your side. He's not going to treat you like this anymore.

You climb on a stool and scramble on your knees onto the island. You stand and lean over him with your heartbeat vibrating in your chest, and you're flinging the words at him in a steady shriek, forcing them out through the sobs—each sentence a semi-automatic burst: "We've never had any money because you're stupid! What a failure you are! What a joke! And you're short! And *you're* toast! And you're...IMPOTENT!"

He picks up a stool and swings it at you. You jump back from its reach.

Air.

Freefall.

Black.

Left. Right. Left. Right. Left. Right. Left. Right. Left. Right. Left. Right. Left. Right.

"What number do you feel?"

The question jolts Mitch's eyes open. "Nine," he says.

"Oh."

"I think I'm done for today."

"Not exactly. We need to do this for a while and your number should decrease as a consequence of the—"

"I'm exactly done for today. Really. Sorry."

"I really must propose that we give it a few more minutes," Bremseth says it like a pleading question.

"And I must counter with a proposition that we're done."

The green light goes off with a turn of the doctor's wrist. "Anyway, this has been a good start. Some strong initial work accomplished," Bremseth says.

Mitch stands up and says, "Psychotherapy doesn't seem to be a good fit for me. Nothing personal."

"Er...this isn't psychotherapy. I'd strongly encourage you to reconsider."

"I can't do it, doctor. I apologize."

"The first few sessions are always hard until we develop a rapport."

"I think you're really good at your work. This is nothing to do with you, I promise. I'd better get a receipt. For the insurance company."

"See my receptionist on the way out about that matter," Bremseth says, drumming some fingertips on his chin in oddly veiled frustration.

"I'd wear a full-visor helmet next time. The ones they have now don't fog up," Mitch says and taps his nose.

"Well, oh, yes," Bremseth says and runs a thumb down the bridge of his nose. "Hope to see you again, Mitch. I think we can make great progress together. But we'll need to get to the source of that darn anger, won't we?"

"Existential angst, Doctor. No antidote for that," Mitch says and walks out to the foyer, wallet in hand.

SEPTEMBER

Mitch often visits Mom on Saturday afternoons, and today is no exception. He's stopped at Shop 'N Save to get some fresh carnations for her. She loves it when "a handsome man brings her flowers."

He gets to the large, open produce area, which is flanked by the floral section on one side and meat on the other, and there, studying a package of ground beef, stands Kylii Tikkanen. Mitch turns around and walks to the next aisle, and he stops and stares at a jumbo box of animal crackers. *Walk away, Mitch.* Then he inhales deeply, gives his head a vigorous shake, and walks towards the meat wall. He takes an empty shopping cart on the way, and then moves in quietly from behind and whispers, "Make sure it's extra lean." Kylii startles for a second and turns quickly, and then she smirks.

"Well, Mitchell, I usually get regular, but why do you think extra lean? Are you saying I need to watch my weight?" She holds a grocery basket in her left hand and leans against the meat shelf with her right. She lifts her eyebrows at him.

"No, no, no. I was just trying to be funny."

You're a regular Robin Williams, genius.

"I know, Mitch." She laughs and slides a finger across the edge of her bangs. There is a long, painful silence, and then Kylii makes a motion to turn back to the beef.

"Doing groceries?" Mitch asks.

Seriously? That's the best freaking conversation starter you can come up with? Get your flowers, and hit the road.

"It's that time again," she says.

"What is it that you make? Uh, what are you making?"

She tells Mitch about a new, healthy kind of shepherd's pie and how to prepare it. Clinique Happy drifts into his nostrils. She is wearing black tights tucked into black flat-heeled boots with a long grey sweater that is snug against her Finnish curves.

Buxom, Scandinavian Viking curves. He begins to smile to himself about the word *buxom* and camouflages it by putting an index finger between his teeth as if he is listening intently as she speaks. In mid-sentence, she turns to grab a package of tenderloin and Mitch sneaks a half-second glance at the profile of her breasts, and when she turns back to him, he stares at a spot beyond her to make it seem like he hasn't been staring. He thinks she might've caught him, but she gives a soft smile. He can hear his own breathing.

"Do you do the groceries in your family?" she asks.

"Sometimes I do. Sharelle sure likes it when I do."

"I bet she does."

"I get tired of the same thing all the time. I like to mix it up. Sharelle wants to know what is happening when and wants to predict everything. In food, in everything." The words lay thick on his tongue, and it's work to lift them off and out.

Oh, that's perfect. Now you're whining to her about your wife.

"Sounds like some room for improvement there."

"Can't get much worse. The trajectory is due south."

There's an awkward silence. Mitch notices a tall green can of "Steel Juice" in her basket. An energy drink. He thinks energy drinks are the biggest, dumbest rip-off imaginable. "Steel Juice, huh," he says. "Cool."

"You ever try it?" she asks.

"Totally. I'm totally into energy drinks."

"They seem like kind of a waste of money," she says, "but a friend of mine told me they really pick you up in the afternoon. You know, like around 3:00 when you need a lift."

"Awesome," he says and then listens to himself launch into an explanation of the twilight zone between the wearing off of lunch and the dinner hour.

Twilight zone? You have got to be kidding.

Kylii nods while he bumbles through, and she smiles in that really cute way she has of turning her head slightly sideways and expanding her eyes—eyes that are olive and underlined by the freckles on her cheeks, and he feels like he's swaying. Though the handle is oily with sweat, he's grateful to have the cart as a physical buffer. He leans his weight on the handle and makes the front wheels lift slightly as if popping a wheelie, and then he eases it down to earth. Then he crosses his arms and rests them on the handle—which has the double benefit of steadying him and projecting confidence—but an arm slips off and he bangs his shoulder on the cart. It jolts forward and hits Kylii in the knee. She goes rigid with laughter—a whole melody of ins-and-out synchronized with the shaking of her breasts—and then there's a popping sound because her thumb has punctured a hole in the tenderloin's cellophane package.

"Oh no, I am so sorry! Are you okay?" Mitch says and starts to reach to touch her knee. She stiffens, and he jerks his hand back.

"Are you kidding? You always knew how to make me laugh. What am I gonna do with this meat?"

"I guess you just bought it."

"I guess not. Here we go." She hides the package under some pork chops. "Don't tell anyone. Our little secret," she says. He has to mentally tell himself to breathe.

Our little secret.

Kylii says, "Thanks for the laugh. I gotta get going. See you in class, Murphy."

"It's not Murphy, it's Michelle. Remember?"

"Right. Ciao, Michelle," she says and walks away to the poultry section. Mitch finds himself analyzing how she ended the conversation and why. He can still smell her and see her eyes and freckles.

What are you doing? Stop this.

He wants to walk over to where she is again and find an excuse to be near her but decides that is weird, and he should hit the road. He leaves the cart standing in the aisle, picks out some carnations, and walks to the checkout. On his way, he notices that boxes of macaroni-and-cheese are on special, so he scoops up an armful.

Kylii is paying for her food a couple tills over. Above the conveyor at his till, there's a small cooler filled with cold drinks for the impulsive buyer. He reaches in and grabs a can of "Steel Juice." He glances over at Kylii a couple times until she catches his eye. He holds the can upright and makes a toasting motion to her. She smiles and raises a thumb.

Mitch walks to the Civic and puts the bag of groceries in the hatch. As he does, the can falls through a hole in the bag onto his foot, and he rests against the car for a few seconds and lets the pain subside. The can has rolled under the car, so he goes down on his knees and reaches under, and of course it's at the exact mathematical centre. With the flowers held upright in his hand, he bends down and snags the can with the tip of his index finger. It rolls back to him. Then he gets up, and Kylii is standing there.

"Go ahead, laugh. I won't be offended," Mitch says. Kylii fires off one quick in-and-out. "Don't worry, I got it. Wouldn't want you to pull a muscle helping me."

"The lengths a man will go to for his energy drink," she says.

"I wonder if sometime a bunch of us should go grab a coffee."

Take it back.

Her smile puckers slightly. "Um, yeah. Or just you and me. Sometime. Lots of memories to troll through."

What have you done?

Mitch can feel his left leg wobble slightly. "What are you doing right now?" Kylii asks. Now both legs are wobbling.

"Going to my mom's."

"That's who the flowers are for, huh? Flowers for Mom. That's so adorable, I can hardly stand it."

Heat rises in his face. "I'd better get going. She's making lunch, and I'm a little late."

"Pitter patter. Women don't like to be kept waiting."

Mitch shuts the hatch and then opens the passenger door and sticks the flowers between the passenger seat and the console. He lays the can in the fold of the seat. He'll put it on the staff room table; someone will take it. He shuts the door and turns back, and Kylii is gone.

An hour later, Mitch is helping Mom with the breakfast and lunch dishes. He always washes, and she dries. Shards of pain stab the fingers of his left hand. He pulls a plate out of the scalding dishwater and, as the throbbing slowly subsides, gives it a quick scrub with the brush. His hands are both dark pink. This is the way Opa did dishes too: Make the water so hot you can only dip your hand in for a second. Let the dishes sit on the bottom of the sink for a few minutes to let things loosen. The water does the work for you.

Since the bus trip, he's been racking his brain and just can't remember. So, he asks, "Mom, do you remember where Dad and I camped that first time?" Mitch asks.

"Don't forget the glasses on the table," she says and walks over to the stove to retrieve a soup bowl. "And this." She hands him the bowl. He puts it upright in the sink and lets it float. Then, he presses one of the sides down and watches it take on water. It slowly sinks under the suds and disappears.

"That time when I was really small, and it was just me and him."

"Did you get enough to eat?"

"Do you have any idea where we went?"

"What makes you think of that?" They're down to the cutlery, which Mitch takes out of the sink in two fistfuls, rinses off, and stuffs in the drain board. He reaches down and unplugs the sink.

"It's the only time I can remember doing anything with him one-on-one," Mitch says.

"I have no idea."

"There was a small lake and lots of trees."

"That narrows it down," she says and flicks her fingers at him, sprinkling suds on his face.

"I'm serious. I was thinking about that recently," Mitch says, taking the dish towel out of her hand and wiping his face.

"That's disgusting! Boys!" she says. She grabs the towel back, pulls it tight by the ends, and winds it tightly with a circular motion. "We need more discipline around here." She snaps the towel at his leg, and his shin prickles with the sting.

"Come on, Miss Memorial Scholarship, search that brilliant mind of yours."

Mom winds the towel around her left hand. "I am brilliant, aren't I?"

"Yes. Do you ever think about if you had gone to university?"

"Yes."

"Trevor spoiled that, huh?"

"It wasn't Trevor's fault."

"What did Opa think about all of that?"

"What did he think? It upset him, of course."

"I don't think he liked Dad."

"They seemed to like some of the same things."

"Like fishing?"

"Like fishing."

"They went together a lot."

"Anyway, I don't know where you camped. It was a long time ago, okay?" She hangs the towel on the counter. "Mitchell, thank you so much for those carnations! I just love them."

"My pleasure. I think I'm going to take a little nap in the family room. Do you mind?"

"Of course not. That's your modus operandi. I'm going to read my book in the living room," Mom says. She leaves the kitchen and Mitch walks to the sink. There is a paring knife sitting on the bottom of the drained sink, encased in white suds. Mitch rinses it off, wipes it on the towel, and puts it away. He blots the little puddles of water on the counter, wrings out the towel, and folds it in half over the metal towel rack on the counter. He puts away the drying rack and then turns, and Mom is standing in the doorway.

"Mitch, why are you so curious about an old camping trip?"

"I like clarity. You forget so much when you're young," Mitch says.

"Memories aren't always reliable. We all have our own perceptions of things that happen."

"You mean of what happened with Dad?"

"I mean with everything."

"We never talk about Dad. About how things were," Mitch says.

"I know," Mom says, walking forward and giving him a nudge on the shoulder. "Sometimes the hardest part is just getting on with it."

"I guess," Mitch says.

"My book is beckoning."

"Okay. Maybe I'll go fire up the old Bell and Howell."

"To admire how cute you were, eh?" She tweaks his cheek.

"Yep."

"I wouldn't mind watching some with you."

"Sure. Let me find something interesting, and I'll call you over later."

"It's a date."

Mitch turns and walks down the hall towards the family room. He has seen a home movie of that camping trip before. On the old projector. When he gets to the family room, he combs through Mom's closet full of old technology. There is a cassette player and hundreds of cassettes and VHS tapes piled in rows. In a box at the back are a dozen old reels of 8 mm film. They still have Dad's printing on them. Mitch goes through them. "Disneyland 1973." "Christmas/New house 1969." He continues searching, and then he sees it: "Summer/Fall 1974." He takes the reel over to the coffee table.

Mitch pulls out the grey Bell & Howell projector, puts it on the table, and lifts off the front cover. A puff of dust sprinkles into the air. He mounts the film reel on the projector and threads the tip of the film through the rollers and onto the empty take-up reel. He goes over to the closet, removes the old movie screen, and assembles it. He plugs in the projector, and it starts with a whir. The ribbons of film are pulled from the first reel, squeezed through the rollers and across the surface of the lamp, and recaptured on the empty reel. 8 mm video: Mitch loves how the burnt metal smell of the projector fills the air, how the edges of the film clatter as they're pulled through the rollers.

The first part of the film shows Mom picking peaches in an orchard. She is quick at it—reaching up, grabbing each peach, and placing it gently in a bucket at her feet. The rhythm of this motion is like a disco move; it's almost funny. There is more orchard footage and some scenes with the family at the beach. Then there is a scene on the side of a road. In it, Mitch is posing beside a sign that says, "Zephyr Bay Provincial Park." The camera zooms in on his smiling, freckled face and then pulls back and pans across some treetops. The next scene is Dad's panning footage of their campsite, Mitch in his lawn chair, and then the ocean in the distance with a small, brown wooden sign in the foreground. White letters are carved into it: "Site 14." With the grainy, washed-out visuals and the absence of sound, it's a totally different scene than what Mitch remembers. After this, the film moves on to scenes of pumpkin carving, driveway hockey games, and leaf raking before it finishes and the reel spins uninhibited. *Zephyr Bay Provincial Park. Escape.* The small of his back is tingling. *Zephyr Bay?* A flapping noise jolts him. The released tip of the film is knocking against the table at the bottom of each rotation of the reel. Left unimpeded in its freedom, it will continue to spin in a loop and smack against the table for as long as it has power. Mitch turns off the projector.

SEPTEMBER

It's the Friday of the Labour Day weekend. Mitch woke early to pack the camping gear into the trunk. Sharelle got up with him and made some scrambled eggs, which they're now eating in silence. "A little getaway will be good for us, right?" she says finally as they're clearing the dishes.

"Totally. To refocus."

"To reset."

"Any idea what the forecast is?" he asks.

"Overcast."

"Sucks." He rinses egg yolk remnants out of a bowl.

"I know."

"Sunny breaks, I hope," he says, leaving the bowl to soak.

"I hope. Long trip. Sure you want to go that far? Gotta be six hours."

"Seven with the ferry."

"Still worth it?"

"I think so."

"Ready to head out?"

"Yup."

After three hours of highway travel, they are moving west through the mountains towards the coast, where they'll get a ferry across Meridian Strait and then on to the campground on Eckhardt Island. Mitchell has to say it.

"You know how I feel about that letter from your friend and this fertility guy."

"Rebekah? Yes, I'm skeptical too. What's the danger, though? The first round is free."

"The danger is that Dr. Muzillo is a nutbar who dices you into perfectly symmetrical cubes and then uses his acupuncture needles as toothpicks to serve the cubes at a party and—" Mitch stops following this thread. At one time, Sharelle would have laughed, and he would have carried the hyperbole to the outer limits.

"Just once, Mitch. We're here anyway. I'll drive the hour to Chamberlain, hang out with Rebekah, check out this guy, and come back. Rebekah has gone to him before." She rifles through the CDs in the console.

"Rebekah has rheumatoid arthritis, not blocked fallopian tubes. What's Muzillo going to do, poke the tubes open?"

Roughly, Sharelle bangs the console lid shut with a snap. "Mitchell, stop. It's not rational that I can't get pregnant, so maybe the solution isn't rational either. Can we just try it without analysing it to death? You wanted to camp at Zephyr Bay anyway. I'm just along for the ride."

"Fine."

They decide to pull over at a rest stop and eat. Sharelle sits on top of a picnic table and munches on a banana, while Mitch pours himself a bowl of Raisin Bran. They don't have any milk, so he adds a little water from a tap. He walks to the table and sits at a 90-degree angle to Sharelle.

As he's finishing the last spoonful, a lady in her sixties strolls over to the table. Her make-up reminds Mitch of the wax Margaret Thatcher sculpture he saw at Madame Tussaud's when he and Sharelle were in London. She asks him if he's familiar with the dinosaur museum in Drumheller, Alberta. Are there tours? Do you need a reservation?

"Sorry, never been there," he says, "but I can check online for you." He pulls out his phone.

"Don't trouble yourself. And you remind me of my son, by the way," she says. Her voice is warm and lilting. Mitch likes the rhythm, the meter of it. Texas. She points at the Dallas Cowboys sticker on the back bumper of his car. "Oh my. Another Cowboys fan way up here!"

"Through thick and thin," Mitch says, sliding his phone back into his back pocket.

"I'm Irene." She calls to her husband who is leaning against a small RV, "Stu, come on over here!" Stu has tiny tufts of hair above both ears, and his face is clammy, but he is beaming and pumps Mitch's arm vigorously, slapping him on the back. "A brother in the Cowboys. That makes you a friend. Name's Stu."

Irene and Stu talk at length about their trip so far. They're returning from a small town on the Olympic Peninsula and driving across Canada. Irene is an "inexhaustible" fan of some vampire book series that Mitch disdains, and she begins to describe some of the points of interest mentioned in the books. Mitch reads the riboflavin content on his cereal box.

"Gotta keep the little lady happy, so I let her drag me along," says Stu.

"Lucky you," Mitch says.

"Speaking of that, I'd say we're lucky to have found a man of your calibre. Didn't catch your name by the way," says Stu.

"Mitchell. Why are you lucky?"

"We didn't pay enough attention to the gas gauge, and she's empty. Coasted on fumes to the rest stop here, and we don't dare try and make it the twelve clicks to Woodruff. Chances of you giving me a lift into town to fetch a jerry can? Slim to none, and slim just left town?"

"Aw man, that's a letdown, eh," Mitch says.

"Didn't want to ask just anybody. Have to be careful these days. I know it's backtracking, but it'll only cost you a half hour, tops. There's a fiver in it for your troubles."

"Oh, I couldn't accept your generous offer," Mitch says. Wildly generous, he thinks, and stifles a laugh.

"I could keep your lovely wife company," Irene says.

"That'd be just fine," Sharelle says. "We have time, Mitchell."

Mitch rubs his eyes with both hands in a way that shields his eyes from the couple and offers Sharelle a quick, apologetic grimace. "I'd be utterly delighted," he says. Stu hops in with him in the car, and they drive east.

"So, you have a last name?" asks Stu.

"Van Laren."

"Is that Dutch?"

"Yes."

"Your father's Dutch?"

"Both sets of grandparents came from Holland," Mitch says.

"The Dutch are good folks. Sturdy folks."

"I guess."

"They know about honour and respect."

"Oh."

"You close with your folks?"

"With my mom," Mitch mumbles.

"You seem like a good son. Bet you make your daddy proud."

"Not so much. He's been—"

"I had it all laid out for my boy. He was gonna work with me in my trucking business, learn the trade, and take over when the time was right. You know what he did?"

"No."

"Pissed it away."

"Shame," Mitch says, turning on the air conditioner.

"That's right, pissed it away. You want to know what he's doing now?"

"Okay."

"Sociology. University of Connecticut. Connecticut!"

"New England is nice," says Mitch.

"What's he gonna do with a sociology degree, huh?"

"Probably teach," Mitch says.

"Teach. Yeah, and his students will end up teaching sociology too. The cycle will continue. Round and round we go."

"Exactly, right?" Mitch laughs.

"A father's dream come true," says Stu. He sniffs. "What do you do, Mitchell?"

"I'm a teacher."

"I'll bet you're a fine teacher," he says. "Hey, Mitchell. I wasn't knocking teachers. It's just that sometimes—"

"You don't have to explain, Stu. I get what you're saying," Mitch says.

"He told us to mind our own business. Said we didn't support anything he did. Can you believe that?" Stu says.

"No. He was lucky to have a mom and dad that loved him."

"Haven't talked to him in a year. Broke our heart."

"Hmm, a year," Mitch says.

"You're a man of few words, huh Mitchell?" Stu says.

"No, I'm only...tired."

"You need me to drive? I hauled freight for over thirty years."

"No thanks. I'm fine."

After five minutes, they get stuck behind a minivan that is sticking religiously to the speed limit. "Good to see somebody who's driving sensibly these days," Stu says.

"I wish he'd speed up," Mitch says.

"We're fine where we are, son. No need to hurry," Stu says. There is steady traffic from the opposite direction, making it impossible to pass. A sticker on the van's bumper reads, "Keep back! Honour roll student on board." Mitch starts to tailgate, and the driver brakes lightly from time-to-time in protest.

"You're following too close, Mitch. Settle in and stay the course," Stu says.

"I'm tired of this," Mitch says.

"If you're tired, I said I could drive."

"No, I mean I'm tired of—"

"It's no shame to let another man drive your car," Stu says.

"I'm fine. Just...I'm fine." The van finally accelerates, and they follow at a normal distance. Stu gives a contented sigh. Mitch glances at him and his eyes are closed.

A sign ahead says, "Woodruff, 5 km." Suddenly, the van slows down again, and Mitch hits the brake pedal. It doesn't move. Something is underneath it. He swerves to go around on the shoulder, but they start to fishtail. Stu gasps as they slide sideways down a small, mild, grass embankment. Mitch cranks the wheel, and the car spins two full rotations and comes to a stop, facing the road.

There is silence for a few seconds. Mitch tries to figure out what's happened. Then he feels under his seat and his fingers close around the can of Steel Juice. He looks over at Stu who seems fine because he is yelling. "You freaking fell asleep!"

"I didn't fall asleep, I—"

"You were snoozing!" Stu's cheeks are blown up like a puffer fish.

"Something got stuck under the pedal. I actually kept us from hitting the van."

"You could've killed us!" he says. "Why didn't you let me drive?"

"Stop it! Quit your yelling!" Mitch grabs the can and sticks it in Stu's face. "Look!"

"Why didn't you listen to me when you had the chance?"

"How didn't I listen?" Mitch asks.

"I told you to let me drive."

"You told me a lot of things!"

"Open your freaking eyes and ears!"

There is a rush of blood to Mitch's head. The words grind their way from his larynx. "This isn't my fault, you cockroach piece of shit! No wonder he screwed off to UConn and never came back!"

Stu stares at Mitch and opens his mouth to yell but then stops. He sits back. Mitch gets out to check the car while Stu stays inside. The honour roll van pulls up in the opposing lane. The window rolls down and a man with an oily, pockmarked face rasps, "You guys okay?" He lifts a baseball cap off his bald head and scratches his scalp.

"There's definitely room for improvement, but yeah we're okay," Mitch says.

"Not sure why you were tailgating me like that."

"Wasn't tailgating. A can got stuck under the...we're fine. Thanks for stopping."

The van does a U-turn and carries on eastward. Mitch stands back from the car and gives it a once-over. There's dirt and grass caked under the front wheel wells, but there doesn't appear to be any other damage. He pries out a chunk of mud with his left thumb, and the knuckle gets gouged against the edge of the wheel frame. A raw flap of skin starts seeping blood, and he sees that it's hanging by a thin string. He pinches the flap between his teeth, jerks it off, and spits the piece into the dirt. Then he sucks the knuckle and tastes the blood's coppery brine.

He pulls off another chunk of mud with his right hand and flings it as far as he can into a stand of trees. "You never gave me a chance!" he screams after it.

He grabs another chunk. "You never shut up long enough..." He hurls it into the trees. "...to get to know me!"

He sucks on his thumb again and feels his mouth fill with the blood's alkalinity. Then he jettisons another mud chunk into the trees. "You acted interested so long as it suited you!"

Another. "You just listened for an opening, so you could talk about how fucking *great* you were!"

Another. "Who gives a shit how many years you've hauled freight. It's *pointless*!"

Another. "You couldn't be bothered with me! Thirty years hauling freight! What *difference* does it make?" He picks up one last chunk of mud, tosses it in front of him, and punts it towards the trees. Then he looks through the windshield at Stu, who is frowning at him and cinching his seatbelt. Mitch continues to blot the blood with his tongue and gets in the car. They pull easily out of the ditch and drive in utter silence for the five minutes to Woodruff. Stu stares through his side window, slumping low in his seat.

When they pull into a Texaco, Stu gets out and buys a jerry can. As he screws on the lid after filling it, he motions for Mitch to unroll the window, which he does but only a crack.

"I can take a taxi back," Stu says.

"No taxis in a town this size. I'm sorry. I didn't mean to unload on you like that," Mitch says.

"It's okay, honestly." Stu shakes his head, tightens the lid, and gets back into the car with the jerry can on his lap.

Mitch turns on the radio for the awkward trip back to the rest stop: an old-time-favourites station. He turns the volume to three. Stu moves it to five. Mitch doesn't object. They drive west.

When they return, Irene and Sharelle are engaged in a lively discussion. Mitch hops out and nods gravely at Sharelle. He still feels washed out from the accident. "We'd better go," he says.

"Everything okay?" Sharelle asks.

"Tip-top," says Stu. "Other than your husband's failure to follow basic road safety rules."

"Let's go," Mitch says and climbs into the car.

Sharelle accepts a hug from Irene. "You're gonna be okay, girl," Irene says, rubbing between her shoulder blades.

"Thank you, Irene. Safe travels," Sharelle says and gets in the car.

"You take care of that gorgeous woman, Mitchell," Irene calls out through the open passenger window. Mitch lifts a hand, starts the engine, and they drive back on the highway.

"What was all that with the road safety thing?" Sharelle asks.

"Fifty percent misunderstanding, and fifty percent me being an asshole."

"Okay." She doesn't press it.

"Irene made quite an impression on you."

"Irene is an amazing listener. Yes."

Within two hours, they're standing at a railing on the upper deck of the ferry and churning across Meridian Strait. Mitch is gazing out over the water with his hands in his jacket pockets. Sharelle has her back against the railing facing the opposite way. Despite the open water, there is only a slight breeze.

"It's about being tethered," Sharelle says.

Mitch pivots to face her. She seems to be studying something straight ahead, so he looks for the object of her focus. A life preserver is hung on the wall in front of her.

"Let's try that again, but with some semblance of context?" he laughs.

As Sharelle starts to respond, a child's cry pierces the air and a father walks between them carrying a screaming girl with a thin line of blood trickling from her scraped knee. Sharelle stops and waits for her wailing to recede. "Having your own child ties you to this earth."

"Okay. Are we sure it has to be a biological child?"

"That's the tether. Yes."

"I don't completely get that."

"I so badly want you to."

A seagull's cry slices the air above Mitch. He puts a thumb in the crease of her elbow and says, "You are loved."

"I know that."

"Whether or not you can have a baby won't change that. You're enough," Mitch says. He lifts her hand and puts it on his shoulder.

"You're a good man, Mitch. It's complex stuff." She removes her hand and pats his heart. "It's good to have this little respite, yes? I'll drop you off at the campground, go to Rebekah's for the night, get chopped into cubes by Muzillo tomorrow morning, and be back in time for supper. Okay?"

"Alright."

And she says, "Remind me again why you want to camp at the park and not stay in Chamberlain."

"I camped at Zephyr Bay once with Dad. I just need some tranquility and reflection."

"No, you want some space."

"Not space from you."

"Let's go to the car. We're docking soon," she says and they descend the stairway to the car deck.

Once they're on land again, the road winds its way through the ferry port and out into the wilderness of the island. As the road descends into a valley, the thinly spaced hemlock trees and subalpine meadows on either side of the road give way to primeval rainforest. The traffic has thinned to almost nothing. They are entering the rainforest, and it is only Mitch, Sharelle, and the road. Before long, the Zephyr Bay Park sign appears, which is now a large arch that spans the entire road. Mitch follows the signs for the campground, turning down a narrow access road.

A canopy of Sitka spruce trees along the sides creates a tunnel effect. Its thickness makes the road dark and damp. Sharelle rolls down the window and sticks out her hand to feel the cool heaviness. Mitch turns his wipers on to wick away the condensing air. Spike moss clings to the bases of giant spruce and red cedar trees, whose branches are painted with lichens. Ferns spring from the stumps of nurse logs. The forest floor is a carpet of moss and oxalis.

They enter the campground and follow the site number signs. Site #14 is at the end of the road. It is not the same site that he saw in Dad's old film. He drives around the entire campground and unsurprisingly nothing is familiar. Finally, they choose an empty site and Sharelle helps him set up his tent.

After the tent is assembled and he's putting the empty tent bag into the back of the car, he sees a bungee cord curled in a corner and the idea comes to him. He folds it into a tight ball and stuffs it in his pocket. He grabs two lawn chairs and brings them to the side of the fire pit, parking them next to each other. Sharelle says, "Now that you've carved out a little piece of paradise for yourself, I'd better get going to Chamberlain."

Mitch sits down and pats the seat of the empty chair. "Just five minutes," he says.

"You know I don't like driving in the dark."

"Come on. Please? Five."

Sharelle sits down beside him, and Mitch pulls the bungee cord from his pocket and loops it around their adjoining arm rests.

"Right. If you're suggesting some sort of bondage role play, your sense of timing is way off."

"I'm tethering you. I'll be your tether. Always." He puts an arm around her.

She reaches back, pulls his hand off her shoulder and in front of her mouth, and kisses it. "Thanks for saying that." She lays his hand on his lap.

"And if you want to let go, you're the one who has to unhook it," Mitch says.

"I really do need to go." She unhooks the cord. "You okay out here in the wilderness?" She stands up.

Please don't untie me. As he rises from his chair, she walks to the car.

"See you tomorrow night, Mitchell."

"Stay safe. Hands at the ten and two o'clock positions." He tries to construct a grin. "See you tomorrow night. 'Girl.'"

He watches her drive away and then finishes setting up the campsite. After he's spread everything out and organized the tent, he sits down in a lawn chair and cracks open a beer.

It's starting to get dark. One site over, a family of four is putting together their tent. The daughter, who seems about six, is trying to fit the ends of two poles together. Her dad has his arm over her shoulder, showing her how the tongue-and-groove ends work. It is agonizing to watch. She can't quite line them up, but he lets her try again and again. He has a gentle, creased smile on his face. He winces every time a pole slips out of her hand, but he sets her up again, and they eventually get the poles assembled. The mother and a young teenaged boy are organizing firewood in a pyramid inside the fire pit. As the boy bends over to place a piece of kindling, the mother whacks him in the butt with a sapling and laughs. Mitch thinks of when Sharelle snuck up on him when he was standing at the grill and zapped him with the bug zapper, and he reflexively slapped himself in the forehead with the spatula. She said she lost all bladder control that time from the laughter. "My water broke," she said.

"Mom, seriously," the boy says, trying to sound cranky but unable to contain a grin.

"Mom, seriously," she says in mimicry, and he gives a stifled laugh. She tweaks the brim of his baseball cap.

A park ranger comes to the family's site and collects their camping fee. Then he comes to Mitch's site. He's like an elderly werewolf: sharply pointed ears with sprigs of white hair growing out of them, a grey handlebar moustache, mutton chop sideburns. He takes Mitch's money and writes a receipt.

"Is there a small lake near here?" Mitch asks.

"Yessir, there's one. Spinnaker Lake. The trailhead is down that way." He points to Site #52. "About a half-hour hike. Not many people know about it, though."

"I came up here as a kid once, about thirty years ago. My dad used to talk about that lake. He pointed it out to me once. Is that the only lake nearby?"

"Yup."

"He talked about building a cabin there." A skinny guy with long, coarse dreadlocks walks by the site. He's wearing a small backpack and has yellow gloves on. He glances at them and nods. Wolfman nods back and then looks at Mitch and smirks.

"Check out that guy. A walking dead man, if you ask me," he says.

"Huh?"

"You know what free soloists are?" he asks.

"Free soloists?"

"A type of rock climber," he says. "They choose large boulders or rock walls to climb, for the sheer sake of overcoming the difficulty. No protective equipment. The focus is on technical difficulty and exploration of the terrain."

"I'm not into rock climbing."

"Free soloists usually end up falling and bashing their brains out. Selfish, if you think about it. They worry so much about what they are, instead of who they are. Yeah, sure, they're free soloists, but they forget they're also fathers, mothers, somebody's kid. At some point, other people are counting on them to arrive. To finish the climb and come home in one piece."

"Thanks for the directions. I should start cooking supp—"

"Don't know nothing about a cabin, but there is a pretty interesting building down at the lake. I won't ruin the surprise for you, but it's definitely one of a kind."

"Does anyone live there?"

"Like I said, you'll have to find out for yourself. Safe travels." Wolfman closes his receipt booklet, offers him a salute with it, and walks back down the road.

Mitch gets up at first light the next morning and finds the trailhead. He begins walking on the path. There is a warm breeze, and the grass blades click together from it. He walks through a grove of spruce trees. His only companion is a rabbit bustling through a natural hedgerow and a woodpecker swooping for ants in the moss beside the trail. He winds his way through giant moss- and lichen-covered trees and century-old cedars—some lying like fallen giants on the forest floor. Finally, he sees the lake at the end of the trail. It's really a large pond. As he gets nearer, he can see the clear reflection of the trees on its motionless surface. The end of the trail takes him to a clearing at the edge of the lake. It is completely silent, like he is in a vacuum. To the right, there is a building sitting at the edge of the forest. The sun is popping out of the clouds above it, and Mitch has to shield his eyes to clearly see it. Jutting from the tall grass that surrounds its foundations, the small rectangular structure is about the size of a one-car garage. Its weathered outer walls are covered with a thin coat of white paint, the grains of the cedar wood showing clearly through. On the roof above the entrance is a crudely shaped grey stone cross.

The chapel's front door is ajar, and he creaks it open to find a large green candle standing on an old oak table. Clustered around it are smaller green candles, all melted into the shape of ears. A box of matches sits waiting at the edge of the table. Along the walls, three other tables proffer extinguished pieces of candle in various states of depletion. Wax ears. Venturing in, he palms an ear. It is very hard, and vertical hairline cracks run from top to bottom. He runs his thumb along the inner lobe. It leaves a thin line of soot on his thumb, which he rubs off with his fingers. He moves over to the main table, takes a match, and lights the big candle. It crackles and sputters, and then a steady flame appears. He stares into it.

A year ago, Sharelle and Mitch went for an afternoon walk the day before one of their Phone Calls, wanting to get out of the house and talk about something other than making babies, to remind themselves that there was life outside of egg fertilization. They walked down Phelbin Street and ended up at a small parish. They walked in during the afternoon vespers and shuffled across the chalky floor and found a pew. Filtered sunlight peeked through some of the stained-glass windows on the west side and illuminated medieval figures in paintings on the eastern wall. Mitch could tell they were medieval because the human figures were not quite to scale and their foreheads were overemphasized. There were halos transposed over them, everyone somber and appearing to be in some sort of painful state. Mitch tried to have peaceful, calming thoughts. *Everything is okay.* His mind wandered, and he closed his sweaty hand around Sharelle's fingers to try to focus on praying but also to quell the tremors in her hand.

The soothing, deep bass and rhythmic melodies of a Gregorian chant thrummed off the stone walls. For a thousand years, one generation of monk after another had continued the recitation of these tones. In a nook at the side of the sanctuary, there was a small table with lit candles and a glass bowl beside it with unlit ones. Half an hour in, Sharelle stood and pulled Mitch up off the pew. They walked to the nook. Sharelle wanted to light one candle together and put it on the table. He told her they should each do their own, to double their chances. She seemed disappointed at this suggestion but agreed. As he lit his candle, he held it too close to his index finger and felt a searing dart of pain. They placed their candles on the table. Sharelle bowed her head and whispered something; Mitch stared into the flame. Afterwards, they walked home in silence.

The next day at noon when they made the Call, Sharelle lay on the bed and buried her head in a pillow. Mitch remembers that the skin on the side of his index finger was pink from the burn, and he ran his thumb over it as a hushed voice on the other end sent an icy draft through him: "This cycle has failed."

This cycle has failed. Mitch leaves the candle lit, and he moves to leave. The broad shadow of his body along the wall narrows as he gets to the door. He closes it behind him and walks back to the pond's edge, where he sits down on a boulder that is cantilevered over the water. He stares at the silhouette of the chapel against the sun. Then he turns around, leans forward with elbows on his knees, and watches his image in the lake. The vibration through the rock from his movement makes the water undulate for a couple seconds and then settle again.

It starts with a tingle in his lower back, which soon becomes a tremor in his arms and legs. His upper lip presses on the bottom, forcing it outwards. He feels little pools forming in the corners of his eyes and then the first droplets spilling from the reservoir, sliding along the walls of his nose to tickle his upper lip. One shivering bead after another. He wipes them with the back of his hand. He takes a few deep, shuddering breaths, and he sits. The cumulus clouds move, clearly and perfectly reflected on the glassy surface of the pond.

Then the first falling tear plops into the water, and the tiny ripple makes the clouds' image vibrate.

There is nothing to extinguish. I will never find him. I want him to stand here. I want to hold him to account. Why did he give up why did he walk away from us why did he have to leave me and why couldn't he take deep breaths for me and for us and I would have listened and would have been a really good boy and kept my ears open so why didn't he want to take me fishing why was he too busy chasing great things and why didn't he have a gentle smile and put his arm over my shoulder and teach me about tent poles and all things because I would have listened and that's how life goes and I want a child to take fishing and teach all things to and I will let the child put the poles together I will wait hours and hours but the cycle has failed from start to finish from alpha to omega but why God why God why God I would have listened with ears open and have someone listen like you did Opa and I miss you Opa it is not my fault the cycle has failed.

Why did you take me camping if you didn't love me, Dad?

Head between knees, hands tugging on bunches of hair. Heaving and weeping with deep breaths. So many sets of in-and-out. Then resting back on his hands, he closes his eyes and lets the water stream from his face—some of the beads running into the corners of his mouth, and he's slurping at the hot, salty globules.

And then Mitch bends over to the pond, scoops a pool of water with cupped hands, and releases it over his head. It runs over the crown and walls of his skull, the tufts of his sideburns, across his temples, and down his cheeks. And he is a globe, the face of Earth: icy water streaming down from the northern zenith—across the surface of the world and clinging to the underside of its orb, the entire sphere drenched in it, the excess plinking down to begin again one day.

How will he begin again? He's run out of cycles, and there are no new lives—no frozen embryos waiting to begin.

And then he raises his head from the pond and turns towards a dark shape to his left, and Sharelle Annette Van Laren is watching him from the base of the trail. As she walks towards him, he blinks rapidly to clear his vision. The trees cast a series of tall, narrow shadows and Sharelle walks in and out of the sunlight as she moves closer. Light, shadow, light, shadow. Then she is standing beside him. She slides next to Mitch on the rock and wipes his eyes with her fingertips. She says nothing and pulls the red-and-blue-striped bungee cord out of her pocket. She feeds it through the belt loops of both his jeans and her shorts.

"What are you doing here?" Mitch asks.

"I came back."

"So I see. Why?"

"Because I stayed up till midnight last night listening to Rebekah's view of life."

"And?"

"Rebekah is a robot. She's reading from a script that I doubt she really believes."

"So you ditched the needle guy."

"I ditched Rebekah too." She shrugs and stretches her lips in a grimace. "I asked her if she really believes that we're never given more than we can bear. She said that she believed that. So, I said, 'Then in that case, the conversation is over. Because you don't get it.'"

"And you walked."

"I slept over and left early while she was still sleeping. I'd rather be tied up in bungee cords with you."

Mitch feels the burning crimson of his face. "I need you," he says.

"So do I." She clasps his shoulders, and he surrenders into her arms. "Your face is so red and puffy, Mitchell."

"Allergies."

"Spring allergies are a bitch. Especially in September."

He searches for more to say as she holds him. Then he feels something rise through his legs and bowels and stomach and then into his eyes and forehead like nausea; it makes him shiver and tremble.

She pulls back and takes his head in her hands and kisses his forehead and says, "I'm here." With an index finger, he squeegees the pooling tears from the corners of her eyes and tries to breathe deeply. His exhales are gasps. She smiles and takes him by the hand.

"Do you really want to be tethered to me?" he asks.

"In knots, Mitchell. There's shit to work out, but I want to be shackled to you," she says. "Will you let me?"

"I will," he says.

Sharelle moves closer to him. "I've been gone for a long time, Mitchell," she says. She leans her cheek against his and strokes his hair. "I haven't been giving you my best."

"You deserve *my* best. I need to find it for you," he says and takes her into him fully, his hands stretched around her shoulder blades.

"I want a baby, Mitchell," she says and sobs into his neck, and her body trembles, and he holds her as tight as he can, a fortress to steady her shaking.

"I want it too," he says.

"I don't want to be left behind."

"I won't leave you behind." He pulls back and lifts her face up to meet his. "And I need you to see me again."

"What does that mean?'

"Save me from walking out on myself. Find me again," Mitch says. Water is streaming down the sides of her nose, trickling into her lips, her doing nothing to dry them, letting them run, run, run. This laid bare and publicly harvested woman with the heart and spirit of a girl—this broken and battered soul—is weeping into him with her head perched on his quickly dampening shoulder.

Mitch cups her cheeks in his hands and the words pour forward. "Look up and see me. When we come to the end of the last possible cycle, and there's nothing to show for it, I'll have everything because you'll be there. I just want to be with you, and I want you to need me. When you're on your knees and every last part of yourself seems harvested, look up and you'll find me. I haven't gone anywhere; I haven't walked away."

"I know, I know. Neither of us is walking away." Sharelle seizes his head in her hands and holds it to hers, their tears intermingling.

"I'll give you as much life as I can, Sharelle. Until your last breath, I will love you. That's all I can offer you: every part of me," Mitch says.

"I want your baby so bad, Mitchell. I really do," she says.

"You're enough, Girl."

"I'm not. No."

"You've always been enough."

"I don't feel like I am."

"Then we'll work through that together. You are enough."

"I want a baby. My own little baby." She buries her head deep into his neck. "But I don't need a baby more than I need you." And now their sobs thunder—a thousand stampeding horses out of the gate—indistinguishable from each other's. Hot, shallow breaths. Utter, wet release.

A gust of wind through the evergreens. A distant baby seagull cries, in search of its mother.

Until the end of all things, don't slip away. Never leave me here.

Sharelle stands and dries her face with the front of her shirt. She unhooks the bungee cord, threads it out of their belt loops, and holds it coiled in the palm of her left hand and outstretched towards him. He stands and stretches his right hand over her palm and the cord and grips them tightly. Then, she leads him along the pond and up the trail. As they enter the spruce grove, Mitch sees through his bleary lenses a tiny, trickling waterfall to the left he hadn't noticed on the way down. In a few months, it will freeze over. Then in the spring, the melting snowpack will unleash a deluge of water, and it will gush across the rocks between the trees and down to the pond. And the cycle will begin again.

At the bottom of the waterfall, the rustling fronds of an overhanging fern send ripples across the stirring surface of the pool.

It's time to go home.

REPLACEMENT

SEPTEMBER

School is back in session. Mitch has had a good first week of the year, with Esther checking in on a daily basis. She's even shown some humour about it all by asking him to include drywall in his classroom budget form for the year. He knows his leash is short, however. "You'd be amazed at the crap that people around here are dealing with in their personal lives," Esther said. "But we are held to a high standard. You work with children. They are watching, listening, and looking to you for how to find their way on this planet. Don't let them down again." He won't.

It's Saturday, and Sharelle is babysitting Rachel at Trevor and Megan's. They've gone to Calgary for a conference on "Poststructuralist Skepticism of Metanarratives." Sounds like a riot, Mitch thinks. He did some lesson planning this morning, and now he's driving to their place to hang out with Sharelle and Rachel.

Mitch pulls into their driveway and sees Norman and Audrey's Corolla. Immediately, the familiar wave of resigned irritation oozes in. For life, these are his in-laws. Year after year, the same frustrating, unchanging walls of resistance and incomprehension of one another—the helpless fury of not being fully known or understood. But there's something else Mitch feels too—an anger that pulses from his groin and surges into his torso. It feels controlled but strong. It's an undeniable feeling that things have to change. He can make them different. He can walk inside that house, and things will have no choice but to be transformed.

Mitch drives past their place and circles back to his house. He leaves the car running while he searches through the file cabinet to find the glossy 4" x 6" photo. He walks back to the car, puts the photo on the passenger seat, and drives back to Trevor and Megan's.

He springs out of the car, puts the photo in his back pocket, and walks along the sidewalk and up the steps. His feet seem to fall heavier on the steps—not in fatigue but with purpose. Yet, he is also nauseous with anticipation. When he gets to the top, he can see a little face in the window peeking at him between the drapes. He enters the house. "Hey, Rachel!" he yells.

"Hey, Rachel." Silence. "Don't make me come and get you!" There's a little giggle from the front closet. "If I have to come and get you, I'm going to spin you like a helicopter."

"I'm not listening," the little voice says. Another giggle.

"Last chance," he says and thumps his shoes heavily on the floor in front of the closet. A splutter comes from the closet. He yanks open the two swinging closet doors, and Rachel shrieks and tries to run between his legs. Mitch grabs her and cradles her like a baby. "Baby, want a bottle?" he says and she laughs. He spins her around and sees Sharelle standing in the doorway of the living room. She is wearing that yellow-and-blue plaid skirt and white tank top she wore when he first met her parents. "What an old romantic softie," she had said when Mitch insisted on asking their blessing. He gives her a tight smile and shifts his eyes to look at the shards of sunlight bouncing off the Corolla's windows outside and then back at Sharelle, who has that resigned expression that says, *What can I say? I can't change them. They're my parents, and they're here.*

He puts Rachel down. "I'm going to come upstairs for another party with the stuffies, Rachel. So why don't you get them all set up on the floor in your room, and come get me when they're ready. Maybe you can group by color again."

Rachel springs up and down on her tiptoes and runs upstairs.

"Where are they?" he says to Sharelle.

Sharelle jerks her head at the living room. Mitch pulls off his shoes and puts them by the door. "Love that skirt," he says. He does a high-step march up to Sharelle and gives her a tight hug, grinding his hips against her. She kisses him softly and then jabs her tongue into his mouth and he pulls back in reflex.

"For frick's sake, did you find any cavities?" he says, wiping his mouth on his sleeve.

"Lower left bicuspid. Plus, you have some gingivitis along the top. And I think you broke my pelvis. Ever heard of foreplay?" she whispers and laughs. She takes his hand, and they walk into the living room. Norman and Audrey are sitting across from each other playing Scrabble at the table. Audrey's back is to the door. Sharelle sits down at the far side of the table.

"You guys are so quiet. I didn't know if anyone was home," Mitch says.

"We were just talking about you," Norman says, without looking up, and moves a tile on his board.

"All good, I'm sure," Mitch says. Silence.

"Sharelle was telling us about your little getaway while she was in Chamberlain," Audrey says and sniffs.

"Yes. Had to check some things out," Mitch says.

"Did you have to...find yourself?" Audrey says, turning and peering at him from the corner of her eyes.

"I knew I shouldn't have told you about our breakthrough, Audrey. Thanks for mocking it," Sharelle says.

"In a manner of speaking, I did have to find myself," Mitch says.

"In a manner of speaking," Norman says and picks up two wooden tiles, clicking them together.

"Let me ask you something, Audrey." Mitch straightens his spine, aware for the first time that his head barely clears the doorframe.

"You could call me Mom. That's what sons-in-law do."

"I have a question for you, Audrey. So, I need you to put down your Scrabble tiles and give me your attention."

Audrey turns around with lifted eyebrows and twitches her puckered lips.

"Okay," she says.

Mitch walks over and stands behind Sharelle, putting his hands on her shoulders. "Do you have any idea what kind of woman this is?" His voice is low and calm.

"I know that a gentleman watches his tone," she says.

"There is no tone. I'm asking you a question."

"If you're going to frame it so rudely, I won't be answering any such question from you," Audrey says.

"I'm not framing anything. Here's another question then: I wonder if you've ever considered what it's like to desperately want a child, to watch your sister and your friends and everyone else with a uterus give birth, while you yourself are unable to. To ache for something you can't have. I wonder if you've ever experienced that."

"Mitchell, maybe this isn't the right place or time for this," Sharelle says.

"Uterus! How awfully crude," Audrey says.

"That's kind of the point, Sharelle. There will never be a right place or time for this. Your parents have helped make sure of that. But I'm not leaving you to deal with it all by yourself anymore," Mitch says, taking his left hand off her shoulder and putting it in his pocket.

"That wasn't a question you posed, Mitchell, it was a statement," Norman says, clicking his tiles again and pretending to study the board.

Audrey stands up. "Who do you think you're talking to, Mitchell?"

"A woman who my wife wants to love and prove herself to and wants to be loved by. A woman who I want to love, but who needs to earn it. Because I'll tell you right now, Audrey, you haven't done enough to earn our love."

"Now you watch your mouth right there, Mitchell. You have no right to talk to my wife that way!" Norman stammers and sits upright.

"It's alright, you don't have to be the protector. Just listen," Mitch whispers and nods at Norman and offers him a smile. "The thing is, Norman, I have the same question for you. Both of you don't realize what Sharelle—what we—have gone through. We need you guys."

"We've always been there for you!" Audrey yells and wags a finger in the air. "We've called and visited and done the hard yards. For you!"

"You may have given us some of your time, but you haven't given us yourselves. That means listening, caring, and trying to imagine the perspective of another hurting human being. You haven't done that, and that's not good enough anymore."

"Sounds threatening!" Audrey says.

"So, I'll put it in the form of a question then. For Norman," Mitch says. "Do you know what kind of a woman Sharelle is?"

"Mitch, that's enough okay? This isn't the time," Sharelle says.

"It's the perfect time. Couldn't be better," Mitch says.

"I think it's the perfect time for a...double letter score!" Norman says and puts down the word *belabour* with enormously exaggerated enthusiasm.

Mitch reaches into his back pocket and plops the photo on top of Norman's word. It is Sharelle's sonogram.

Sharelle reaches for it. "They don't need to see that," she says, but Mitch presses his fingertips on her arm, and she stops.

"This is a sonogram of a woman with bilateral fallopian hydrosalpinx," he says. "Note the sausage-like shape of the blocked tubes. It's a textbook case. But this woman is not textbook. And neither is her husband, who incidentally, struggles with impaired spermatozoan motility."

"That is totally inappropriate and a complete—" Audrey begins.

Mitch continues in an even softer voice. "This woman, however, is not defined by the bilateral fallopian hydrosalpinx. She is, in fact, defined by the beauty of her character. This is a woman who forces me to call my brother on his birthday—a brother I can barely stand sharing the same city with. That's called kindness."

"We know she's kind, for pity's sake," Norman says. He slides the photo to the side of the board.

"I *am* sitting right here, everybody," Sharelle says.

"And that's all I want you to do right now is sit and listen. You're not alone in this," Mitch says. "This is a woman who ruthlessly mocks soap operas and then watches them when I'm not home."

"What?" There's no way I'd—" Sharelle sputters.

"The PVR is full of them, my dear," Mitch says. "This same woman also steals my razors to shave her legs and then acts confused when I confront her about it. That's called being mischievous and hilarious."

"Husbands don't share those kinds of inappropriate details. Indiscrete." Audrey's lips are twisting to the side in steady rhythm.

"She listens and cares and laughs and dreams. That's who she is. And she hurts," Mitch says. "She hurts all the time."

"No point exaggerating now. All the time?" Norman says, his head bent over the game board again.

"All the time, Dad," Sharelle says.

Audrey grabs her Scrabble bench and tosses it into the box. Then she frantically picks up the tiles and throws them in. "I'll be in the car, Norman."

"And we need to borrow $7000 for our next round of in vitro, and we're not going to feel bad or bashful about it. We need your support in this. Please," Mitch says.

"Good one," Audrey says. "I'll get out my checkbook ASAP!"

"And we'll pay you back as soon as we can. We're good people. We're honest and loyal and loving. We're solid together, and we are committed to this. You're on this journey with us, whether you like it or not. It's time to acknowledge that," Mitch says and rubs one of Sharelle's triceps, and she puts her hand on his hand. Audrey walks out of the room and makes a raucous production out of putting on her shoes in the hallway.

Sharelle stands up, and she and Mitch step into the hall with their hands held. Mitch offers his most soothing, hushed voice: "I want to call you Mom, Audrey. I really do. But that's a title you're going to have to earn. And that process starts with appreciating and honouring this royal woman here for who she is."

Audrey stands upright after tying her shoes. She sweeps her right foot behind the left, bends her knees, and holds the edges of her skirt out from her body with her fingertips—a full curtsy. Then she glares at their interlocked fingers and bows her head, like she's mentally slicing their hands apart. She turns, marches out to the porch, and slams the door.

Mitch and Sharelle return to the living room. Norman is gently putting his tiles and bench into the Scrabble box. He walks over to them, and Mitch prepares for a punch to the kidneys or some other assault. Norman kisses Sharelle's forehead, ignores Mitch, and heads through the hall towards the door. Mitch follows him. Norman pulls a shoehorn out of his back pocket and pries on his shoes. "Things can't go on like this. We need them to change," Mitch says.

Norman scratches his ear with the shoehorn. "There's something you'll need to learn as a man, Mitch. Things don't really change. You choose your love and you love your choice. That applies to family too. You show respect and forbearance. We're fine the way we are, and your life is fine the way it is. Yes, things will get thrown at you, but you accept the limitations. Your life has a pre-ordained plan, and there's no sense fighting it. Settle in for the ride." Norman scans him up and down, smiles to himself, and calls out, "Thanks for the game, Sharelle."

"I suppose that's the point, isn't it?" Sharelle says. "This isn't a game anymore."

"I don't recall ever saying it was a game."

"Things are going to be different, Norman," Mitch says.

"You've clearly ensured that this afternoon," Norman says, and Mitch walks past him and opens the door.

"There are three words I think you need to learn how to say, Norman," Mitch says, one hand holding the door ajar.

"*I. Love. You.* Right? Thanks. That makes all the blues go away," Norman says.

"We're done with sarcasm too. That's not good enough anymore," Sharelle says.

"No, the words are, *I don't know*. Put away your blueprints, Norman, and start imagining a God who isn't made in your image. Even for a second."

"Such food for thought." Norman walks through the door and reaches his hand back to pull it shut. Mitch sticks his foot in front of the door, and Norman's eyes pan up Mitch's body.

"Think about what I said. Don't close doors that don't need to be closed," Mitch says.

"Whatever chip you've got on your shoulder today, you'd better learn how to grin and bear it. That's something *you* need to start imagining, Mitchell."

"Food for thought," Mitch says and pulls back his foot.

"We're going to talk about this, okay Dad? I'll call you tonight. Mitch is right. We're going to have to adapt to each other and let each other evolve. I'm not spinning in circles anymore," Sharelle says.

Norman shakes his head slowly and then pulls the door gently shut.

Mitch stands at the door for a moment and softly drums his index finger on it. He feels Sharelle's fingertips on his shoulder and pivots towards her, but then he feels a tugging on his pant leg and looks down at Rachel, who peers up at him.

"I've been waiting in this hallway forever. The stuffies are ready for the party."

"Perfect! I can't wait for the party to start," Mitch says.

"Your eyes are sad," she says. "How about a group hug? That's what we do around here when somebody has sad eyes."

Mitch reaches down with arms out, and she gives his left arm a quick hug and pulls away. She turns around and hugs Sharelle's leg and smiles shyly at Mitch. Rachel darts her head back and forth to peek at him and then giggles when he crouches down and makes a tickling motion at her. She runs over to the living room with Mitch in pursuit and hides behind the loveseat, giggling. Mitch lifts an end of the loveseat and peers at her underneath. She runs over and grabs hold of his leg, and he pretends to try to shake her off in mock exertion as he lowers the loveseat to the floor.

"Easy on the furniture," Sharelle says, walking over and splaying herself on the seat. She throws her arms outwards dramatically. "Furniture is for ravishing, not for hurling through space."

"Are you implying that some ravishment needs to happen around here?" Mitch whispers down to her.

"What's *ravishing* mean?" Rachel says. Sharelle jumps up, kisses her on the forehead, and then pecks Mitch on the cheek.

"Before you two have your party, how about some ice cream, Rachel?" Sharelle asks. Rachel smiles, and Sharelle walks to the kitchen. Mitch tickles Rachel under the neck, and she fights him off with one hand but stays fastened to his leg with the other. Sharelle returns with three ice cream cones. Butterscotch ripple. "It's claustrophobic in here. Let's enjoy the sunshine. It'll be winter before we know it." Sharelle carries the cones to the porch, and Mitch limps outside with Rachel bonded to his leg like a barnacle.

Sharelle and Mitch sit in chairs across a rattan wicker table from each other.

"I'd say our chances of borrowing the money from them are somewhat precarious," Mitch says.

"Doesn't matter. We'll find the money somewhere else."

"I got some moneys in my jewels box," Rachel says. "You can have it."

"That is super kind, Rachel. We'll be fine, though," Mitch says. He stoops across to Rachel and tickles her neck. She traps his fingers between her neck and chest, and he howls in pretend anguish. She relents and giggles. Mitch sits upright. "So, I didn't mean to disrespect your parents," he says to Sharelle.

"You were perfect," she says, licking around the edges of the cone.

"It can't be easy to hear someone talk like that to your parents because they've raised you, and despite it all they are your parents, and that's loaded with all kinds of nuances and —"

"Shut up, Mitchell. It was unbelievably great."

"*Shut up* is a mean word," Rachel says, narrowing her eyes at Sharelle.

"Sorry, Rachel," Sharelle says. "*Shut up is* a mean word, and the last thing I want to do is be mean to your Uncle Mitchell." Rachel smiles and sits on the floor with her legs in a V, her left hand perched flat for balance. Then she licks her sweating ice cream cone and sucks the liquid seeping out of the bottom. From the porch, they watch as the wind blows through the hanging prickles of the Chinese chestnut tree.

It blows across the valley and into the horizon.

Until your last breath, I will love you.

OCTOBER

Mitch is sitting at his classroom desk grading social studies projects. It's 5:00 on a Wednesday afternoon. Most of the kids' paragraphs contain mistakes that he's been working on with them for months: comma splices, sentences that run on for half a page without a pause, misspellings. He keeps his head down and plows through them one by one. Sharelle is coming by soon to pick him up for an impromptu dinner out.

Deep breaths.

A soft voice interrupts his concentration. "Look at you working so hard." Kylii is leaning in the doorway with her arms folded and her head cocked slightly to the side. She has a backpack on her shoulder.

Mitch's neck feels stiff as it turns towards her voice. He can't help feeling a tremor in his ribcage. "Oh, hi," he says with a steeply rising intonation and then lowers his voice to an unnatural bass: "Hello." He starts to rise from his chair and then sits down again.

"Whatcha doing?"

"Grading projects."

"The life of a teacher, eh?"

"It pays the bills. What brings you here?"

"I was in the neighbourhood. Thought I'd drop by."

Mitch plays with the clicker on his pen. "Not much excitement here," he says. He inspects his papers.

She has to go.

"Depends on what you call excitement. Maybe you could use an energy drink," Kylii says. She slides the backpack off her shoulders, which draws his eyes back.

"Yeah, I kinda don't drink those anymore."

"You'd be in luck if you did."

"How do you figure?"

"I happen to have a little treat with me." She opens the backpack and shows him a can of Steel Juice. "Kept it cold for you."

"I was kinda fibbing at the grocery store the other day when I said I liked them."

"Oh. So then, were you trying to impress me, Mitchell?" she asks, zipping the backpack shut again and sliding it over one shoulder. "Because you knew I liked them?"

"I don't know." He smiles politely and plays with a staple on one of the projects.

She needs to leave.

"I just wanted to stop by. I learned from Gina about the patterns of passivity I was trapped in with Steve. So I decided to get more agency and initiate things with people."

"It's super nice of you to stop by. Thanks."

"You teachers work pretty long hours, huh? How do you find the energy?" Kylii says.

"I feed off the energy from the pupils."

She laughs. "Pupils?"

"Kids. Students."

"You must be awesome with kids."

"I like kids. Usually." He takes a new project and circles a missing capital letter in the first sentence.

This is not a good scene. Please go.

Kylii pulls a chair from the wall behind Mitch and slides it into position at the side of his desk. She lays her backpack on the floor and rests her elbows on the desk, face in hands. "Haven't seen you since the assertiveness class," Kylii says.

"Nope. Been busy asserting myself."

"I know, I'm so assertive now, I can barely contain myself."

"Glad it worked for you."

"You mentioned coffee last time we talked."

"I did? I did, yes. Coffee break sometime to talk shop. Compare notes."

"Still waiting for a call."

"I just kinda meant with the class," Mitch says. He shuffles some papers.

"That's why you blush and stutter when we talk, huh?" She gives a short gasp of laughter. "Seriously, where you been?"

"A lot on the go. Teaching, trying to start a family. You know, standard stuff."

"Oh," she says. "You mean like making babies?"

"Uh, yeah. That's probably on a need-to-know basis, huh?" He blushes.

"That's okay. I like openness. That's pretty rare," she says. She reaches under one of her sleeves and adjusts a strap on her shoulder. Then she locks eyes with Mitch. "In a guy."

"I think I gave you the wrong impression. That is so my bad."

"I guess I thought...I didn't realize...That's okay," she says with a trace of irritation.

"I'm sorry, Kylii, but Sharelle is picking me up for dinner and—" Mitch stops, hearing footsteps down the hall.

"Yes, some wires got crossed here," Kylii says. The footsteps get closer and then Sharelle appears in the doorway.

Mitch instantly stands up. He can feel that his face is red. Kylii flashes a polite smile at Sharelle and looks towards the outside window. "Hi there. You," Mitch says. He walks over to her. "What brings you here...you?"

"Did you forget we're doing supper? Then again, I can see that you have a visitor."

"No, Kylii stopped by. Have you two met?"

"No, but hi," Kylii says.

"Hi," Sharelle says, staring at Kylii without expression. "Mitch mentioned you on our camping trip. That he used to have a crush on you. That you've recently had some interaction again."

"Mitch and I were in the assertiveness class together."

"You seem to have no trouble asserting yourself."

"Yeah, we learned a lot in that class. We were usually in different groups, I think, eh Kylii?" Mitch says.

"Sometimes. Mitch was the star student," Kylii says.

"Mitch is always the teacher's pet. It helps that he's cute, doesn't it?" Sharelle asks.

"Is he?" Kylii asks.

"I don't know, is he?" says Sharelle.

"Uh, I should go," Kylii says.

"No, please stay. He's adorable. He's got that 'Aw shucks' kind of thing going on, where you just want to take care of him like he doesn't know what's going on."

Kylii leans forward, picks up the backpack, and slides on one of the straps. "Sorry to bother you, Mitch."

Sharelle sits on the desk between Mitch and Kylii and turns to her, arms folded, peering almost directly downward. "But he's super smart and funny and kind, and that makes it even more effective. I get it. I'd forgotten, but I know. I'd be coming back for more of that too. He's like cocaine, huh?"

"This is all on me. No one's fault but mine, okay? Let's grab our supper," Mitch says. He hurriedly grabs his papers and puts them in his bag. Kylii stays seated as she leans to the side away from Sharelle and pretends to unjam a zipper on her backpack.

"When you talk to him one-on-one, you feel like the only woman on earth. Don't you agree?" Sharelle crosses her legs and leans in closer to Kylii. "He's fabulous. One-on-one, especially." Sharelle closes her eyes and strokes her hips with the back of her knuckles.

Mitch walks past Sharelle and out into the hall, looking back at the two women. "The janitor needs us to go so he can buff the floors," he says. "And I'm the asshole in this."

Sharelle brushes her hair around her ears. "You seem totally nice, Kylii. So no offense, but you have no idea where you're playing. We may be broken, but he's mine and I'm going to take him home and we're going to fix us."

"I'm only saying hello. Not trying to find a project."

"I think I heard him next door. The janitor. He gets cranky if we're here past six," Mitch says, trying to even out the papers sticking out of his bag.

"Forgive me, Kylii. It was a thrill to meet you." Sharelle reaches out and shakes Kylii's hesitant hand. Then she gets off the desk, walks to the classroom light switch, and turns it off as Kylii rises to leave. "Guys like Mitch only happen once in a lifetime," Sharelle says into the darkness. "I don't plan to let him fall away."

Mitch steps back into the room as Sharelle leaves it. He flips the light back on. "I apologize if we had some confusion and misunderstanding before. See you in class, okay?"

"See you in class, Mitchell. Yes," Kylii says. She walks past Mitch at the door without looking at him, takes a wide detour around Sharelle, and then shuffles down the hall. Mitch and Sharelle go the opposite way, out the exit door, and into the sun-bleached parking lot.

OCTOBER

The next evening, Mitch tells Mom that he's walking over for supper. His treat. Sharelle has to work extra late tonight, anyway. He buys some fried chicken and two side salads, which they devour together in relative silence in the kitchen. It's funny that Mom eats as quickly and voraciously as he does. Afterwards, they sit back and view the carnage of stripped, sinewy bones and seeping ketchup packets. It's stuffy, so Mitch opens the kitchen window to let in a breeze through the screen.

"I guess all his stuff's been sold off now, eh?" Mitch says, sitting back down.

"A lot of it."

"How about the shoelbak table?"

"Yup, even got rid of that."

"Somebody bought it?"

"Somebody bought it."

"Trevor didn't mind?"

"Do I need Trevor's approval?" Mom says.

"No." Mitch picks up a wing and gnaws on the remaining meat tucked in between the cartilage. He puts it down. "I know you don't like talking about this, but I know that you suffered a lot," he says.

"Losing Opa was tough, but I wouldn't call it suffering."

"You know what I'm talking about, Mom."

She rubs her thumbs together.

"I know what Dad was like."

"We've come through fine."

"You know things I don't. So does Trevor. Very...difficult things you probably won't tell me."

"I heard you went to Eckhardt Island," she says.

"Yes, I did."

"Did you find what you were looking for?"

"Why do you think I was looking for something?"

"Your father is gone, Mitchell."

"I know that." Mitch can feel that blood has drained from his face. Outside, there is a sudden gust of wind and they both stare at the swaying chestnut tree. Some of the prickles fall to the ground. "Mom, why didn't you go to university?"

"Family became our priority."

"His priority or your priority?"

"Times were different."

"That must've hurt."

"Yes."

"You had a gift and could never use it."

"Yes."

"There must have been a lot of...disappointment." Silence. "For Opa too."

"Yes."

"Accumulated over time."

"Yes. But you and Trevor aren't a disappointment." She gets up, grabs the overflowing garbage can, and shovels all the debris into it. Then she puts the can back under the sink and leaves the room.

Mitch pulls the can out, closes the bag with a twist tie, and takes it to the garbage can in the garage. When he returns, Mom is sitting at the kitchen table. In front of her is an old tape player. "What do you have there?" he asks.

She smiles at him and presses “Play.” He hears the whirring background of an old cassette, and then the voices begin:

“Um, so...uh...what’s an important world event and how did it impact you?”

“You wanted me to talk about the moon landing, right?”

“Um...you said you would talk about 1969, so yeah, that would make sense.”

“But you told me you wanted me to discuss the—”

“Alright, so how did the moon landing impact you?”

“Should we start over?”

“Mom, it’s okay. The moon landing. 1969. Go. Expand, please.”

“You were born in 1969. I want to talk about that.”

“I’m not a world event.”

“You are a world event.”

“What was it like to see Neil Armstrong’s first step for mankind?”

“Mitch was an absolutely gorgeous baby. He is still my gorgeous baby.”

“You’re sabotaging my project.”

“Then let me sabotage it.”

“This is due tomorrow.”

“You get a low mark on this, and the teacher can talk to me.”

“Why are you doing this?”

“Mitch barely cried. He just gurgled and cooed and laughed.”

“I give up. Let me know when you’re done.”

“He was and is a beautiful boy, and he will grow into a wonderful young man. Mitch is like this coral reef. He’s just bubbling with colour and passion and richness, but you don’t realize it because it’s all going on underneath. He overflows with all those things, but he’s too busy keeping the lid shut on himself.

“I’ve known loss and destruction—of dreams and gifts especially—and the end of things I will never get back. Yet I’m left with the legacy of two boys I love. And Mitchell is one half of that legacy. The gift is in the pain, my father continues to say.

"All his self-deprecation won't keep Mitch hidden. And one day, I know that Mitch is going to be this incredible man who will change everyone he meets. He has something inside him, something in his blood, that is...transcendent. Yes, that's it. He will walk with his head high because he is Mitch Van Laren, and there is no one like him. Nor will there ever be.

"So what impact did Mitchell's birth have? Everything. And he will impact the world around him."

"Thanks, Mom. You realize I can't use this, don't you?"

"You need to use this. Just not for school."

"Okay."

"All the time. Use it always."

"I'll keep it, I promise."

"Take it into your lungs. Like the air you breathe."

"Alright. I will keep it with me. Yes."

"It's how I feel about you. It will never change."

"Thanks, Mom. Let's start over now, alright?"

Click.

Mitch presses the "Eject" button and pulls out the tape. He studies it for a moment and then says, "Wow, you kept this. Very cool, Mom."

"It's how I feel about you. It's never changed."

"Thanks, Mom. Seriously."

"Why didn't you keep it with you, Mitchell?"

"I must have forgotten to."

"No. You didn't lose or forget things."

"Then I must have...not believed it enough," Mitch says softly.

"Yes. That's exactly right. You didn't. Do you believe it now?"

"I think so."

"Good." Mom pulls the cassette from his hand and drops it into his breast pocket. "Everything I did, I did in your best interests, okay?"

"Okay."

"Mitchell, sit down. Only listen." Mitch sits across from her. Mom takes his hands in hers and squeezes them so hard that it hurts. "Everything was for you, and it was all worth it."

"Alright, Mom. I get it. I'm pretty perceptive, actually."

"You are." Her right hand lets go and reaches into her back pocket. She pulls out a flat, brown object and drops it down on the table between them with her hand overtop, like she's about to reveal a poker hand. "And you're right. There are things I can never tell you." She lifts her hand off to reveal the faded, buckskin wallet—the one with the large orange stitches.

"Zo gaat het in het leven," she says and lets go of his other hand.

Mitch's head is buzzing as he walks back towards his house. When he gets to his street, he stops and stares at the lights of the hospital rising above the houses. Renfrew Memorial Hospital: where he spent the first three days of his life. And one other day. When he was ten.

Lying in the hospital bed. Your head burns. Dad hurt you. He was so furious. He's smiling at you now. He's standing beside your bed, and his hand is on your shoulder. The other hand is stroking your hair. *I shouldn't have called you a loser.* Trevor and Mom are standing at the foot of the bed. Trevor is patting your foot.

Mom's face is white, eyes red. "You'll be out in no time, Mitchell," she says.

Dad's voice is friendly. "Gave us a scare, you little rascal. Always climbing trees. I tell you, they say girls are tough to raise. But boys, they're always pulling crazy stunts."

"Just horsing around," you whisper.

I won't tell on you.

"Bet you're glad you only had one boy, eh Clarence?" Dad says and winks at you.

Opa is leaning against the window sill, hands in pockets. He walks to the other side of the bed from Dad, ruffles your hair with the thick fingertips of his left hand, and then folds his arms and gazes down at you and breathes a heavy sigh. He's so serious. He looks across at Dad, the veins in his forehead bulging. Red face. Opa runs his hand through his thin wisps of hair, a rooster tail poking up from the top of his head. You stare at the thick ridges of veins on the back of his right hand as it moves towards your face. He strokes your cheek, and then he rests his lips on your forehead for a second and kisses it.

"Been on the lake lately, Clarence?" Dad says. So cheerful and light.

"No." Opa's voice is low and strange.

"You and I really should get out there." Silence. "Maybe I can convince you to try a new lake."

"No."

"Sometimes a change is good, you know. Great new things can be around the corner."

"No."

"Will I ever convince you?"

"You will not."

"Who knows? Someday I could drive your truck for a change. I'd pretend to drive to Crenshaw, then go somewhere else to fool you."

"You will never fool me."

"Of course, I don't know if I can leave Mitchy alone anymore." He tries to tousle your hair. It makes your head hurt more. "Mitchell, my little tree monkey. He's trouble with a capital *T*, isn't he, Opa?" He nudges your shoulder. So gentle.

Opa sticks his hands in his pockets. You hear him breathing deeply through his nose. He walks to the mirror across from your bed, and you watch his reflection as he stares at himself. He decisively pats down the rooster tail and runs a comb through his wisps. Above the bridge of his nose, there is a triangle of wrinkles—a furrow.

Not those little ones, Tony. Not on my watch.

Sleep tight, father. I know where you are now.

OCTOBER

On his forty-seventh birthday, Mitch wakes to the alarm clock at 6:30. He reaches for Sharelle, but she isn't there. Instead, sitting on her pillow, is a plain green gift bag. He opens the bag and finds an object wrapped in red tissue paper. Opening it, he finds his old knitted wool hat and headband. There is also a small bottle of lighter fluid and some matches. He puts on the hat and then the headband, lining it up with the ends of his hair, and feels its claustrophobic constriction around his scalp. He hears a little half-sneeze from the doorway and looks over. Sharelle is standing in the doorway with her arms folded. She is smiling widely at him. "Familiar?" she smirks.

"Where did you get these?"

"Your mom, obviously. She had them in the attic."

"Did she know what I used to do with them?" "What do you think? She told me she called it your 'Flathead Phase.'"

"Ah, memories," Mitch says.

"You must miss these. They'd make you look so freaking hot."

"I tell you what, Baby. I had sweet hair in high school with this little treatment."

"I've seen your high school yearbook, Mitch."

"Oh. Yeah." He takes them off and twirls the headband around his index finger. "So, judging by the incendiaries, you have some specific intentions for this stuff?"

"I think it's a fine day for an exorcism."

"That's what you call a gift? Destruction of my childhood memories?"

"Something like that."

"The burning's a little dramatic, wouldn't you say?"

"You ever try to shred a polyester hat, Mitch?"

Sharelle pulls him out of bed. She slips a bathrobe on him and leads him downstairs to the living room with one hand, holding the gift bag in the other. There's a table set in front of the fireplace with orange juice, coffee, an omelet, and bacon strips. Sharelle sits him down at the table, then sticks the headband inside the hat and lays them on the fireplace grate. She squirts lighter fluid in diagonal lines across the hat and holds the matchbox in front of Mitch's face, striking a wooden match and winking at him. He starts to object, but she puts a finger to her lips and throws the match into the fireplace. The polyester fibers curl and shrink, releasing an acrid stench, and soon there's just a pile of soot.

"You are enough, Mitchell."

He gazes into her eyes, over at the smoldering ashes, and then back at her. Her eyes are soft and gentle.

"You are more than enough for me. But you are enough for you too. You always have been."

"Thank you, Girl." He takes his orange juice, holds it against the light from the window, and drinks it down. Then he says, "For all of it. We've been working hard. On us. It's gonna be worth it, okay?"

She takes a sip of her orange juice, and not once does she take her eyes off of him. "Hey, Mitchell," she whispers. "It already is."

Sharelle Van Laren is sitting across from Mitch, and she is the most astonishing woman alive. She is wearing plaid flannel pajama bottoms and one of his old, baggy T-shirts, and her hair is a mess, and he wants to devour and be devoured by her so desperately that his legs wobble. In the end, the insatiable dreamland of carnal fantasy rooted in his romanticized memories and bottomless insecurities will do nothing to fill Mitch up. He won't spend a raw, empty afternoon fucking it all away with Kylii—simultaneously screwing the pain and heartache away for a while and breaking the seal of his soul's alliance with his wife forever—and in its place he yearns for a fully formed night of sacred hunger between two entwined and fully known lovers where he presses his lips under Sharelle's chin, explores her throat with his tongue, feels her breath quicken with faint gasps, and rides the slowly rising waves of rhythms and sighs into shaking, shivering release. Then deep, dreamless sleep and a sunlit morning ushered in with the milky hue of her back and her golden hair spilling over her shoulders, first stirring and then waking together below a headboard of dancing leaves and tree branches and underneath a bedspread checkered in earth tones.

Mitchell doesn't know if they will ever conceive a child together, let alone carry it to term. And he doesn't know if they'll ever have the money to adopt. Maybe a year from now, his birthday will be different. Maybe he will be a Daddy. Maybe he will lie face-to-face with the helpless child his soul has ached to meet. Maybe he will stare into its eyes and let it speak to him without a sound, its irises rippling outwards in an endless, kaleidoscopic cycle.

Or he will continue to stand on the sidelines and watch Rachel go to kindergarten for the first time, run home with her report card, be walked down the aisle by Trevor. Maybe he will continue to bear this grief, raging against this curse of nature—this darkness that has suffocated and drowned the joy from the eyes of this beautiful woman he's always loved, as her chances for motherhood slowly slip through her fingers.

Whatever happens will have to be enough. They will have to make it enough. They will claw through the dirt and murk, and they will howl into the wind to find heaven on earth—to find the way and to find each other. They will rage against the blankets of familiarity that are laid over them over time—the small predictabilities and unfulfilled expectations that can dull their hopes and their libidos. They will fight through, pushing the branches aside and clearing the fog, to see each other in this story they've created together. And now, sitting in this plainly carpeted living room and gazing across at this majestic woman who's chosen to spend her life with him, Mitchell knows something. He's known it all along; it's just taken all this time to solidify.

And here's what it is, Mr. Powell McAllister—you who eviscerated him, a fatherless boy at the most vulnerable point in his life, in front of his classmates, in front of the exquisite girl he so desperately wanted to impress. This is what he's figured out, Porter:

The failure? The coward? The impotent eunuch in the classroom that day?

It was you.

NOVEMBER

He answers on the first ring. "Hello?"

"Congratulations, Dr. Van Laren."

"Thanks, Mitch. I'm not a doctor yet, though."

"Megan said you passed your dissertation defense. So, you are a doctor, my boy."

"Thanks a lot, Mitch. I appreciate your support."

"Yup."

"That's all you got? No "Big But" jokes? No snarky teacher-student circle of life comments?"

"Just a guy being proud of his brother."

"It isn't that big a deal, though, I promise you."

"You've been through a lot, Trevor. To get to this point."

"I just had to chip away at it."

"All this time. You've carried a lot." Silence. "How did you do it?" Silence. "How did you function?"

"You take deep breaths."

"You've known all these years what happened. What Opa did that day. Not the details, but you knew. I was oblivious."

"Sometimes we only listen to what we want to hear."

"True that."

"Opa baited him, Mitch."

"Maybe a bit."

"He baited him."

"That didn't change the outcome."

"I know that. Now."

"He loved us. He thought he wouldn't be around later."

"Yes. And I walked away from you, Mitchell. I apologize for that."

"You were surviving."

"I guess I was. I did visit him, you know. The night before he died, I went to his room. He was totally out of it. Said nothing. I squeezed his arm. I said goodbye."

"I'm glad. That was a gift to be able to do that. To you both." Mitch winces and holds the phone lightly between his index finger and thumb as he says, "Trevor, there's something I never tell you. Have never told you."

"Okay."

"I want you to know that I compassionately regard you."

Long silence. "It's nice to be regarded. I mean, I accept your regards."

"And regards to your beautiful family, Trev. It's a gift too. Never, ever forget that."

"I know. So is yours. You'd be a great dad. You know that, right?"

"Yeah, I think I would."

"I know you would," says Trevor.

"So, give that family of yours my regards then."

"I am regarding them as we speak."

"We're pathetic," Mitch says.

"Yes, in that regard. We are, aren't we?"

"Yes, a couple of English majors without the words. Well, kind regards then. Later, Doctor."

"Like I said, still not a doctor. Soon, very soon."

"All But Ceremony. Only a small 'But' now?"

"Shut up, Mitch. Enjoy the day, okay? Go easy on the drywall."

"I promise."

When Mitch's online order comes in the mail, he removes it from the shipping box and then wraps it in some plain yellow gift wrap. He puts it in a bag and takes it to Coffee Break, and he orders his usual extra-large dark roast, double cream. He grabs a tray and sits down by the window. He takes out the box and leaves it on the tray. With permanent marker, he has written on the box in big letters: LARSON. Then he walks into the parking lot and watches through the window to make sure only Larson picks it up. A couple minutes pass, and then Larson comes to the table, stares at the box and looks around the restaurant. He takes the tray, and he disappears into the back with the box.

Mitch gets in his car and drives towards school. A mile down the road, he imagines Larson opening the box filled with the complete first and second seasons of *TJ Hooker*, six DVDs in all, and he smiles to himself.

We all have moments we wish could have been different. As Mitch drives with his coffee in hand, he imagines that he's walking to school on the track again. Planting one sure foot after another firmly onto the path. In his periphery, a distant shape is moving towards him. Mitch doesn't speed up to reach the corner house, and he doesn't pretend to be distracted. He turns and waits, ready to walk and talk. *Thanks for walking with me, Larson:* that's what he should have said. Every single time.

We all have moments we wish could have lasted forever. Mitch remembers grade seven. He's playing street hockey in the middle school parking lot near the end of lunch hour. Opa has stopped by on his break, and Mitch keeps looking for his red plaid shirt to make sure he's watching. As Mitch's legs pump furiously with his adrenalized lust for Opa's approval, he wills the ball to come to his stick. Up and down the side he runs, urging the ball to pop loose and find him. He glances over to see Opa, who smiles at him and taps the face of his wristwatch with a shrug.

Almost time for him to go.

Mitch runs back to help out on defense. With another glance, he sees Opa walking slowly backwards towards his truck in the parking lot, his eyes flashing between the game and his watch.

Please don't leave yet, Opa. Let me show you what I can do.

Shot by an opposing forward, the orange ball ricochets off the goalie's extended left foot and settles on Mitch's stick, and he is flying up the left wing with the ball rattling against wood as he weaves around the first defenseman and then through the feet of the second, the blade gliding in a twirling dance along the pavement. His hands squeeze the stick as he closes in on goal, faking a forehand and rolling to his backhand, flipping the ball in an arc over the goalie's shoulder and rustling the nylon mesh in the top right corner of the net. In jubilation, he hoists the stick above his head like a spear and turns and scours for the red shirt.

Did you see it? Where are you? I'm not ready to say goodbye.

There is no red giant anywhere on the sidelines.

No, no, no, no. It wasn't supposed to end like this. Why did you go? I just needed one more minute.

Then Mitch hears it coming from behind his own goal. Ping. Ping. Ping. Ping. And there Opa stands, his wedding band clattering with the slap of his left hand on the net's rear crossbar. Then arms raised in a *V*, Opa throws his eyebrows to the sky with mouth agape, hollering, "THAT'S...MY...MITCHELL!"

My Mitchell: the biggest man I know. Do you believe that, Mitch?

Yes, I finally do. Goodbye, Opa. You were my oxygen.

GENESIS

"Then a mighty angel picked up a boulder the size of a large millstone and threw it into the sea, and said: 'With such violence the great city of Babylon will be thrown down, never to be found again.'"

–The Book of Revelation

Crenshaw Lake is cold and very deep. It sits at 7600 feet, and the fishing season only lasts from May to mid-October. The rest of the year, the lake sits covered in ice, and the road buried in snow. There is only active life there for a few months, and then most every living thing is entombed in dormancy.

Clarence prided himself on getting in one of the last fishing days before the winter freeze. He knew that by the second week of October, there wouldn't be a soul on Crenshaw. It would be bitterly cold, but they would go one last time. He and his son-in-law.

As they pull out of the driveway at 5:00 a.m., a hand rises and gives an unseen wave from the upstairs bathroom window. It is the hand of a boy whose almost-thirteen-year-old bladder can't quite make it through the night—whose orange soccer shirt sits neatly folded on his night table, ready for the day to arrive. A boy who, from this day forward, will know.

Once on the lake, Clarence sits bundled in his winter jacket with one freckled, muscular hand on the throttle of the old McCulloch. Once in a while, he swings his arms back and forth in the frozen air to keep his circulation going. The icy afternoon gales whistle across the surface of Omega, but he endures. He sits at the stern behind him. His fist clenches the chain handle of his lunch box, filled with cement the night before. An aluminum nameplate is riveted to the front of it: *Clarence*.

In his mind, he has visualized himself lifting it high and then the torque of its arc. He knows that a tremendous final effort will be needed by his sapped arm and shoulder muscles to hoist and set the pendulum in motion, that the parietal bone will shatter, and it will be over in a second. He releases the handle and fishes until they have a total of seven. He takes a few deep breaths, and then his hand reaches down again, and he does what he has to do. A bad thing. A very bad thing.

Afterwards, with nausea hovering at the base of his throat, he wraps a chain around the neck, down between the legs, and back up to the neck again. He padlocks the lunch box to two overlapping links, leaving a few excess links hanging loosely down. The iron bolt threads through and clicks into place, and the weight droops from the neck in a lunchbox bowtie.

The nameplate faces forward. *Clarence*.

Convulsing with gagging shudders, he lines up his stiff fishing knife and punctures the lungs and stomach to prevent them from ballooning with gases later—closing his eyes right before each plunging injection of the knife. Then he jettisons him over the edge, careful not to capsize, and watches the rigid cocoon sinking and then disappearing into the darkness, the loose ends of the chain swaying and undulating with the downward fall, each rung twisting and following the other down into the depths.

He motors to shore. He gets out, tips the boat on its side, and uses the piss bucket to wash the spatter from the boat's sides. He transfers his gear into the bed of the truck, placing the two fishing rods carefully so they don't snap. He sheaths his knife. He hauls the boat on with the winch.

Clarence secures the load. He takes one last sweeping look around to make sure nothing has been forgotten. The air outside is thin, and he takes an extra breath of oxygen. He climbs into the cab and turns the ignition. The engine cranks over a couple times, and then the big V-8 starts with a throaty roar. He lets it idle for a minute until the engine subsides into a contented drone, and then he shifts into first gear and the truck begins its creaking journey home. He winds through the water-logged potholes and arteries that are glazed over with gelatin skins of ice. He can mostly steer between them but sometimes he has to plow right through.

As the lake disappears in his rear-view mirror, the rows of fir trees march along the side of the road. Their dense trunks thrum with the wind that, on the lake, was a shriek but is now a low Gregorian hum.

Onward, Clarence labours the creaking pick-up across the merciless terrain of the access road and then shifts into second gear onto the washboard of the gravel highway. The hums of the tree trunks join the drone of the truck's engine as the struts of the suspension groan across the punishing gravel and finally find the highway asphalt, and he shifts into the third and final gear now—the V-8 opening up, RPMs rising, pistons surging and falling in concert, tires whining with the friction—and the sheets of rain stream from his feverish crown and swollen tear ducts in a torrent, his spinal fluid crackling with an electrostatic buzz, and the atoms of his malignant, rapidly dividing cells leaping in expectation of new life.

Alone on the road, he is descending into the Valley.

Clarence has reached his limit.

The tribulation is over.

Acknowledgements

Rain has been a twelve-year journey. What began in 2005 as feverishly scribbled notes on scraps of paper in a Vancouver fertility clinic parking lot has evolved into a manuscript born from hard experiences and hard work. My skin is decidedly thicker after bringing this novel to life.

Publishing *Rain* has been a truly international endeavour. To Connie May Fowler, thank you for your immense generosity in helping me craft this book. You never gave up on me or it, despite the complexity of the story and its subject matter. Thank you also to my other mentors at the Vermont College of Fine Arts: Laurie Alberts, Robert Vivian, and Clint McCown. In your diverse and caring ways, you have all taught me so much about the craft of writing fiction.

Thank you to the supremely generous writer and teacher Robert Boswell, who first saw the skeleton of this story in 2009 at a conference in New Mexico and informed me, "You're going to graduate school for creative writing. Any questions?" I owe so much of this to you, Boz.

A big thank you goes to Jennifer Cohen for the rich insights and unrelenting encouragement she provided on this long road. Your influence is all over this book. Thank you, Mathieu Cailler, for your belief in me and the work. You have been a great friend and advocate on this road. Kali Van Baale and Donald Quist, thank you for your inspiring example and your unconditional friendship. I am proud to call you friends and colleagues in the craft.

To the Circle of writers from VCFA who have given me so much insight into my worlds—creative and otherwise—I want to thank Deb Baldwin, Mike Blair, Catherine Buni, Courtney Ford, Phillip Garcia, Christina Gustin, Jane Poirier Hart, Greg Hill, Mandy Holland, Leah Kaminsky, Jackie Kharouf, Hollie Loveless, Amanda Silva, Shawn Dallas Stradley, John Taylor Stout, Lee Thomas, and Ian Wallace.

To Maggie Morris, an editor of the highest order, thank you for the multiple ways in which you made the book better and have advocated for it since.

Thank you to Peter O'Connor, the best cover designer in England (or anywhere for that matter).

Lorna Lee was an absolute professional and a joy to work with in the complex task of formatting the manuscript. Thank you, Lorna.

Many thanks to Janice Johnson, who never stopped believing in the larger vision for this book and was an ever-present support.

To the many New York and Toronto agents I approached who gave generous feedback and urged me to persevere, thank you. To those who dismissed the manuscript with, "No one publishes new literary novelists anymore," thank you for the motivation to bring *Rain* into the world myself.

To the sneering agent I met at the PNWCA conference who told me, "Nobody cares about a guy who can't have kids": It turns out people do care. It's not them, it's you.

To my parents, John and Joan Antonides, thank you for letting us kids tinker and explore and chase our dreams, and thank you for loving and believing in me and this project.

Thank you to my sister and brothers for their enthusiasm and example of humility and hard work: Ev, Dave, Doug, and Rob.

A special acknowledgement to the numerous women and men I have met who struggle with infertility. It is my hope that you will recognize in this novel at least some aspects of the agonizing road you have walked.

To all those who pledged and gave support to the publishing campaign for the novel, thank you so very much.

And finally, to my wife Monica and my sons, Daniel and Zachary. Thank you for walking with me on the precarious road to publication. I love you. This is *our* book.

91641633R00173

Made in the USA
San Bernardino, CA
23 October 2018